MW01609054

BRETHREN OF ACADIA
a Second Face in February

An Oscar Phelps novel
By David B. Green

authorHOUSE®

AuthorHouse™
1663 Liberty Drive
Bloomington, IN 47403
www.authorhouse.com
Phone: 1-800-839-8640

This is a work of fiction. Places are in the main accurate. Names, characters, events, incidents
and situations either are the product of the author's imagination or are used fictitiously. This
story while entirely fiction based, does carry factitious elements. Any resemblance to actual
persons, living or dead, businesses, companies, events or locales is entirely coincidental.

David B. Green has asserted his moral rights.

First published by AuthorHouse 1/24/2011
ISBN: 978-1-4567-1733-9 (sc)
ISBN: 978-1-4567-1734-6 (e)
ISBN: 978-1-4567-1735-3 (dj)
Library of Congress Control Number: 2010918919

Printed in the United States of America
This book is printed on acid-free paper.
Any people depicted in stock imagery provided by Thinkstock are models,
and such images are being used for illustrative purposes only.
Certain stock imagery © Thinkstock.

Published with the financial underwriting participation of Amsterdam based PR & Media
Group - Molitor 5901 Boekerij in conjunction with 32-Red Productions. – Brethren of Acadia
– is available electronically and in paperback and hardback editions through our commissioned
publishing house; AuthorHouse in the United States, who manage distribution worldwide
through the Ingram Book Group. Available online at Amazon, Borders, W H Smith, Barnes &
Noble, Dymocks, Magrudy's, Waterstones, Booksense, Bookworld Espana, Chapters Indigo Books
and through major accredited retail outlets throughout; United States of America, Canada,
UK, Spain, Gibraltar, France, Australia, New Zealand, UAE & SAR Hong Kong, PRC.

David B. Green

Brethren of Acadia
a Second Face in February

AN ENTERTAINMENT

Foreword

It had long been an ambition to visit the revered cricket grounds of Australia. Ever since as an enthusiastic teenage prospective Nottinghamshire cricketer, I would listen to the exploits of the English (MCC) tourists of the day, battling away far from home in pursuit of the Holy Grail, engaged in the only International Cricket Test Series that really matters. The *Ashes*.

The SCG, the GABBA, the MCG, the Adelaide Oval and the WACA, were mythical venues to me. Botham, Willis, Gower, Gooch, Lamb, Boycott, Amiss, Brearley, Randall, Old, Knott, etc were the English principals of the era.

The closest I thought I would ever get to these cricketing antipodean Mecca; bastions of the victorious and relentless Aussie march, was courtesy of the BBC TMS radio broadcast.

My first and most memorable experience was the *middle of the night* TMS coverage of *The Centenary Test* match held at the MCG from March 12 to 17 1977.

Remarkably, after a valiant and hugely entertaining 174 from our own (Nottinghamshire's) Derek Randall, made against an Australian attack led by the great Dennis Lillee, to whom he famously doffed his cap after narrowly evading a savage bouncer, stating "No good hitting me there mate, nothing to damage." ...and when finally dismissed left the ground by the wrong gate and found himself climbing up towards the Royal enclosure where Queen Elizabeth II was watching the day's play... Australia still won by the exact same 45-run victory margin as the First Test match 100 years previously.

However, it was during a day-night game at the GABBA in Brisbane almost thirty years later, that I first arrived upon the premise for ***Brethren of Acadia.***

The Commonwealth Bank Series was the name of the One Day International cricket tournament held in Australia for the 2006-07 season.

It followed immediately the *Ashes* series debacle.

This was Match 4: Australia v England, 19 January...

I was stood at the terrace bar at the Watermark Hotel, Wickham Terrace, Spring Hill, Brisbane, drenched from the sweltering humidity and quaffing down a XXXX... *'It's Queensland for beer'.*

In the distance, I could see the GABBA and the floodlights illuminating high into the clear night sky. England were getting a beating yet again and I could not bring myself to attend. So close and yet so far.

Soon after, came the ICC Cricket ODI World Cup in the Caribbean and with it the *Bob Woolmer* affair. RIP.

Former England Test Cricketer and respected Pakistan Coach Bob Woolmer was found dead on 18 March 2007, one day after his team's defeat to Ireland had put them out of the running for the World Cup. Jamaican police performed an autopsy which was deemed inconclusive.

The following day police announced that the death was suspicious and ordered a full investigation. Further investigation revealed the cause of death was "manual strangulation" and that the investigation would be handled as a murder. The Jamaican police then rescinded the comments that he was murdered, and confirmed that he died from natural causes.

With these catastrophic events set in my mind and a recent visit to *Katrina* ravaged New Orleans to reference upon, allied to wonderful TMS memories of 2005, tours to New Zealand, the Sub-Continent and the West Indies and again the *Ashes* in the Summer of 2009. I had the background and the story for *Brethren of Acadia,* the next in the **Oscar Phelps** series of international crime fiction novels.

To Henry Blofeld. (Aka **Blowers**) National Treasure & H*ero.*
To TMS...National Institution.

Long may you continue...

DBG September 2009
Niagara-on-the-Lake, ON

Critical acclaim for the previous novels of David B. Green

"You certainly know how to string words together David...I expect this'll sell well…"
- International Weekly Telegraph – London

"I think you have created a very intriguing, complex character and a highly entertaining read." – Bentley Productions, Pinewood Studios, England,
Producers of Midsomer Murders

"32-Red" is a classic crime mystery thriller with all the ingredients of the genre...containing beautiful and sensual women, explicit sex mixed with a good dose of violence and action. Oscar Phelps, reminds us of Patricia Highsmith's Mr. Ripley – so suave and perfect in every move."
– Costa del Sol News, Andalucia, Spain

"With so many twists and turns, I couldn't put the book down. And when the story was finished I really missed the characters. David Green created such a great story. Stylish, with psychological depth and insight. Insanely readable. A contemporary Ripley. Hypnotically haunting. The detail is dark and somewhat disturbing."

"I write this note on the same day that the great Nottingham author Alan Sillitoe is pronounced dead. Sillitoe of course is known for his ground-breaking novel Saturday Night & Sunday Morning, which was subsequently made into the film starring Albert Finney in 1959. I have always thought the Phelps stories to be naturally cinematic - classic Bond territory with a little anti-hero edginess thrown in for good measure."
– Papplewick Arts. Dreamtargets & Headland Media. England, UK

"The rotating cast of characters are interesting, but Phelps is truly the one who comes alive…a quick and enjoyable escape into another world."
– Vancouver News Mirror Group, Victoria, BC. Canada

"I love the characters…"
- Andrew Pearson, Screenwriter. The Nike Girl. Los Angeles, CA

"Anti-hero charms in thriller novel"
- Robin Wark, Vancouver News Press, Canada

"Good Luck with "32-Red" and with the next books as well"
— Robert B. Parker. Boston, Massachusetts. US Celebrated Author —
SPENSER Novels — Jesse Stone novels — Sunny Randall novels

"a real choice item"
— Gibraltar Chronicle, Europe

"a thoroughly absorbing and riveting read "
— Maurice Boland, OCI Radio, Marbella, Spain

Oscar Phelps: A Fictional Contradiction

"Oscar Phelps is a fictional character who has traveled the world over, not necessarily seeking murder and mystery, but they somehow always seem to find him. He is a rapscallion and anti-hero in the classic mould, the fictional centre of The Enigmatic Mr Phelps."
— Niagara Magazine, ON. Canada

"The Enigmatic Mr Phelps is fast-paced, jam-packed with mystery, violence, sex and action which take place all over the world...filled with interesting and sometimes menacing characters."
- The Standard, ON. Canada

"Oscar Phelps was usually the indefatigable host. He exuded characteristics of the suave and cynical, whilst obviously highly sophisticated and infinitely debonair. He was a combination of consummate villain and unmitigated blackguard. His appeal was indisputable."
- The Standard SPECTRUM feature Arts & Entertainment article "Dreaming Big" Ontario, Canada

"David Green is an interesting character himself..."
- The Gibraltar Chronicle, Europe

"David B. Green insists he is not the flesh and blood equivalent of his creation Oscar Phelps, the shadowy international killer at the centre of the author's reality-based thrillers The Enigmatic Mr Phelps and Brethren of Acadia. I am not so sure..."
- Bernie Dowling, WEEKENDER Reading supplement, Northern Times, Brisbane, Queensland, Australia

"The story rattles its way through several international locations and shady goings on."
- Radio Sol de Almijara, Nerja, Spain

"Phelps' escapades promise great entertainment, excitement and a truly enigmatic read..."

- H! Society Magazine, Marbella, Costa del Sol, Spain

"Oscar Phelps sounds like a Hollywood goldmine!! No wonder you are having so much interest from LA!! I actually agree with your initial thoughts for Oscar, Ralph Fiennes would be perfect..."

- S J Evans – Producer/Director Pillay-Evans Productions, Wales.

"British Author Lives out His Own Adventures"

'If you have ever taken a fancy to International Crime Fiction, David B. Green is a name you will not want to miss. David has established a place for himself in the literary world…'

- The BritishCanadian.com Vancouver, BC. Canada

"I have perused your very comprehensive and interesting stories, and admire the range of your travels and attainments. It goes without saying that I do wish you great good fortune getting Oscar into film. Merton Park holds a special place in my heart and memory, representing as it does a more innocent social period and pleasurable friendship with some fine actors. We shall not see its like again. I wish you great success and I had great fun back in the 70s promoting the Tobin novels. Very little in life compares with the joy of hearing someone tell you that your books have given them pleasure. It never ceases to amaze me that words I've put down on paper have affected people's lives. Once again, I shall keep an eye out for news of Oscar's progress."

"I think your choice of James Spader is spot on - a very good actor, good-looking enough to be likeable and attractive, yet with the quirky streak necessary to portray the sociopath that is Oscar.
Can't wait to see the film!
Two tickets, please, in the balcony.
What is more cinematically appealing than a likeable rogue?
The best of good fortune with Oscar. I'm rooting."
Stanley

- Stanley Morgan actor in the James Bond movie **Dr.No** playing the Concierge in the casino who first introduces Sean Connery as James Bond and author of the ***Russ Tobin*** series of novels and of TRANCE.

&

"David… Are you Oscar Phelps?"

- Radio Europe Mediterraneo FM, San Pedro de Alcantara, Malaga, Spain

Brethren of Acadia

The Oscar Phelps series
cover designs
by

Karen Ann Green

Front Cover Photograph by

Andrew Orth III
New Orleans, Louisiana

Courtesy of
Joseph Fein, III
Owner

The Court of Two Sisters Restaurant
613 Royal Street - French Quarter
New Orleans, Louisiana 70130

http://www.courtoftwosisters.com
+1 (504) 522-7261 United States
Fax +1 (504) 581-5804 United States

Crime Writer - David B.Green

"Brethren of Acadia"

A Second Face in February… an Oscar Phelps novel. (2010)

COMING SOON…the next in the Phelps series:

"Where King Meets Queen…" an Oscar Phelps novel. (2011)

I've always been interested in people, but I've never liked them.

– Henry James

Live all you can - it's a mistake not to.

It doesn't so much matter what you do in particular, so long as you have your life. If you haven't had that, what have you had?

Henry James, "Ambassadors", 1903

"The test of a first-rate intelligence is the ability to hold two opposed ideas … and still retain the ability to function."

- F. Scott Fitzgerald

"Crime is a protest against the environment…"

Fyodor Dostoyevsky: 'Crime & Punishment' 1866

'Never underestimate the capability of friends and family to disappoint.'… 'The only thing wrong with having hope, dreams and ambitions…is that once fulfilled, there is very little left.'

- David B. Green 2009

"Everything in writing in a sense is down to memory…in Producing it is all about connections, leveraging upon relationships and pulling in favours."

David B. Green 2009

"Achievement & Success are really just a matter of perspective… I want reality and authenticity, but I don't want to present it in a realistic way"

David B. Green 2009

"If you have a friend on whom you think you can rely, you are a Lucky Man!"
- Alan Price 1973 O Lucky Man! (Lindsay Anderson / Malcolm McDowell)

"Never underestimate the English, for they invented cricket"
- Michael Collins, Eire.

"When to the sessions of sweet silent thought, I summon up remembrance of things past, I sigh the lack of many a thing I sought, And with old woes new wail my dear time's waste."
- Shakespeare.

"The power of accurate observation is commonly called cynicism by those who have not got it."
- George Bernard Shaw

"You're maudlin and full of self-pity. You're magnificent! That I should want you at all suddenly strikes me as the height of improbability. But that in itself is probably the reason: You're an improbable person, Eve, and so am I. We have that in common. Also our contempt for humanity and inability to love and be loved, insatiable ambition, and talent. We deserve each other.

We all have abnormalities in common. We're a breed apart from the rest of humanity, we theatre folk. We are the original displaced personalities."

"The mark of a true killer: Sleep tight, rest easy, and come out fighting."
- Addison DeWitt:

"I am not one of those people who would rather act than eat. Quite the reverse. My own desire as a boy was to retire. That ambition has never changed. I don't ask questions. I just take their money and use it for things that really interest me. I was beastly but never coarse. A high-class sort of heel.
I never really thought I'd make the grade. And let's face it, I haven't."
(George)

"Oscar Phelps, much like his creator is a character profoundly antagonistic to ordinary domestic life..."
Anonymous

There is so much weariness and disappointment in travel that people have to open up — in railway trains, over a fire, on the decks of steamers, and in the palm courts of hotels on a rainy day. They have to pass the time somehow, and they can pass it only with themselves. Like the characters in Chekhov, they have no reserves — you learn the most intimate secrets. You get an impression of a world peopled by eccentrics, of odd professions, almost incredible stupidities, and, to balance them, amazing endurances. "

— Graham Greene, The Lawless Roads, 1939

"Morality comes with the sad wisdom of age, when the sense of curiosity has withered."

— Graham Greene

"Anyone who lives within their means suffers from a lack of imagination."

~ Oscar Wilde

"Writers are manipulators of the soul..."

Anonymous

In reference to the SPENSER novels;
"I make this stuff up!"

- Robert B. Parker

In reference to the PHELPS novels;
"I can't make this stuff up...I have to live it."

- David B. Green

For Karen Ann.
The center can hold, and does.
No matter what…

Brethren of Acadia
A Second Face in February...
An Oscar Phelps Novel

By David B. Green © 2010

Dedication: To Christina A. Hunter (Steen)...she kept us together when all the rest of our world was falling apart...

Synopsis

"Take that you bastard!" said Oprah, her strong little fist exploding upon my chin...

The England cricket team had just lost yet another *Ashes* series down-under.
An International cricket coach of repute, had just lost his life.
A beautiful naked blond had just plummeted to a very messy death from the balcony high atop an Oahu hotel, overlooking Waikiki beach...and *Oscar Phelps* had just received a credit to his bank account of more than $70 Million Dollars!

He remained a dear, dear boy!

The English fraudster, impresario, raconteur, wit, sociopathic killer and friend, returns in this, the third entry in the recent series of international crime fiction escapades, resident within his exciting, enticing and dangerously mythical world.

Embarked upon a global quest to track down the origin and rationale behind the multi-million dollar transfer in favour of one of his US corporate accounts, Oscar finds death at every corner and a distasteful connection to his passion for the game of international cricket and links back to his former friend and arch nemesis; the late; *Rt. Honourable Eric Armstrong-Jones.*

Manipulating events from beyond the grave.

Oscar is almost completely divorced from his former life of corporate crime. Drawing income from his investments; legitimate *below the radar* SME businesses on all continents, properties and consulting fees, dividends received from a network of associates who continue to flourish within the organizational structure designed and orchestrated by their mentor.

Continuing to benefit from a series of annual stipends and directors fees for his trouble.

Still operating effectively within the area of illicit enterprise, but not as exposed as he once was. Less of a chancer. Mellowed with age.

With his trusty associates from the earlier stories in the trilogy; *32-Red* and *Berlin by Christmas* providing unfettered support. Phelps unravels a web of deceit which takes him from the North Devon coast of England to Auckland, New Zealand. To all parts Australia, to London, the French Quarter of New Orleans and the Old Port of Montreal, before returning to Continental Europe, his favourite haunt - the city of Amsterdam - and ultimately back to *32-Red* in Nerja.

His business empire and the very fabric of his life are now threatened by previously stalwart characters on whom he once thought he could rely.

A secret society of manipulative business people - the *Brethren of Acadia* - with whom he had once enjoyed a lucrative third party strategic alliance, has now turned the tables and is actively seeking retribution.

Shadowing Oscar's every move, inflicting punishments and creating hazards to hinder his progress, demonstrating their strength of purpose and testing the *Phelps* resilience as he traverses the globe in search of answers, solutions and ultimately revenge.

Oscar must go to greater lengths than ever before to protect his interests, his associates, his reputation and the noble game.

His veneer of respectability, his resolve, his fortitude and his loyalty endear, but are tested to the full as obstacles are faced head on, threats carried through and barriers to decorum and fair play established. People it soon becomes clear...will just have to be made and seen to be accountable.

Despite their contrition. Some will inevitably have to die.

Fast-paced, crammed with intrigue, violence, explicit sex and an intensifying & refreshing eccentric honesty, this leads often to the characters of menace evolving to become an ensemble of people for whom you will wish to cheer.

The consummate villain, beguiler and unmitigated blackguard. All represent the Enigma that is...*Oscar Phelps*. Often haunting, dark and disturbing. His appeal is indisputable...

Contents

...Passion of the Talented. Envy of the Underground. Murder in the Game.

...relentlessly moving towards the date with death that would rock his world.

...It's better to be a fake somebody than a real nobody.

...In a story this treacherous, what a good man needs is a diversion.

... *Brethren of Acadia*; **Murder, intrigue and fabulous twists in both time and tale.**

Dedicated in Memoriam
to Robert B. Parker

"I have two great vices - writing and gambling. Writing enriches the soul; gambling depletes the bank account."

- Anonymous

"I watched him. He ignored the traffic lights, walked diagonally across the wide wet road, then ran after a bus and leapt safely on to its empty platform. And I with my books have not seen him since. It was like saying goodbye to a big part of me, forever."

- the Decline and Fall of Frankie Buller, Alan Sillitoe

"Murder is the bloodiest of the creative arts,"

- Robert B. Parker – extract from Walking Shadow 1994

Prologue

PROLOGUE

Yesterday was a foreign country…and Oscar didn't live there any more.

It had taken thirty five years to realize, but his most persistent obsession had been that it took great courage to move forward and take risks in life, whereas the truth was in actuality, quite the opposite. His obsession had been a sham. An exhaustive, painful and excessive sham. The real courage was in standing-still. In accepting your lot. In having the courage to not only face it, but to survive it. To endure.

To accept this was a real trial and tore at his very fibre. But deep down, Oscar knew it to be true. It so riled. Perhaps risk didn't reap reward? Either way, it was much too late now.

He had long since been accused by friend and foe alike of always looking to make good an escape from the world in a constant search for something more. Something better. Something of greater value. Something different! Unconventional.

At this point in his life, Oscar had reconciled that it was not the seeking that was important. It was the being.

The air was always damp and cold at this evening hour.

Everything about this place was thoroughly miserable. Dank. Desolate. Wretched. Sad.

If environment really did shape expectation, then at this place there was quite literally, no hope!

Capstone Hill, Illfracombe, North Devon, England. Oscar's thoughts turned to matters Bostonian.

Funny how those so anxious to preserve their good name, usually deserve the worst reputation. Supplicants.

Oscar was at the summit of the hill, stood in the oppressive damp and enshrouded by the harsh bitter cold late January wind, right between the Union Flag and the memorial to Ekaterine Frolov (Kate), who had fallen tragically to her death at nearby Hillsborough Head these five years or more ago.

Way down deep below, he could hear the heavy swollen waves of the cruel and heavily foreboding sea periodically crashing and eroding harshly on to the mass of hideously deformed rocks that littered the area like a series of carefully formed giant troglodytes holding guard at the base of the landmark. The waves were seemingly uniform in relentless pursuit of their quest to swell into the natural bays and swathe with white wash before dispersing for another attempt at an assault on the natural devonish coastline.

Oscar had on his Shark Black & Citrus Bollé goggles with the double polycarbonate lens. He was also protected from the wind by his Canadian Harricana Sport Aviator brown leather Musquash hat.

As he peered down in a panoramic sweep, in the distance through the rose-red lens and on to what he knew were the gray hotels, gray houses, gray church, gray Landmark Theatre lay down deep to his right on Wilder Road, gray skies, he could see only emptiness and despair. He could taste the despondency. Smell the desperation. The place, the people, the sense of being and of usefulness had been exhausted, spent out during the Thatcherite years. All that was left were the remnants of a bygone age, which had faded into memory and decay along with the remainder of what Oscar had romantically perceived to be…his England.

This sweet festering cesspool.

This England had become the polar opposite of the image of the stereotype so typified by the jingoistic Cool Britannia symbolism depicted in the movies of the early new millennium. Of New Labour. Of a country living in a state of Multi-National and tribal harmony, of no racial divide and sympathetic to all matters of ethnicity. Which deep down everyone knew as being an absolute myth, though few would have the guts to acknowledge as such. A corruption. A joke and a dangerous one at that. Neither clever, private nor appealing. Movies which at first had both attracted and intrigued Oscar and then with the starkness of a cold wet, deeply biting reality, had served only to repel. Confirming his suspicions. It had become a very sad enlightenment, but not completely unexpected. It made him feel like weeping.

His thoughts drifted to the old maxim proffered by the late Neville Cardus. That... 'if everything about England was destroyed except for the laws of cricket, then life in this country could be recreated.' Oscar now doubted the validity of this assertion, though it hurt him to do so.

England had degenerated in to a system run by amoral and chilling men and women who appeared to have amalgamated both in significance and indeed gender. Perplexing. Perfect manners had long since departed, as had decorum, exploration, imagination, adventure and wit. Each person encountered had so lost any kind of basic humanity, not to mention idealism or joy.

Business organizations, Oscar had discovered to his frustration, engaged in a series of ritualistic gatherings in anonymous conference rooms or endured an almost endless and meaningless roundelay of witless, joyless and witheringly, caustically charged dinners and webinars. It was a world of cramped, monotone impersonal decor, generally sucked in by shadows, so that you cannot even be sure of what you see.

A world of men who had collectively risen to become over the years, a virtually paralyzed, blubbing cloud of eponymous and ridiculously vacuous outcasts in the making. Populating an infinitely drab world where life, vigor and colour had seeped away, or simply went by un-noticed. Where jokes are unsophisticated, bitter and grim. Where the 'in conference' notifications discharged by voice messaging systems ultimately signaled a wider, more fundamental malaise.

This was Oscar's idea of hell. You see all the people you thought were dead and all the people who deserve to be dead and after a while, you start to think that you might be dead, too.

Part 1

Anatomy of the Talented

Chapter One

There had been an abdication of responsibility. It had been subtle, though distinct.

Much pressure had been brought to bear as a result. It had not escaped Oscar and his associates.

Down, deep in the ever darkening distance, Oscar could hear the sound of shutters being rolled down to cover the rows of terraced plate glass showcase shop-front windows and make them secure from both vandals and the elements, both of which at night appeared that much fiercer. It was almost the last thing he had grown accustomed to hearing each day at this time. He listened instinctively for the comfort it would bring him. The reassurance. The surety. The security held in boredom. In sterility.

The slow rattle of the engine from the truck that moved off with apparent reluctance from the curbside next to the now closed *Maddy's Chippy* fish & chip shop. Driver having tooled up with the fruits of the briny, consoled no doubt by the hot food housed within the heavily vinegared golden brown package held, was a constant, as was the belching cloud of black diesel released from the exhaust pipe as it left St. James Place in its wake.

He saw her white coat flap open in the distance as she turned the corner and approached the telephone box across the road from the low stone walled church yard. Oscar wondered if she had been engaged in an embrace, delivering a long and hard, deep, flickering-tongue probing, bottom fondling farewell to her boyfriend. He wondered if the boyfriend had deserved it?

Everyone deserved a modicum of pleasure.

Then the taxi with a rear break light out, drove off with a lurch in the direction of the small harbour nestled over to Oscar's left. Footsteps pervaded now from heavy hob-nailed boots. It was time to move on.

Meanwhile, in a very Northern European heraldic city, Helene Kvakheim was waiting along with her girl friends for supper to be served; Ariana Danielli, Dalia Lundberg, Veronica DeMarco, Babet Dubuclet and Mrs. Hillary Robinson in attendance, were ravenous.

They were seated and were becoming quite loud, raucous and animated, at a long corner table at the Potetkjelleren Restaurant in Bergen, Norway, located just off the main Vågen harbour up on Kong Oscars Gate.

The Potetkjelleren had a warm and cozy cellar atmosphere as befitting a restaurant found below ground - in an actual cellar. A potato cellar.

The ladies had perused the menu and in the main went for selections favoured by the Vikings. There was nothing about the concept of the VIKING that Hillary Robinson didn't like.

Her fire had been ignited.

Meals containing oysters, mussels and sometimes with mutton, cheese, cabbage, apples, onions, berries and nuts were evidenced. While Helene had ordered moules avec frites, her friends had opted for either reindeer or whale, which were house specialties. Hillary, not surprisingly, had gone for the whale.

When it surfaced, which was often, Helene had an unfortunate laugh; capable of bringing down a fleet of small light aircraft at some distance…the dinner would be a good one.

The all night lesbifest planned to take place in Hillary's suite at the Clarion Collection hotel would be even better and in all probability take significantly longer to conclude.

The peel of the bells were soon to ring out from the close-by Korskirken, 17th century church…

Ariana Danielli knew of course that they would also be soon to relent. It was not a happy thought.

Oscar had taken to carrying in the left side pocket of his charcoal chinos, a red handkerchief of cotton, complete with a small embroidered cross of St. George in one corner. He carried it habitually, for the 'Luck' that it would bring him.

He had long since recognized the inevitability of it all. That in his life and relationships, there would always be a time when those closest to him would see their feelings toward him turn to stark hatred. He would be ostracized and castigated by the people he loved and held dearest. A precedent had been set. Poor Eric.

In his rapidly approaching dotage, it was something that had become somewhat troubling. Try as he may, he could never quite find just cause. It made Oscar sad. Morose even.

Oscar had recently, while back in Niagara, ventured through the cemetery at St Marks, the bastion of the Rev. Jephcott Proudfoot-Wason and found immediately to the right of the Carnathan-Baur crypt, a young lady dressed all in gray. She was laid prostrate and was completely ignorant to his presence. She had a small paperback book laid open at her fingertips nestled on the ground and her eyes were closed as she listened intently to her headphones... Oscar had moved a little closer. The book was a guide to North Devonshire mysteries...

To England; where the vernacular of the populous had crassly degenerated to that of the east end barrow boy. Oscar had found it appalling! Depressing. What had happened? People had learned to be happy with and accept so little from life. They appeared to esteem their lives so cheaply. Contentment in mediocrity.

As Oscar moved steadily down the unforgivingly steep serpentining pathway to the main road next to the Landmark theatre, the cut of the wind began to diminish.

It was replaced however by something much more menacing. Something that would prove to be altogether something else. Altogether something very sinister and something very terminal. Oscar found himself lapsing into invisibility and of no consequence as he moved through the narrow streets back towards the harbour. Things had gone wrong, more often than he could accept. Life had become for Oscar, one long and lovely suicide and he was not sorry that it had. There had been so many contingencies. So much angst. So much grace.

He had contemplated that there was no time quite so remote, as the recent past.

As with the Brethren of Acadia and the guest's of the Queen's Royal hotel in Niagara… the guest who never arrives, seemingly, is always welcomed back. Oscar's thoughts drifted back to the poignance of his first love.

He was ready for whatever lay ahead.

Chapter Two

Reuters Newswire: February 20th 200X; Oscar Phelps former friend and business associate of the Rt. Hon Eric Armstrong-Jones KBE, reported 'found dead' in the early dispatches of the Boston Herald.

Era es verdad.

His body had been discovered in the cold dark early morning by an ICS bicycle courier who was taking a short cut through the Public Garden in Boston. He had been found fully clothed and rigid in elegant and expensive gentleman's winter attire by Barbour. He had on a full length Drovers-cut long length wax cotton Stockman coat in golden brown, He was seated upright on a bench (ironically) and carried as identification a drivers permit issued curiously in Louisiana which had been folded in to an old receipt from the Le Pavillon hotel of Poydras street in New Orleans, and which had been further secreted within the pages of an old paperback book which was heavily soiled with a solution of tar and was lay flat at his side. His shirt was made by Turnbull & Asser, his heavy silk tie was broad and dark blue with logo by R. M. Williams, Australia (the Bush Outfitter), his black cotton socks by Rodd & Gunn, black trousers by Eddie Bauer and he sported Edward Green shoes. Excepting the tie, they were all mainly products of the Old England department store in Paris. A store Oscar was known to patronize.

The novel was called 'Red Lights' by Georges Simenon and a stamp on the inside front cover indicated that it had been the property of the Nerja Bookshop in Spain and the Illfracombe public library.

It was past due...

Chapter Three

After having given the matter some real and extended consideration and very serious thought, his conclusion though drastic was inevitably the only viable recourse. At the very least, it would buy him some time and allow Hillary and Trent to complete their various missions under marginally less scrutiny.

Staging his own death was the correct decision.

While it would make the required journey down-under a little more difficult to manage, it was doable and while he found it a bore, the rewards from the risk involved where clear in his mind. It had to be this way.

Relatively speaking...He was in the pink!

Trent Alexis was seated at the bulkhead in an aisle seat in row 1 (front); seat D of the 7.01am WESTJET flight en route from Toronto to Vancouver. The flight was 45 minutes into its journey. They were approaching 37,579 feet and had a cruising velocity of MPH541.

The route was taking them across the US, high above Traverse City in Michigan, before swinging back north into Canada at the far western North Dakota/Montana border.

Trent was bloody annoyed. He had things to do. They wouldn't be pleasant.

The WESTJET flight attendant seated opposite, slightly forward and to the left of Trent, who had been strapped in for take-off in the cabin seat adjacent the main entry door to the aircraft had caught his attention. She wore a short jacket of turquoise with logo positioned just above her left breast, a white blouse with an ornate frill at the neck, a partially zipped up black cardigan and long dark pants which looked good and pulled tight when she crossed her legs. Her auburn hair was pulled back into a short ponytail and she had a high tapering forehead and large eyes of green. Her face was almost Egyptian looking, but not quite and her complexion was olive and unblemished. Her eyebrows were sleek and somewhat sculptured. She had taken care and had made a nice job. She perhaps had applied a little too much mascara to her lashes, which were long. She looked as though she had recently applied a good moisturizer. She wore wide black oblong-rimmed eyeglasses, which gave her a certain distinction. She had dainty pink earlobes protruding just below here hair, which held small diamond stud earrings. They looked inexpensive. She had large, though even white teeth and her smile, when occasioned, served to brighten the day. She was prim. She carried a certain sex appeal. She was eating a green apple. Trent sat back into the four and a half hour flight, closed his eyes and started to mentally undress her.

Chapter Four

It was bloody cold and the Court House in Niagara on the Lake was open at its side door entrance and waiting for the ambulance which was expected imminently. The punters at the Olde Angel Inn, circa 1816, had gathered outside the front door to see what had caused the commotion across the street. The skies were dark yet somewhat obscured and showed few signs of the appearance of a star. The air was chill and as Oscar stood in the shadows of the car park, stogie in hand, he could see his breath first extend, then hold and finally dissipate in front of him as he waited along with the now massing crowd to see if the fall to the bottom of the stairwell had been enough? Her neck had looked twisted and broken and certainly she had not been moving as her body lay skewed and prone, sprawled upside down along the final decline of the last few steps. Her facial expression had not held any promise. It had hardly been a very Dostoyevsky-like executed solution, was Oscar's thought. He hadn't broken into even a tremble, let alone a cold sweat. The whole episode, short as it was, was completely devoid of panic, anxiety or confusion.

She had annoyingly given him a quite dreadful laugh, almost a guffaw, which disclosed villainous yellowing teeth as she had been speaking and she displayed an altogether childish lilt which was unseemly. Her mouth had been slack right before the event, then as Oscar had gone about his business, her eyes had screwed up and her brow had become furrowed, betraying a violent and nauseating pain.

Still, Oscar justified in his own mind... if it meant one less car in the street, one less voyeur in a gallery and just that little less noise for all to suffer, then all was well.

The music from the wedding party one flight above the scene was still banging out relentlessly with vigour and showed no sign that it would be abated.

Oscar was thinking back to the Oscar Wilde line with amusement as the ambulance, lights flashing and siren sounding turned the corner from Queen Street and swung a hard left bypassing the Olde Angel.

"Sausages and women…if one is to enjoy them both, one ought never to see either in preparation".

The ambulance pulled in hard, crackling on to the apron next to the car park designation and the doors swung open in silence and the two paramedics, a man and a woman came to the rear of the vehicle with haste. The entrance to the Court House theatre stood grand a few metres away. The two white wooden entrance doors were pulled outwards to fully open by inquisitive bystanders looking to help and the impressive stone portico that lead to the entrance of the building, the staircase and the elevator, extended as a small colonnade with a flat roof supported by two rounded columns, which was structured over the short walkway and was ready to bid them entry.

Oscar stood slightly round shouldered and head bowed. His cigar, a MonteCristo 'Edmundo', hecho en Habana, Cuba, fell to the hard ground and bounced somewhat, scattering a few embers before dying.

We are all racing towards death was Oscar's conclusion and no matter how many great, intellectual conclusions and discoveries we draw during our lives, we know that they're all just man-made, like God.

Oscar began to wonder where it all might lead? But concluded that you can do very little except do what you can do, as best you know how. In this he drew some comfort. Profound.

He found his thoughts drifting to "32-Red", to his precipice, to his friends and to things Mediterranean. It was a form of catharsis.

He was distracted by events unfolding in New Orleans and further south in Buenos Aires, which were not as they should be. He then began to visualize a waterfront hotel on Victoria Road in Devonport, a short 10 minute ferry ride courtesy of Fullers, from Auckland harbour on it way to Rangitoto Island in the Hauraki Gulf of New Zealand. The old world charm and Edwardian architectural and the alluring ambience of The Esplanade Hotel, was beginning to pull at Oscar from afar. Perhaps he would venture south, but first he must attend to matters in Memphis, Tennessee, where a young paralegal had discovered, nay stumbled over, items of a nature that could only serve to annoy and frustrate.

It was time to reacquaint himself with the hotel which had spawned years earlier, an altogether entertaining encounter with the now long deceased nemesis; "Buffalo" Bertram Keelan. He of the Peabody Duck tie. The Peabody Ducks being five North American mallards - one drake with white collar and green head, and four hens with less colorful plumage. They had become a tradition. Somehow, that seemed very apt.

This was going to be a difficult one.

Oscar had never seen life as simply an exercise in survival. That was something for other people. His idea of survival revolved around getting by each November 11th armistice day ceremony in the Olde Town, unscathed by the attempts at local tradition and occasionally upon his life. He so loved and looked forward to his Remembrance Day anniversaries. They served as the launch pad in to another year of promise, discovery and adventure. Oscar had long since considered that there was more to being a great man... than simply the willingness to commit and get away with a crime.

Oscar began the next morning with a determined optimism. He awoke early and dressed in old but still stylish comfortable clothes – after taking in his suite, a pot of delicious 'Seattle's Best' coffee and sweet morning rolls. He had taken his first cup black to wake himself up – he then made his way through the narrow corridors passing by the Vintages Wine Bar and Lounge and in to the main reception area of the Pillar and Post Inn. It was just after 7.35am and the broadsheet newspapers, the Globe and Mail, the Financial Post, were already on the rack and the fireplace was generating heat.

To his left taking pride of place on the wall next to the men's room was a photograph of the Queen, strolling through the very same corridors some years earlier. This somehow seemed inappropriate.

Time for a sojourn.

Oscar had chosen eight o'clock in the morning as the time for his promenade down King Street before turning left through and on to a wintery Queen Street, simply because it was his favorite time of day in Niagara. He loved the quality of the crisp morning cold, the sprinkling of layered snow and ice and the invasive sunshine that made him squint. He had grown to love the sounds that began and made the day's activity.

Early traffic in the street, doors opening and closing, sidewalks being scraped and hosed down with hot water by industrious town workers with their red liveried trucks parked nearby and displaying in near silence a keen sense of sobriety. The increasing footfalls on the sidewalk, which steadily increased in volume as the day commenced, the filling up of the parking bays with good and close access to shops, which would lead in quick time to the inevitable encounters with the 'Parking Nazis' who patrolled the town with vigilance post Ice Wine Festival and Winterfest seasons..

As he peered into the window of the "Because I'm Worth it" store located almost opposite the Royal George theatre at 80, Queen, looking at a shaving cream by the 'Art of Shaving' company, he caught in the storefront window's reflection the image of buxomish young blond girl with tight firm flesh who appeared somewhat underdressed for the season. She had brawny limbs and her hair was disheveled as if she had been engaged in a battle. As she lifted her arms to smooth down her tresses she turned slightly to reveal enormous milky white breasts the shape of huge industrial light bulbs which clearly sought liberation from the loose fitting garment in which she was scantily clad.

Oscar observed that she was young, not many years past twenty, quite tall and slim but surprisingly curvaceous, pretty, nervous, ghostly pale in complexion and cold. Her dress which had a Calvin Klein signature label was peppered with wet icy sludge and as she became aware of Oscar, she instinctively closed her arms across her breasts.

The ingénue was staring at Oscar, almost despairingly. She took out a white handkerchief and wiped her nose and eyes, twisting her hands and tugging at her fingers in what was fast becoming a paroxysm of anxiety.

She frowned once more and then after a moment, she smiled, quite invitingly with large blue inquisitive eyes and pulled over her head a tightly hand woven knitted lime green toque and hurried along the street in the direction of Simcoe Park. It had been an unnerving smile which served to cause Oscar concern.

He had lapsed in to a state of mind with which he had grown familiar. Like he was in a daze. Conscious of his surrounds and circumstances and indeed the history, but without attaching any real significance to it. Without making an effort to place people or things in time or space. It was a quandary.

"An artist is a fellow who can hold two fundamentally opposing views and still function…"

A man can never truly love, until he has despised himself completely and Oscar had known love, known love so very true and so complete.

Chapter Five

Hillary had arrived into Bergen a matter of a few days earlier. She was expanding her network into Scandinavia at Oscar's behest. She had found this city of the Viking to be a little bit of a Noah's Ark.

A gathering ground for everything that lived and breathed. A veritable cornucopia of an opportunity for matters sexual and of commerce. Her first impression was that it was a place apart. Neither horrid nor tawdry. Stimulating. Invigorating in fact. A place that warranted a hasty visit to the bathroom and a brief encounter with a new toy...

Vågen had embraced people from all corners of the world. Germany, Holland, Britain, the Americas. Seamen, traders, craftsmen, artisans, writers, poets and entrepreneurs. Hillary was open to having sex with all of them. She showed little prejudice and did not discriminate. It was, as she approached middle age, one of her more defining, consistent and redeeming qualities.

Bergen, the capital of fjord country. Open to all. Mrs. Robinson would take advantage and learn all she could about the lovely Ariana, her confidante the vivacious though disturbingly secretive Babet and the relationship with the Doctor in Argentina. It was good for her to have a purpose. Oscar would like her for it, which pleased her.

Babet Dubuclet, B.Sc. (Agr.) LL.B Barrister & Solicitor, had recently served 66 days in jail and was on 3 years criminal probation. She was a lawyer who had practiced in the region of Upper Canada since being called to the bar in 1995. She had fled Haiti as a child with her family from Dictator François Duvalier's regime in 1968. Her Grandfather, from whom she was estranged for many years, was a philosopher who had been tortured under Papa Doc Duvalier's regime.

Her Father went in a completely different direction; exiled from Haiti to Barbados and later Jamaica where he became involved in sports and did whatever he could to support his daughter's habits.

She had lived in New Orleans's before settling further north in Canada.

She was allowed to continue unsupervised, the practice of law while on probation. She was to face further LSUC corporation charges and charges relating to a sexual personal relationship with a clients spouse. She was also under investigation for excessive billing, having had an action filed against her and her firm for legal bill of $25,000 which had escalated to $223,000

She had needed this distraction in Norway.

The spouse she had shared impropriety with was Dr Carlos Leonardo Tagliapietra of Buenos Aires, Argentina. She was the perfect mark.

Chapter Six

I

As the aircraft was preparing to land in Vancouver BC, easing into its final descent and circling the city and the sea, Trent Alexis was reading the Globe & Mail and catching up on the latest developments in a story which covered a Politician suspected as being behind a murder in Russia.

Anna Politkovskaya had been shot dead on her doorstep.
It was a name with which Trent was familiar.

The article said;
"The murder of Russian journalist Anna Politkovskaya was ordered by a Russian politician", a defence lawyer has said.

Murad Musayev was representing four men charged over Ms Politkovskaya's murder at a trial in Moscow, which had now been re-opened to the public. Mr. Musayev had told reporters that the unnamed politician, based in Russia, was mentioned in the case files.

"Ms Politkovskaya, a leading critic of Russia's policies in Chechnya, was shot dead outside her Moscow house in 2006.

Ms Politkovskaya's supporters believe state security agents were involved in her murder - and for that reason, they say, there will never be a fair trial at Moscow's military court." was the general contention.

It was indeed a shame. Trent remembered vaguely a dalliance with this woman which he had been encouraged to forget.

Trent believed that all of his life, what he was unconsciously doing was struggling against respectability. Perhaps Anna had suffered similarly?

That was his bête noire, his raison d'être or whatever the fuck you call it.

He put down the newspaper on the empty seat beside him and picked up the book that Oscar had recommended he read.

'NOBLE HOUSE' by James Clavell.

Trent had read the first five chapters with difficulty, but at least the effort had been made. Which is what he would tell Oscar when next they were to meet and break bread. The story was somewhat beyond his limited capacity for managing intricate detail and not greatly compelling. He didn't have a clue what was going on and he didn't like Hong Kong pre or post 1997. He saw the recommendation as possibly a private joke. The best kind, as he had been taught.

With a bump, the plane landed. Trent deplaned without incident.

His mission he knew would be a potentially dangerous one. He was en route to a rendezvous with Oscar at Le Pavillon hotel in New Orleans via first Victoria on Vancouver Island and then Carefree and Cave Creek near Phoenix, Arizona. Trent had become the veritable world traveler.

As he walked through the main airport terminal building after collecting his luggage at the small section of carousel, he heard at the taxi stand the tones of a song which appeared familiar, but he did not know why. He did not know from where it came. It bothered him.

It was a strange song and not in the usual Alexis mode when it came to favorites. But it somehow intrigued and in a vexing way was somewhat haunting.

Trent listened intently as he waited in line. The melody lurched and there were trumpets and string instruments in support, but the vocals were the key to its resilience.

…A Sunday smile you wore it for a while.
A Sunday mile we paused and sang.
A Sunday smile you wore it for a while.
A Sunday mile we paused and sang…

As Trent took his seat in the heavily promotional Vancouver 2010 liveried taxi, bound for the main harbour float plane terminal, the sound petered away. Trent still could not trace the origin. His door slammed shut and he was speeded off in his continued task slightly more in hesitant and cautious mood.

At the small terminal for West Coast Air, Trent alighted and made his way in to the main scallop architecture designed seaport - departures building. He did so quickly as it was beginning to rain.

An hour later, Trent was taking off rather noisily and abruptly from the surface of an increasingly rough Pacific ocean in Vancouver's inner harbour, in a small white and yellow single wing float plane bound for Victoria harbour. The aircraft appeared resolute but the shaking and violent vibration that ensued at take off was a little uncomfortable for Trent who grimaced and held on to the seat arms for dear life, his knuckles visibly whitening. The pre-flight briefing and safety address had been given competently by a young man whom Trent initially believed to be the chief steward, who had at the end of the speech suddenly turned around in his seat, affixed his captain's hat and made ready for take-off. After the customary radio checks and the signing off of documents on a clipboard, both pilots interlocked right and left hands, holding down the lever in the high front console of the plane which appeared to govern the actual flying of the plane. This was worrying.

Trent decided that if this was to be 'it'. Then sobeit. He had little choice but to put his faith along with that of his fellow four passengers in the two kid's at the front who at the requisite altitude swung a hard left and leveled off and then clipped on what Trent assumed was the auto pilot. They then began the process of deciding who would have which sandwiches!

Trent looked over at the well dressed and obviously moneyed old lady occupying the seat directly behind the kid captain. She appeared in some kind of trance. No doubt she was one of the "tweed curtain" set that Oscar had told Trent about who populated the Oak Bay area of the former nation's capital. He then looked out of the window, could see very little because of the clouds which they were just about breaching.

It began to get very cold.

For the comfort that it would bring him, he opened up the complimentary oatmeal raisin cookie that he had been given on entering the plane. It was very good. He then cast his attention to the Times Colonist newspaper. Nothing in about the Russian…

II

Trent exited the floatplane with palpable relief. It was still raining at the Victoria harbour dock and he was going to get wet. He brushed aside the offer of an umbrella and made his way quickly up the white floating deck and in to the arrivals building, which was little more than a prefabricated hut with a nice coat of paint. His luggage delivered, he walked out of the building, across the car park and up the short incline to the main road. The rain was relenting.

Across the road was the magnificent Fairmont Empress hotel. It was impressive. To his far right over past the main harbour was the Governmental Parliamentary building, again impressive.

To his left he could see in the not too far distance a hostelry.

It was a Milestones restaurant. He made this his destination.

Suitably refreshed after a jigger or two of Black Bushmills Irish whiskey and a plate of fries, well cooked prime rib and onion rings he was ready to get things done. It was almost mid-day and the sun was making an appearance.

Trent paid the bill, passed by the gold covered real-life statue performance artist who was positioned outside of Milestones waiting to be rewarded for standing still by a milling crowd and made his way over the level crossing on the 'Don't Walk' instruction in the direction of the 'Empress'. Trent was feeling indestructible.

Luggage stored with the bellman, he then asked for and was given the directions he required at the concierge desk and was on his way, direction Beacon Hill Park.

III

Trent strolled to the entrance to the park and stopped only when reaching the petting zoo. He crossed the road and walked with purpose through the putting green and looked over at the stretch of water that was the 'Juan de Fuca' straight. There was an Alaskan cruise ship preparing to dock. He navigated his way passing by children playing with Frisbees and baseball catcher's mitts and balls and couples courting, some quite passionately.

At just before 12.40pm he could see the basin that was home to Victoria Cricket Club. It was edged by trees around its oval boundary and was a very picturesque setting. It was just as Oscar had described.

To the far end of the ground was stood a Pavilion. It was aged and had character and for Canada was a little out of place and time. An anachronism.

Not knowing or caring about the etiquette of cricket, Trent marched resolutely across the field which was a little damp and slippy underfoot from the rain and strode past the middle and the main cut wicket which was roped off. At the entrance to the pavilion he stopped, looked around and caught sight of a middle aged man in cricket whites and a very nubile scantily clad younger lady engaged in a passionate sexual grope which looked consensual. They were in an office of some kind and she was being straddled on a desk and both of them appeared oblivious to Trent's presence. Engrossed in their own particular quest.

Their own particular sport.

Before moving further on into the building he witnessed the scene become even more debauched, as the girl exposed her nipples for sucking and began a very enthusiastic genital massage on the man. Trent had little time for this. It was an extraordinary though not remarkable and did not warrant further distraction.

He walked up the staircase to the first floor and studied the second of the four available closed doors leading off from the main landing. It was marked 'Club President'. He placed his ear to the door and listened.

…A Sunday smile you wore it for a while.
A Sunday mile we paused and sang.
A Sunday smile you wore it for a while.
A Sunday mile we paused and sang.
A Sunday smile and we felt true. (and)…

A moment passed and Trent used it quickly to consider his options.

He entered.

Chapter Seven

While it was a distinct come-down in terms of class, the Vertigo restaurant at the summit of the Mercure Hotel in Auckland held an appeal. It was a little like the personality of a typical North American to Oscar. Completely devoid of any manners, common courtesy and good grace, but still with an amusing appeal. A certain resilience...

Arriving after an exhaustive flight in via a San Francisco stop-over, Oscar had summoned his might and forced his senses to react to the stark contrast of night and began to walk the few meters across the apron from where his cab alighted and through the revolving doors in to the foyer of the hotel. It was quiet, dimly lit and sparsely populated. The reception desk in the far left hand corner was long, heavy, brown and expansive. It was unmanned. Oscar looked at his TAG. It was 5.49am and Auckland was at slumber.

Oscar made for the desk and as he arrived was met by a night porter who emerged from behind a door marked STAFF and who had obviously been busied in some pursuit or other, (if the annoyance etched upon his face gave good indication), the nature of which did not either concern or disturb one Oscar Phelps.

Oscar was hungry. He completed the registration formalities but could not at that hour be allocated a room. "Not until 10am" he was advised, could this be done. Oscar took the news pragmatically but was still bloody annoyed as he contemplated what could be done with the next four hours?

The clock on the wall behind the porter said it was now two minutes before 6am. The other clocks positioned along side showed the appropriate times in London, Paris, Athens, Sydney, Tokyo, Dubai, Los Angeles and New York. How Oscar wished he were in Paris at the Scribe or even Athens at the Grand

Bretagne. It was a forlorn hope. The porter had however responded positively when asked at what hour breakfast would begin. It was imminent.

Oscar approached the elevators as it was almost 6am.

The bank of elevators to his immediate right could be activated by depressing a button which Oscar duly did…Nothing! Oscar looked back at the porter who was stowing the Phelps luggage and showed little in terms of encouragement. Oscar tried again. He could hear something mechanical start to engage. A few short moments later Oscar was the sole occupant of the lift on its way to the top floor of the hotel. A bell rang, the doors opened and Oscar was out and turning immediately right in the direction of the familiar aroma which was wafting its way toward him.

The Vertigo Restaurant and Bar was again dimly lit, but held a certain cache. Welcoming. It offered panoramic views to Oscar's left of the city straight down on to Customs Street and protruding high into the night sky, the Sky Tower, which was lit in what appeared to be blue and white. Over to the right there was Waitemata Harbour. The early hour did not diminish the appeal of this small city and Oscar made his way quickly toward the bar which looked well stocked though closed. It also served as the restaurant reception.

To his surprise a few people were already seated both at the window seats to his left and also in the main restaurant seating area. As he took his seat at the allotted table, he surveyed the many large silver domes, mounted on functionary serving trestles with hot lamps overhead, under which the many and various selections of food were gathered and presented. Hot dishes, cold cuts, various assorted pastries and a bank of fruit juice selections. A host of differing flavours of coffee and hot water for the boil in the bag hot chocolate, which was own branded to the hotel.

It looked and smelled very inviting. As he got up to charge his glass with an orange juice, stir some prunes, select his sausages, poached eggs, bacon, stewed and button mushrooms, bagel, English muffin, toast, plum tomatoes and baked beans and then finally de-bag his hot chocolate, his attention was caught by the occupant of the table in the far left hand corner of the room overlooking the harbour.

It was a familiar and completely unexpected face staring back at him. Oscar took to his seat slowly and deliberately, though never taking his eyes from the lady in question. Shocks are so much better absorbed with the knees bent he had grown to realize.

Antoaneta Chiankova. A Russian. A second face in February.

"I come undone…" Oscar whispered to himself.

Outside, the first strains of daylight began to emerge and cast down on to Shortland Street.

Chapter Eight

Following the breakfast, Antoaneta casually strode over to Oscar's table and asked if he would join her later on in the day. She had something of importance to discuss.

Oscar acquiesced though with a slight hesitancy.

They agreed to meet at the Victoria Park Market Hall of Fame, just up and by the Sky City Casino adjacent the Tower and down on to Fanshawe Street. Difficult to miss.

Jet-lag had set in. It was just after 5pm local time when Oscar awoke according to his TAG. It was already dark outside. He had missed the daytime. His head was heavy and his eyes strained to focus. He dowsed his face in the cold New Zealand water which sprayed soft from the tap. He was trying to remember his last encounter with this Russian woman. None had been particularly striking for creating memories joyous, but when was the most recent? He considered for a moment.

There had been one particular episode of note, in the Four Points hotel in Darling Harbour, Sydney in January of the previous year. The occasion had been the Sydney International ladies tennis tournament and the competitors, save for Sharapova and Clijsters, had been resident in this hotel for the week. Oscar's hotel. He recollected how he had stumbled upon Antoaneta in a compromising position in the grey padded service elevator cell late one evening with a very well known and extremely lithe and vivacious tennis celebrity from Serbia. Oscar thought that this may have been the last time they had crossed paths? The question was, why was she here now and what did she want?

Chapter Nine

There were times in Hillary Robinson's highly volatile and debauched life that her association with Oscar Phelps drew into question whether or not she would have been better off simply having the baby and not taking the money when he had offered it. She often damned the Doctor in Boston for being so convenient and efficient. She also hated the spin of the roulette wheel which had not been kind. There were times when she hated Oscar Phelps and what he had done to her, her friends and her life. Now was not one of these times.

Over the years she had grown to bear the loss of Francesca Luciana, of Enrique de Chesaris and even the initially so detested Lori Kasabian. She sometimes yearned for the early days under the stewardship of

The Rt.Honourable Eric which had served to so exhilarate and then the ultimate betrayal that so hurt her, even more so she thought than it did Oscar Phelps.

Hillary left her suite #516 at the Clarion Collection hotel on Havinekontoret, Slottsgaten 1, with the mark; Babet Dubuclet following on behind in a few days. They had agreed a rendezvous which would be at or nearby the office of Kasper Lundquist in New York at 555, Fifth Avenue.

Hillary had other meetings to conduct, at Rockefeller Plaza near the ice rink and opposite the Sheraton on 7th at the Rosie O'Grady's restaurant before going on to Le Pavillon in New Orleans… She also had a luncheon appointment at the library Bar of the Royal York hotel in Toronto where she had promised herself a Cobb salad in a big white earthenware bowl which would be slanted toward the guest and would be delicious with blue cheese dressing. Hillary expected everything to be just so.

Hillary was now, after 70 minutes in flight, at Schiphol in Amsterdam at the Voyager restaurant inside the Sheraton Schiphol hotel contemplating having a light brunch. She decided against it.

Instead, a 35 minute taxi ride later she was eating a cheese & ham *toastie* with salad julienne positioned on a large white oval plate in the café bar of the Americain hotel at Leidsekade 97 opposite the Leidseplein. As she looked out of the windows she could see workmen busy in renovating the City Cinerama, where she had once given 'head' to Oscar. Happy Days. She was also fascinated by the red & white trams. They had been all yellow on her previous visits,

The Amsterdam Americain Hotel was built in 1900 and officially listed as a national monument. Typical Art-Deco features could be found in the beautiful Café Americain where she was seated, but they were of little interest to Hillary. She was within a stone's throw of the most important places in Amsterdam worth seeing and with the famous "Leidseplein" just in front of the main door. However, Hillary would not be swayed from her task.

Hillary paid the bill and left the *Americain Hotel* through the main entrance. Fully nourished and ready to go.

She was not in the habit of walking the streets of Northern European cities and saw no reason to start now. She sparred for a while with the oncoming trams at the *Leidseplein* which were a challenge, before finally finding a taxi rank next to the blue plastic awnings stood outside of the under renovation *City Cinerama*. The workmen treated her to a series of appreciative whistles and catcalls. Hillary of course ignored them.

She gave the taxi driver, a *Surinamer*, the address and told him to get a move on. She didn't want to be late.

Park Hotel Amsterdam, Stadhouderskade 25, Amsterdam 1071 ZD

The Park Hotel was not to her usual standard, but she was not there for pleasure.

The main entrance opened out opposite (across the tramlines) from a sordid little waffle house which was positioned directly in front of the main city *Holland* Casino at Max Euweplein 62, Hirsch Passage 7. The lobby was small and very *seventies* in terms of decor with long flat black surfaces and lines featuring. There was clearly a movement to bring seventies style back. Very retro. With orbs, globes, plasma screen monitors and ridiculously crass lighting fixtures meant to look like Christmas adornments on the end of long thin metal tubular arrangements which were supposed to be refined and cosmopolitan, but weren't. There were banks of sleek thin computer terminals set on elevated bars much in evidence in the center of the room, catering for the business traveler and a cluster of uncomfortable looking pastel and black patterned fabric rounded contemporary couches (code for uncomfortable) and glass topped coffee tables, around which business people could meet to discuss figures, contracts and trends before retiring upstairs to consummate the deal. It was little more than a souped up Super 8. The 7Eleven of the hotel trade.

She did not bother asking for guidance at the reception desk. She walked with confidence and purpose through the lobby, turning multiple heads as was her way. Ignoring the attention.

She was a stunning package even with maturing years, even more so in fact because of her maturity, and she passed by the small concierge table without giving the attending there a glance.

She made her way through the narrow dark passageway to the main elevator, which was small and more suited to tradesmen than to someone of her bearing. She got into the lift only after ensuring she would be the sole occupant and checked her look in the reflection of the glass with which it was lined. The doors closed. She was as usual, delicious and irresistible. Business suit tightly packaging a delicious content. Perfectly coiffured hair which was blond, bobbed high and which had a gloriously healthy sheen. She depressed the level number 7 and was sped upwards on her way.

As the man opened the door he met with the full dynamic and formidable force of *Hillary Robinson.*

"Do not speak." she said. Her only words.

As he recoiled from the initial blast of charisma and animal sex appeal that she exuded, he decided that it would be most valiant to do exactly as he was told.

Hillary pushed him backwards, flat onto the bed. Not bothering with the formalities of drawing back the covers.

The room had very little natural light, which made the job easier.

She then placed her Cherry coloured patent aqua bag by *Dooney & Bourke* on the bedside table. Kicking off her very expensive black Anne Klein *Portia* sling-back shoes. She took off her *Caraceni* suit jacket and unbuttoned her blouse, leaving on her very sexy burgundy Red *Wonder Bra* which was not really needed and she then sat on the bed next to him. Her skin was smooth, tight in the right places and silky.

Her breasts still youthfully firm and rounded. She was in excellent condition.

She opened his belt at the waist, undid his clip and pulled down his zip. She pulled his suit trousers and BOSS boxer shorts down to his knees. His upper thighs and pubic area were very hairy with matted black and a tinge of grey hair. It was unkempt.

His dick which was fat and substantial, needed some coaxing. It was still limp which she took as something of an affront.

Hillary started to roughly manipulate his organ with her left hand until it was rigid and stood at its maximum potential height and fullest girth. The man was looking hard at the ceiling and holding on for dear life. Inhaling and blowing out intermittently. He was starting to perspire a little. Saliva was dribbling over his lower lip onto his chin as he licked it away with his tongue.

Her head was now hovering above his fully erect penis which she then yanked a couple of times to ensure continued interest. This was never in doubt and at its full extension she realized that it was of a dimension that would perhaps need a saddle, if she were to mount. This would be her pleasure.

She then positioned herself to be comfortable, laid between his thighs. She cupped each bollock in turn and licked passionately, like a dog on heat, before salivating upon his scrotum. And then Hillary started to suck him off. Something at which she was a proven expert and particularly enthusiastic participant. He started to writhe pleasurably and the occasional *yelp* could be discerned, sometimes from pleasure, sometimes from pain.

Her head started to bob up and down, taking in his length, circling the head of his penis, which was a turtle neck, with her tongue. Then she began to take long very slow and deliberate, quite squelchingly audible sucks. She increased the intensity gradually to bring him towards climax. She had most of the full length in her mouth, which pushed out her cheeks and made her face flush. With less than two minutes of Hillary, the man started to shoot his load. He ejaculated first into her mouth and then as she withdrew, continually pumping and jerking his organ with her fist, he throbbed all over the bed and his sperm landed across his right thigh and drained until he was spent.

Room service would not be happy.

The man was lay prostrate; eyes tight shut and could not move. Blowing, almost panting hard. Close to distress. Getting back his breath.

Hillary stood back. Replaced her blouse and suit jacket, slipped back on her shoes, collected her bag and checked her look in the bedside mirror, retouching at her makeup. She took a drink from the bottled water that was on top of the mini bar and rinsed. She swallowed. She then wiped her mouth with a tissue and re-glossed her very full lips before walking toward the door.

The man on the bed called after her a little belatedly;

"Don't I even get a kiss then?"

Hillary at reaching the door, pulled it open, suppressing a smile and then slammed it closed behind her.

In three minutes, she was back outside of the hotel and calling down a taxi.

Chapter Ten

Oscar had changed and was sporting his black 'Eddie Bauer' jeans and had chosen a cotton button down shirt in very dark olive green with a motif etched on to the left breast pocket. The motif was golden and had class.

He walked slowly from his austere room and looked out in to the dimly lit hallway of his hotel floor which was narrow and quite uninviting. Too many concealing nooks and crannies for Oscar's liking.

He soon found himself in the men's room on the Mezzanine level, where he wetted his red George Cross handkerchief and soothed his brow. He then washed his hands carefully with an anti-bacterial hand wash by Health Basic NZ, called Honey and Jojoba before making haste back to the room. He got to work. This woman was a danger. No point being reckless. Over the years Oscar had pulled a lot of crap and made a lot of money, which meant in his eyes he could now afford to be artistic. However, caution still prevailed.

Minutes later he was at street level. He exited the hotel. Turning an immediate right and headed for the street corner. He stopped at the traffic lights and the pedestrian crossing. Looking out toward the main shopping area on Queen Street, he could see the small tourist class shops and a number of local ANZ, Westpac, BNZ banks and forex windows on either side and he recognized the clamour which was building, hordes of commuters leaving the city. He looked up and to his right at the Quay Tower which stood impressive. The sign on the address and occupancy board standing outside on the main concourse said that Aon New Zealand occupied the 16th floor. Oscar made a mental note and then crossed the street and duly got caught up in the rush. Though chilly, he began to perspire. He looked up. Bungee jumpers were still busied in the pursuit from the top of the tower and wore green luminous suits. Bungee jumping was clearly a nocturnal event. The road to the rendezvous would be easy to navigate. Just after the Rodd & Gunn designer menswear store to his right he took a turn in to a small alleyway which smelled of Kebab meat. There was a discharge of some sort on the ground next to his feet, several chards of broken glass, a mirror perhaps and also a discarded whisky bottle of a brand with which he was not familiar.

Oscar stood with his back to the street in silhouette and pulled from his pocket a long nylon cable tie garrote which he had last used in the men's room of the Court of Two Sisters restaurant in the New Orleans French quarter on rue Royal.

He tested it for tension on his wrist. It seemed to have integrity. He was ready if need be.

It was time to go.

Fleetingly, Oscar looked down and caught his reflection in a larger piece of the broken mirror. It did not hold, but it was as if his temperament were being reflected. Oscar considered himself extraordinary. It was impossible to repudiate himself from the notion. It was perhaps fallibility. A weakness.

"Wish me luck as you wave me goodbye…"

It was starting to rain. Just drizzle, but enough to get wet. Oscar turned around facing the street and took a left, bowing his head to go under some low standing scaffolding and started back down the street toward the crossroads. A drop of water from the scaffold hit the back of his neck, exploded and coursed down the inside of his shirt causing Oscar some discomfort as he stopped rigid and then after gathering himself, carried on. Relentless pursuit. That was the Phelps way. He then made a left up the hill, passing by the Acadiana Eyewitness News 10 KLFY TV studios and then the old public baths housed in an impressive looking older building to his right. Within minutes he had crossed Hobson and Nelson streets and was on Fanshawe and headed for Victoria Park.

He stopped briefly at Victoria Street West to look in the window of the Kathmandu store which was of some mild interest. It sold all manner of things for the great outdoors, clothes, tents, equipment of a high quality and there was a sale on – 50%. Oscar thought that his long lost friend Enrique de Chesaris would have enjoyed this, as he had always displayed inclinations in this direction, when not fully occupied with copulation pursuits. It was indeed a crying shame that he was no longer alive.

Oscar was nearing the appointed place. As he saw the collection of odd shaped and multi-entranced buildings, which looked like an old factory site from nineteen-fifties England, he came upon the entrance to the Celebrity Walk of Fame. He stood at the beginning of the inclining entrance walkway which had a canopy its full length leading to the main doorway and looked in to the general commercial courtyard. The complex appeared to be filled with rather tired looking artisan and art galleries, small coffee and sandwich shops, stores with stalls outside which held tightly compacted rail upon rail of cheap clothing which all appeared to be connected with the New Zealand ALL BLACKS rugby team.

Oscar turned to the signage on the wall high to his left.

It said; New Zealand Celebrity Walk

The Celebrity Walk of Fame was opened by Sir Robert Muldoon on July 12 1984. Originally it was the old horse ramp that leads between the Stable buildings and the courtyard. Since its opening many outstanding New Zealanders have been honoured by placing their hands, feet, or a combination of both, in cement. Some of the famous personalities and sportsmen and women have been Sir Edmund Hillary, Dame Kiri Te Kanawa, Billy T James, Sir Robert Muldoon, John Walker, Rachel Hunter, David McPhail and Jon Gadsby to name but a few. Their imprints attract visitors who can't resist comparing their own hand and footprints with these great New Zealanders.

Oscar would look for Sir Richard Hadlee. It was galling to him that Sir Richard did not take centre stage.

As he walked in, he came across what he considered an odd bunch of miscreants who were clearly custodial in their respective duties. None appeared too keen to venture unsolicited guidance and Oscar did not seek it. Other things preoccupied his mind. It was after all a fleeting visit with a purpose.

Once outside, he strolled over in the rain which had now become a light drizzle, toward a small gallery which was positioned in a corner next to a confectionary shop. The small pictures featured were numerous, colourful and busy looking and by a local artist who went by Diane Vassey. Oscar went in.

Five minutes later he had purchased a small tabloid picture on board by Vassey depicting Auckland City.

It was a vivid effort with a stark contrast of orange and blue being the dominant colours. The tower was pre-eminent and it was signed on the reverse. Oscar bought it with his Nerja residence in mind. He knew just the place for it.

He exited the gallery and turned in to the confectioners. He bought a chocolate bar, the first one he saw, for the strength that it would give him. It was a Super Peanut Slab of Milk Chocolate made by Whittaker's of Porirua. The foil wrapper was of gold with burgundy scripted writing and looked olde world, which was not exactly the source of the appeal to Oscar. Inside was a heavy slab of hard dark chocolate. The same slab which had been produced since 1896 and was no doubt always as sickly...

It was close to the appointed time. Oscar after taking a couple of bites, discarded most of the chocolate in a nearby garbage bin and made himself ready.

He fixed on a nearby square wooden table with two chairs either side. It was part of a Greek kebab concession. He ordered a Cola with lime, sat and relaxed. The rain began to pelt, but he was sheltered by an awning high above. Auckland at this moment was not exactly appealing. There were few other patrons in evidence and most shop keepers were inside their establishments, which Oscar thought of as fortuitous.

Chapter Eleven

The Russian woman approached from his left. As she reached the table, Oscar positioned the chair so that she could sit almost next to him but at a slight angle. Immediately after she sat her dress rode up to mid thigh. It was a convenient accident from which the Russian hastily recovered. A little flustered, a little embarrassed and flushed. She composed herself and relaxed.

She was a symphony of high, thick and very blond feathered hair with just a hint, perhaps more a suggestion of dark roots. Locks cascading down to her shoulder blades at her back and reaching the start of her cleavage at the front, with very even features, more pretty than handsome. Better than he had remembered. Her hair was layered in the way a very sexy Asian would wear it with contradictory messy strands hanging loosely at the front and over her fringe. Bangs of gold without any discernable form. She was very appealing. This was not her 6am breakfast look. She had a wiry, lithe and athletic frame. It was stunning. Her eyes were large and azure blue and she had a button cute nose. Her carefully and expertly applied make-up covered a quite pale complexion. She had a very wide mouth with thin lips and a hint, when not smiling or animated, of an economic downturn at the corners. They were covered by a layer of pinkish-red lip gloss which extended right in to the very corners of her mouth as if to compensate.

A change exploded into life as and when she developed a full on smile, exposing a thing of radiance and beauty, incredible sex appeal, attractive and with very white and even teeth.

Her skin was of near alabaster. Porcelain almost with a slight pinkish hue high on her cheek bones. She was dressed in expensive looking; elegant clothing and she had distinctly rich smelling perfume and a watch in gold crafted in Switzerland by Raymond Weil.

For a moment Oscar wondered about his instinctive thoughts of copulation which at this moment were rife. The possible ramifications of such an act.

He had an erection which was growing hard to disguise. He crossed his legs.

Would it be bad Joss?

It was as if he were two people…sometimes one, sometimes another… conflicting.

She then, as if sub-consciously reacting, crossed her legs slowly and seductively and then stretched back a little in her chair, the effect serving to push her breasts out from within the emerging gap in her coat. They were rounded and firm and her nipples had grown noticeably hard beneath her white blouse. A pleasant surprise. She exhaled and met Oscar's stare full on. A moment which passed in silence, was then broken.

She smiled. The full version. There was a sparkle.

"The last I heard…weren't you supposed to be dead?" she said bitingly with a combination of sarcasm and high degree of cynicism. Her Russian dialect and eastern inflection briefly surfaced in a deepening drawl.

Oscar leaned back into his chair, still distracted by her breasts and with a hand now on each thigh after uncrossing his legs, he retorted;

"Clearly, that was somewhat exaggerated."

"Most things with you, (she paused for dramatic effect)… appear either protracted or exaggerated…" she countered immediately with an even lengthier and sustained drawl in her voice.

The Russian looked somewhat dismissively over and beyond Oscar's shoulder, creating an impression of ambivalence.

It was a somewhat contrived and rehearsed performance. Nonetheless, quite well delivered.

Oscar leaned forwards and met her head on. Eye to Eye.

Her smile began to ebb and the downturn re-emerged.

"Oh My dear Miss Chiankova. Do I detect a note of resentment, masked behind your hurtful tone?"

Oscar had become quite caustic in his manner, which caused noticeable shock in the Russian.

She again activated the smile. This time however, neither as pronounced nor devastating.

"Dr Carlos Leonardo Tagliapietra" she countered abruptly...

It was a Deadly Coda, perhaps mistakenly and carelessly presented. Her body language which lapsed into that of a slight fidget, almost betrayed the bravado of her performance without quite destroying the impact.

Oscar ran his tongue across his front upper teeth, mouth still closed and he breathed in hard through is nose as his head pulled back instinctively.

Oscar considered her words.

It was a strange and unbalanced exchange. She was out of her depth, but appeared set on swimming against the tide regardless. Oscar wondered if he should gallantly throw her a line? It would after all, be the gentlemanly thing to do.

He decided against it. 'Feng shui' was a factor, which he had learned to draw upon on occasion.

Lessons learned from his time in Wanchai.

After a short while, Oscar eased back in to his chair and considered his position. He felt fatigued after the journey and the inadequate period of sleep that followed and had yet to adjust properly to antipodean time.

'Another time', was his conclusion. He remembered now why he did not care for her.

The Russian became noticeably more relaxed, which caused Oscar some little annoyance.

Confidence began to re-emerge after the momentary lapse. She had gained in her own mind a considered victory, Oscar surmised. She stood, shifted her attention away from Oscar and casually walked to the area which was not covered by the awning and held out her hand to see if it was still raining heavily. It wasn't. She sat back down and gave an encore of the re-crossing of her legs performance. Not quite so much breast emerged this time. Disappointing. Oscar glanced over toward the Gallery and picked up his purchase, which he had rested aside the table leg. The Russian waited.

"You have earned yourself another audience." he said. Though in truth, it was more of a reprieve.

With that, he turned his back on her not waiting for a response and strode off with purpose in the direction of the main gate, at which he made a right and strode back up the hill.

The Russian smiled to herself. Her mission clearly accomplished.

Oscar disregarded the rain which had started up again as a mere drizzle; he had other matters to contend with. Matters much more potentially serious. He started back in the direction of town and felt at the form of the garrote in his pocket for the comfort it would afford him. It provided little.

Oscar had learned never to make a fool of an enemy... as it serves only to discredit them as a competitor.

Oscar had also grown to accept the voracity of the female and he decided that it would be to Sydney for the coup de grâce.

Chapter Twelve

His clothes were quite wet. But it was of little matter. As he reached the concourse which lead up to the entrance of the Aon tower he stopped to look into a News Stand that was housed in a small concession just inside the main hallway foyer. He went into the concession and picked up a Trib. It was the last one they had from the previous day according to the publication date.

He then looked in at the store next door which was one short flight of steps down and was the site of a pie & pastry, designer sandwich shop. From the look of the patronage and the servers, they were just about to close for the day. Oscar walked in and took a seat, ordering a coffee with cream, a sausage roll and a glass of cold water from the tap. All the time apologizing for the lateness of the hour as he found a seat. Oscar always maintained his manners, which costs nothing.

His tray in front of him, he sat daydreaming a little while staring blankly out through the shop window at the increasingly busied with pedestrian traffic street corner, where the traffic lights were changing and influencing the flow at efficient and regular intervals. His mind had drifted and had become fixated on a steaming bowl of pasta with Alfredo sauce served up at the ill-fated *Ilio DiPaolo's* **Restaurant** and Ringside Lounge at South Park Avenue, Blasdell, Western New York. Not a million miles away from Buffalo. He was visualizing the restaurant, decorated with hand-painted Italian murals of the *Bay of Sorrento* and had become lost briefly. Almost entranced. Captivated.

Then as the traffic lights changed again from Green to Red he looked down instinctively at the lone sausage roll which lay ominously prone, unappetizingly on the paper plate. He took one bite and then discarded.

His TAG told him it was near time to draw a close on the day. The heaviness of his eyes confirmed this.

The article in the Trib was somewhat disconcerting.

After reviewing the personal column for news and an expected Nordic update from Hillary, which perplexingly was not to be found, Oscar scoured the other global features.

There was a passage about a painting by Pablo Picasso called The Bay at Cannes which Oscar remembered admiring as a callow and innocent youth in a museum in Paris. Oscar enjoyed a flood of reminiscence…

Then his attention was drawn to a feature concerning Somali Pirates living the high life while plundering and reaping benefit from their ill-gotten gains in the Gulf of Aden.

The article read;
"Pirates were benefiting from ever-increasing illicit profits originating from ransoms paid in cash by the shipping companies concerned, many of whom did not want too much attention being drawn to the nature of the cargo that they carried. It was further reported that Mogadishu weapon dealers often received deposits for orders via an "hawala" company, which operated on an informal money transfer system based on the honour system, (which Oscar Phelps was only too well familiar with). Further, and most disturbing of all, the article noted that these pirates did not consider themselves as such, but moreover as "coastguards" and that they were the beneficiaries of seed funding made available by wealthy though clandestine international business syndicates based in Yemen, north of Eyl in Puntland, just across the Gulf of Aden, which was reportedly where the pirates get most of their weapons from."

The feature went on to mention that links to western industrialists were rumoured and that several members of the Quildeberg group had long been suspected as having complicity. Oscar's thoughts momentarily cast back to his friend the Rt. Honourable.

Now this was a very real concern for Oscar as the Brethren of Acadia had it was rumoured, certain established links with Quildeberg.

Quildeberg engaged in annual meetings usually at Harlaxton Manor, a mansion in rural Lincolnshire, England. Built 1837 by Sir Gregory Gregory,

Oscar had visited on various and sundry occasions in relation to pursuits orchestrated by his late friend and associate of the learned gentry.

The house as Oscar recollected was quite monumental and upon first sighting delivered an unforgettable and dramatic impact upon the mind, which would be difficult ever to dispel. Certainly that was the effect on one Oscar Phelps.

The architecture combined Jacobean and Elizabethan features with symmetrical Baroque, massing to create a house more exuberant than any surviving Elizabethan or Jacobean mansion. Few houses to Oscar's mind could match the splendid approach to Harlaxton. A straight mile long drive across a bridge, under a gatehouse towards Salvin's towering façade which whether approached by day or night (when the building was floodlit), was in itself a guarantee of a memorable and mystical experience.

His memories where tinged with certain fettered regret, as he had once had to resort to an ultimate solution in the grounds in connection with matters Nigerian. Matters which had been bothersome at the time.

Oscar however enjoyed the fleeting reminiscence. Though the catalyst for such was much less palatable. By degrees.

He then moved his attention to the international pages which dealt with matters Iberian.

There was little of any real consequence. However, Oscar still considered Nerja his home and there's no place like home. It's where one has a modest function.

Oscar scanned the article relating to the winners of the Christmas lottery. Apparently, they (1,950 of them sharing several billion Euros) were still reveling in their success and doing splendid benevolent deeds. Oscar had been regularly playing the El Gordo National lottery in Spain ever since he first arrived in Nerja and had once shared in a ticket with the travel agency; *Verano Azul* and their modest win back in 1997.

Oscar put the broadsheet down.

He began to consider the significance of what the Russian had said. He remembered Dr Carlos Leonardo Tagliapietra as being portly, bordering upon fat. He had a young face almost without blemish save for a small horizontal scar on his cheek which was hardly noticeable. He had magnificent eyes. He was always richly dressed in an old world style with heavy rings of platinum gold on his fingers and he was, as is the want with the Argentine male, heavily scented. For businessmen in Latin America, the fragrance they wear is as important as their tie, suit or shoe selection. As nothing can be more personal than the way an individual smells. It often conveys a message.

Serious, traditional Latin executives, Oscar had noted, often favoured deep woody scents or stronger citrus aromas. Younger executives were often more likely to experiment with contemporary labels and fragrances that bend the machismo-driven tendency toward stronger more "masculine" fragrances.

The Doctor as Oscar remembered, favored Fahrenheit by Dior. Probably bought from Pozzi on the Avenida Santa Fe. For Tagliapietra was clearly a member of the fashion-conscious Portenos.

Oscar had one other thought on Tagliapietra and that was that no matter what the appearance, he 'couldn't quite cut the mustard...' His deep commanding voice was the ultimate betrayal. It just didn't fit the Argentine.

It was a heartening thought upon which to pursue and hopefully find sleep.

As Oscar made his way back into the reception of the Mercure. He was not without concern.

He took the lift up to his room and slept an uneasy though mind cleansing 18 hours.

He loathed Missing breakfast! Though it was a disappointment he would have to accept. There were greater losses and disappointments with which he had had to come to terms over the years.

To make matters worse, as he slept he had had a strange but recurring dream... he awoke with the following bothersome passage in his mind, which would not go away.

"Child Rowland to the dark tower came; His word was still 'Fie, foh, and fum' I smell the blood of a British man."

It was from "King Lear," Act 3, scene 4

Perplexing.

The Esplanade Hotel and the palm trees that skirted the beautiful orange-tan stone facade at Devonport would have to wait…The following day's afternoon saw Oscar's body clock realign. Just in time to tackle things Australian.

He paid the exorbitant NZ$75.00 exit fee at the Auckland airport and was on his way, Qantas - Business Class, flight number QF44, seat 2F and westward bound.

Formidable, he would have to be.

Chapter Thirteen

It sprang out from nowhere, perhaps ten meters just ahead of her and she was more startled stiff than actually alarmed. Not enough time to get scared or concerned by this large white-tailed deer, complete with an array of ominous looking and clearly treacherous antlers as it bounded in fits and starts down Mississauga Street headed in the direction of the expansive green on the second hole of the oldest golf course in North America.

Hillary was on another mission for Oscar, the kind that the late Rt. Honourable would gladly undertake, although this one she found rather tawdry and wondered if this really was making the best use of her time. After all she was now in charge of all matters European and this place was a little bit off of her patch.

Hillary was stood at the corner of Mississauga and Centre Street in the heritage district of Niagara on the Lake. It was her first trip to the Southern Ontario town, though Trent had spoken very highly of it to her. He had mentioned it in dispatches. She was looking forward to taking in a couple of plays at the SHAW Festival Theatre, to dining at the Stone Road Grill which had been highly recommended and she did at least have Nikki Konopka for company. Nikki had proven herself a very adequate and willing belly warmer.

Hillary had been warned by the amiable and delightful minions at the Harbour House Hotel, where Oscar had insisted she take lodging, that it was not unusual at this time of year to encounter squirrels, skunk, raccoon, coyote, fox and even the odd puma in the more rural parts of town and that she ought not to wonder off too far, but they did not mention either odor from the skunk which appeared to be endemic to the town, nor the deer. She would no doubt reproach someone for both of these omissions upon her return.

As she re-engaged her senses and collected herself, decorum and poise were all, she decided to put the distraction from her mind and set about her task. The walk up until now had gone without major incident, excepting the foul malodorous emanating skunk, from Melville street through the graveyard at the obviously new MacDonald gates entering at St. Mark's Anglican which Oscar had insisted she visit, passing by the Carnathan-Baur crypt, crossing Byron Street and down and through the picturesque Simcoe park on the pathway that carved its way to the left of the band-stand, which had lead her on to Picton street and emerging directly opposite the Prince of Wales hotel. From there she had gamely taken a route as mapped out by Oscar and Trent passing by the Clock Tower Cenotaph and turning a left before passing by the Olde Angel Inn and the Bowling Green.

She then took a right on Johnson street and continued straight on passing to her right the Poste House circa 1935, until reaching the cross street that was Simcoe, where she made a tired left before walking another few hundred metres to the apex of Simcoe & Gage Street and found to her right the St. Andrews Presbyterian Church and the expansive though flat graveyard that lay behind its impressive six white columned colonnade facade.

The sign to the immediate right said; 'To God be the Glory'. Which Hillary found fascinating but reserved the notion that she deserved some element of glory too...

Behind her she could hear the distinct clip-clopping of the Sentineal horse and carriage which was traveling away from her and fully loaded with Japanese tourists and turning from Gage on to Johnson. At which point her cell phone rang out, disturbing the moment.

Oscar had checked his TAG and it was time.

"Hillary, are you there yet?" he asked across a very shaky connection and one which had an annoying echo and about a two second delay.

"Oscar...I'm here and I don't like it." she said in a very hurtful and reproachful tone.

"Did you get the key" he asked ignoring Hillary's mood.

"Not yet, but I'm almost at the house." she said.

"I'll wait." said Oscar.

"You'll call me back in 15 minutes." she retorted and closed her phone in annoyance.

At the graveyard she visited the grave of Christina A. Hunter as directed, sitting for a short while in contemplation on one of the two marble benches which were positioned opposite the final resting place for a very extended family going back almost 150 years.

Hillary had then after gathering her strength and taking a sip from her elegant pewter flask for the strength that it would give her, walked across the short distance to Centre Street and headed down toward the very clearly unkempt and derelict high square looking building on her left hand side which was to be her first destination.

Then the episode with the deer.

Oscar called again.

"Alright Oscar. I'm almost there and I was almost killed!" she reproached scornfully. Ignoring this dramatic pronouncement, Oscar waited, as he had learned to live with her moods and mini-tantrums. He found them somewhat endearing. Still, this was important, so he let her alone and patiently listened for news of any progress.

Hillary, now fully in command and ready for action took an acute left a few steps further on at the end of the building which met the road and saw to her immediate left at the rear of this quite uncharacteristic defeated brown brick house and almost fully obscured by the jungle of foliage, an aged well of stone jutting about three feet up and out of the earth. It begged to be investigated.

Oscar had told her that this was where the key would be. She saw no reason to doubt, but at that moment was not at all encouraged by her quest.

Steadfastly she moved forward with stealth. She was beneath a natural branch layered canopy providing for near silence apart from a minor rustling from the tree branches as they interconnected high overhead.

Hillary continued to tread carefully as she made her way in trepidation a few metres more toward the edge of the well. As she reached the edge, twigs and kindling crunching under foot, she looked hesitantly though carefully around her for more wildlife or perhaps an inquisitive bystander watching her in her investigation. There was no-one and nothing excepting the occasional car going down into town, much to her relief.

She slowly, hands steadying her on the edge of the well, leaned over to peer into the depths. There was a long black cable running down the inside wall of the well and she could see where it hit the bottom and coiled about 12 feet beneath her. Slowly, taking care not to soil her suit, she leaned over into the well and felt down and to her right for the sharp edge of a shelf which Oscar had said would hold the key. Remarkably it took her only seconds to locate.

Oscar waited on 'hold' patiently...

Then he heard a click on the line and with it a series of heavy breaths from Hillary.

"I've got it." Hillary said in triumph.

"Well done" said Oscar, "now you know what to do next." he continued.

a silent moment passed...

"Love you Oscar" she said.

"Love you too." he replied.

Chapter Fourteen

Harbour Garden Towers is one of the most prestigious residential buildings in Sydney's Darling Harbour.

Located at number 28 Harbour Street, Oscar kept apartment #807 which overlooked the Chinese Gardens and off to the acute right from his balcony, laid the intersection of Liverpool and Harbour streets and the short and narrow footbridge which lead across and down to the main promenade of the Harbour and Cockle Bay. The apartment was modest but functional but it suffered from long periods of not being occupied. Still, to Oscar it was a convenience rather than a luxury. Oscar was on the balcony; he had just finished his ablutions, was clean shaven and was carefully rinsing his hands with a solution of Naran Ji by Molton Brown of London.

He had dressed with an understated morning shirt of white cotton accompanied by a narrow sky blue tie from Turnbull & Asser, his shoes from Church's, and his lightweight tan suit from the Italian company Brioni. He splashed his face with Del Mar from Baldessarini. Dapper. Perhaps too much for his location to remain un-noticed. Inconspicuous would be challenging.

His view of Darling Harbour was cinemascopic and extended toward its southern end with Cockle Bay spanned by the Pyrmont Bridge, which was open solely to pedestrian traffic and the overhead monorail. Both looked quite busy. The middle section of Pyrmont Bridge was about to be opened to allow a tall watercraft through to Cockle Bay. As Oscar cast his glance further he could see The Harbourside shopping complex fringing Cockle Bay from the western end of the bridge. Further south of Harbourside stood the Convention Centre, the restaurant complex and the Exhibition Halls.

At the western foot of Pyrmont Bridge was the route one would take to cross the road to the Casino. It had been a road well traveled by Oscar over the years and for his late wife Lori, it had been a favourite haunt.

The monorail which travels directly beneath Oscar's balcony level vantage point and was six stories down, sped by at regular intervals. It was raining again. No time to spend in the long thin rooftop pool was his conclusion and the fitness room was not that appealing. He had things to do.

Behind him on the TV Oscar could hear the loud, lucid and quite inane ramblings of the Seven Network's *Sunrise Breakfast* TV presenters David Koch and the delectable Melissa Doyle. 'Koshee' as he was colloquially referred to as a strained term of Aussie endearment was sharing his insight with regard to matters financial and cricket. In neither niche did he appear all that well versed. Oscar took umbrage with some of his less qualified comments particularly when they referred to the Poms. Men fine and true from Lords. 'Koshee' was tolerable, but in small doses and as long as he didn't take himself too seriously, which appeared not to be too great a risk.

Whereas, when called upon to respond or simply validate her partners assertions, 'Mel' was quite a different matter… and a sight to behold. Oscar turned his head at hearing her sexy Aussie tones which served always to wake him UP for the day, in more very pleasant ways than one. She was what the Aussies would term; 'a bit of a stunner', with a girl next door quality that always held an appeal.

The telephone rang and the concierge noted to Oscar that a letter had arrived for him by hand messenger.

Time to go.

Oscar made his way to the lift and exited directly into the main lobby which featured solid marble floors and an ornamental fountain. The concierge desk was directly opposite the main doors which were security coded.

The lobby was quite empty save for a cleaner going about her business with a mop and dust buster.

She smiled upon seeing Oscar and bid him a cheerful and genuine "g'day". Oscar responded in the customary fashion.

He collected the letter from the unmanned desk;

Oscar Phelps Esq

Harbour Garden Towers
28, Harbour Street
Darling Harbour
Sydney, NSW. 2000

Thank you for your reservation request.

Confirming that I have placed your booking on Saturday 25th March @ Noon for 2 guests at the Tearoom, Queen Victoria Building. (QVB) Level 3, Nth End, 455, George St.

Please note that as we have a large group arriving at 1.30pm, your promptness would be much appreciated.

We look forward to welcoming you to the tearoom soon and would be grateful if you could provide a contact number.

Warm regards
Michel De Martini Pires
The Tearoom

After digesting the confirmation he duly pocketed the envelope and exited the building, casually ignoring the elements, making a right at the end of Harbour Street up the steep concrete pedestrian steps, ignoring the condom wrapper and the used syringe which were gathered in the filth and strode up the hill in the direction of George Street.

He then made a left at the level crossing and began the long stroll in the general direction of Circular Quay and the Sydney Rocks area.

At an outdoor street-side concession just down from the QVB and opposite the HCF Private Clinic he picked up a Cadbury's Cherry Ripe chocolate bar, made of ripe juicy cherries and coconut in Old Gold rich dark chocolate and also a box of ARNOTT`S Shapes Cheesy Puffs - Cheese and Onion flavour, which would be saved for later. Eccentric.

Oscar stood on the sidewalk seemingly oblivious to the pedestrian traffic which was building in intensity but managed to steer clear of him. He ate the chocolate bar more out of duty than pleasure and uncharacteristically let the red wrapper fall to the ground.

He crossed George Street and entered the building at number 403.

Thirty minutes later he exited from the same doorway. He was not moving as swiftly as when he had left his apartment. His face had become markedly strained, a little ashen. He had also just learned that he had lost a little weight. Walking had become a visible effort which as a man of resolve he was determined to work through. His stride lengthened as his slight stoop diminished, passing by on his left the R.M. Williams shop at number 389, which he decided he would patronize later on in the day. He had seen a large red and gold beach towel in the window with an impressive logo which was worth buying.

Oscar had dispensed with his tie. He was getting wet. He clutched the box of ARNOTT's to his side.

Next stop would be a pub for a pint on Argyle Street or perhaps the Fortune of War in the Upstairs bar.

No tinnies or stubbies for Phelps. He would enjoy a JAMES SQUIRE GOLDEN ALE or two, a Brumby's style tear & share loaf of raisin bread, a Cheddermite Scroll, a Cornish pastie, a Lamb Mint & Rosemary Pie and a lamington of the lemon variety and then move on to the 'Ken Done' gallery on Hickson Road, just beneath the Sydney Harbour Bridge for some new culture and to buy a bag.

It would be wholesome and satisfying, if not gluttonous.

Oscar reapplied and carefully adjusted his tie and felt for his handkerchief. His stride became easier with every step and his pace increased.

The day to follow would bring with it a challenge...

Preparation was all.

Chapter Fifteen

It was 11.35am and Oscar had an appointment to keep at the Queen Victoria Building.

Once again he elected to walk, only this time the day was sunny and the temperature rising.

He was dressed in a rather extravagant double breasted blazer in blue with gold and red buttons by G.D. Golding of St. Albans, England, bespoke tailoring representing the finest traditions and by Royal appointment. This was indeed a step too far, but of no matter to Oscar who felt it was right for the occasion. His one concession to good taste was to wear his Eddie Bauer jeans by way of creating a contrast.

His shirt was crisp white and collar button down with small brass studs. His tie was of silk and Burgundy red by RMW.

Oscar made his way briskly into the QVB, stopping only briefly to cast an eye over and across toward the statue of Queen Victoria which was positioned on a light grey stone plinth on the corner of the extended paved apron to the main south entrance. The Sovereign had her back to him. Oscar did not take offence.

Once inside the Romanesque QVB, Oscar strode the length of the ground level floor to a section called Country Road. To his immediate right he looked at the main directory displayed on the wall next to the old fashioned cast-iron griddled lift which upon calling would take him to the Tearoom. He was impressed as always by the impressive staircase that wrapped itself around the lift shaft and the periodic landscape black & white photographs which chronicled the history of the building and documented each stage of development and historical significance. He considered making his way to his appointment by that route, for the exercise it would bring him. The building consisted of four main shopping floors, the top three of which where pierced by voids protected by decorated cast-iron railings. Impressive. Most of the tile work, in the men rooms and especially under the central dome, was original. Oscar waited for a moment when under the dome and admired the sweeping staircase. Underground passageways, the directory noted, lead off to Town Hall Station at the southern end, and to a food court at the north. Worth noting should he be in need of a quick exit and it would probably be busy down there. Congestion could be good.

Oscar walked a few meters back in to the building. A little in awe. The dominant feature was clearly the central dome, which consisted of an interior glass dome and a copper-sheathed exterior, topped by a domed cupola. Stained glass windows included a cartwheel window depicting the ancient arms of the City of Sydney, which allowed light to cascade in to the central area. The roof itself incorporated arched skylights running lengthways north and south from the central dome. This was a great building. Worthy of a Phelps episode was Oscar's thought. This was a fitting setting.

It was 11.50am and Oscar had a few minutes to kill. He wanted to be late. Make the Russian wait. Extinguish the smile…sow seeds of doubt.

He decided that he would pay a quick visit back across the ground level floor of the building to the ABC bookstore situated immediately above his head one story up on the Albert Walk. He had a question to satisfy. He also decided that later, later on in the day after he had tended to business he would return to visit The Royal Clock by Neil Glasser and made by Thwaites & Reed of Hastings in England, that had long been a favourite and shows scenes of English royalty from King John signing the Magna Carta to the execution of King Charles I. He would do this without fail, irrespective of possible interruptions or distractions, or even danger. He would also visit the watch shop on the street level floor and look at the New Year's selection of TAG's. Oscar had a plan for the day. In this he felt contentment. Satisfaction.

The noon hour had approached, been fulfilled and had now passed by. Oscar was ready. He had paid his visit to the bookstore and committed a purchase to memory for another time. It involved John Eric Bartholomew and a reference to Oscar's past, back in the day when he shared good times with Horace Boylan in theatrical pursuits. Long before 32-Red and Blackfriars.

When he had completed his task, he strode outside the store and walked with swiftness to where the directory was positioned and took the antiquated lift to his immediate left, up to the Tearoom on the higher third level at the North end of the building. He was the sole occupant. The elevator doors opened at the Tearoom and Oscar walked out purposefully and made a right to the small receiving lobby which was quite busied by keen patrons and a duo of hosts. He ignored them and walked the few steps up in to the actual revered Tearoom and waited just inside the main double door entrance to be seated. He observed the room opening up in front of him.

There was a buzz of conversation but nothing raucous, as befitting the venue and situation. It was quaint, respectable and had a certain sophistication which delighted Oscar Phelps. A few heads turned as Oscar stole the limelight with his bravado. Some in admiration, some in something less pleasing, but still they had noticed. Oscar wondered if the elaborate, exuberant attire had been a sensible idea. Probably not, was his conclusion.

Antoaneta Chiankova he could see, was already there, seated at a table almost centrally positioned at the large picture book window and close by the grand piano, she was looking frustrated. No doubt annoyed by Oscar's tardiness.

It was the perfect scene.

Chapter Sixteen

The Tearoom was located in what was the original Grand Ballroom and it epitomized unparalleled style, elegance and grace with modern luxury and functional features tastefully secreted within a unique heritage setting.

Oscar took his seat opposite the Russian. She did not make any attempt to acknowledge him and casually stirred her tea which was devoid of milk, as he made himself comfortable. Oscar unbuttoned his blazer. The lining was a deep burgundy red and of rich silk. Some may have found it a little crude or even ostentatious.

There was a brief exchange of what were not exactly pleasantries before the waitress came to serve.

Oscar ordered a Cipriani Bellini mix with Gin. He did not particularly enjoy the taste but it would put him in the right mood. The Russian said she would stay with her tea.

When it arrived, the afternoon high tea was a delight. Quite decadent.

There was a set selection of finely cut finger sandwiches, freshly baked scones, preserves and cream, and a range of delicate pastries, served on a silver three tiered stand with Royal Albert china.

In addition, Oscar had requested for them both a sampling of Fig galette, caramelized onion, rocket and feta accompanied by roast barramundi, tomato and parsley crust, squid and prawn agnolotti. This was then followed by Blue cheese with fig compote, oatcakes and lavoche and a piccolo of French Champagne.

It was an unusual combination. Rather perversely, Oscar did not take tea.

After an hour or so of conversation which was cordial but none the less banal and often had the Argentine medic as the topic, (to Oscar's mind a rogue, scoundrel and thief), he suggested they move from the table to the seating area at the end of the room. Antoaneta Chiankova agreed and was beginning to relax. No doubt comforted by the champagne. They took with them a dessert wine offered by the server. A 2003 Lillypilly Estate Noble Muscat of Alexandria 375ml Riverina NSW, which was just about drinkable. The Russian would drink most of it. Oscar would take a small Italian Hazelnut liqueur of Frangelico. It was a taste he had acquired while in conversation with good friends in Niagara a few years earlier.

The seating available consisted of several groups of four red and beige button upholstered wrap-around chairs with wooden arms of a very high quality. A type that would fit well within Oscar's apartment on calle Hernando de Carabeo in Nerja or even in the Boston townhouse. The fabric was a rich velvet, leather & felt and had an expensive sheen and even length brown tassels hanging from each arm. The chairs were spaced to service a neat and highly polished brown wooden coffee table. The arrangement afforded a degree of privacy. Oscar sat the Russian down and sat immediately to her right. The wine was poured. A moment passed and Oscar turned and looked a little more severely in the direction of his companion. A lady who was clearly not for turning…and who's attitude hung around the mind like latent cigar smoke.

…Oscar leaned over toward the Russian, toward Antoaneta, with a deliberacy, almost a deliverance and touched her lightly on her forearm with his right hand. He held the touch for a few moments and squeezed lightly so that it became a hold as he looked deeper into her eyes. Her reaction was to glance away, which was both instinctive and defensive. It betrayed her mood and at that moment she was in his power.

As the seconds passed, Oscar realized the time was near.

The Russian as if sensing a growing unease excused herself and sped off towards the ladies room, which meant going out of the main room and by the small receiving lobby which was now almost empty save for one host and an elderly man making some kind of nebulous enquiry.

Oscar watched her depart carefully. She had taken her purse.

He called to the server and asked for the bill. He settled it in cash and followed in the general direction of Antoaneta. His passage was marked by creaky uneven floors which signaled each footstep and caused a little dizziness as he moved carefully by the lectern and through the narrow corridor which ran aside the main kitchens. To his right at the far end was signposted a *Mensroom*. Not quite as far down the narrow hall and also on the right hand side, was signaled; the *Ladiesroom*.

Oscar waited for a moment to see if anyone would come out of either facility. They didn't.

He looked behind himself, over his shoulder, and there was no one in either plain sight or earshot, not even from the kitchens.

It was time.

Oscar entered the Ladiesroom very quietly and with a degree of nervousness which usually surfaced at these times.

Though with luck, very brief would be this particular visitation.

His fixated vision became coloured by a crimson hue as he set about his task.

The Russian, who had conveyed an enduring vulnerability beneath the armour-plated exterior had the ligature still intact, cutting deep in to her neck and had bled out profusely from the wound so savagely inflicted by Oscar. This was neither happy nor encouraging news. Her tongue was also protruding which was unsightly. Some of the blood had splattered on Oscar's shirt cuff and on the sleeve of his blazer near his TAG and close to his cufflink.

Blood was always a bother to get out.

Kneeling down, he toiled for a minute or so in an effort to eradicate the stain and some colour came off on to his new Rodd & Gunn handkerchief, which disturbed. Then he stopped. His TAG said it was almost 1.30pm. The significance of the hour did not escape him.

This was not a good situation. It was grave, but not yet dangerous…

Eloquence under pressure.

Chapter Seventeen

Oscar, still on his knees, looked up and directly at the small square windows and had an idea. He had to be patient.

In the corner of the room, next to the row of stalls, there was an ornate notice board just at the top side of the main vanity mirror. It referenced a premium wine cellar housed within the Tearoom and that it was open to the public. Possibilities raced in his mind. So much so that he found himself drifting… drifting in to reminiscence. Remembering a time in Buffalo, New York state and while he tried to concentrate his thoughts on events more precarious, in the here and now, he just couldn't. The pull, the lure was too strong.

He felt nauseous and began to sweat heavily, cold beads on his forehead and his shirt was tightening.

His red tie felt like a noose. His mouth became dry. He opened it wide, trying to suck in air. He demanded of himself that he must not faint. Anxiety must not prevail. He could not succumb. He had to hold it together. A few years ago, this would not have been a problem. Oscar cursed at himself in disgust.

It had been a very cold stark, bright day in Buffalo. Minus 12 degrees centigrade and cooling, with a wind-chill of minus 20. Oscar had worn his dark Real Madridista suit with an expensive red Hugo Boss silk tie.

He had his Oxford Blue overcoat on for the warmth, which was golden in colour and of waxed material to keep off the elements. It had a lagged blue insulating lining. His one none concession to the conditions had been his footwear. He was sporting his burgundy Bostonian brogues. He had resisted the "Spenserian urge' to park on a hydrant and instead more conventionally positioned the black Lincoln in the outdoor ground level Allpro parking lot directly facing the HSBC center, which stood tall at more than 30 stories, but not so elegant. He had then walked steadfastly across the street at the illuminated red DON'T WALK sign ignoring the oncoming taxi traffic.

He made his way down the side of the wind sheltering half tunnel and exchanged a pleasantry with a large black security guard, who reciprocated. At the door of the tower he ignored the central revolving doors and pushed open a side door and made his way to one of the two tall narrow escalators which dominated the foyer area in front of him. The gust of warm air hit him and he undid his overcoat and immediately began to perspire. He noted the plastic transparent Umbrella Sheathes which were offered to all incoming upon mounting the escalator and thought this a worthwhile innovation. The passage to the top which he made alone, as there were no other people going in either direction, was fast.

Once there, he fought the inertia which pulled to turn an immediate left into the mezzanine foyer where the main HSBC banking reception area unfolded and the queue for the Canadian Consulate office had formed, and instead looked to his immediate right and behind him, where stood an impressive, antiquated, elevated bank of shoe shine chairs.

Oscar removed his coat, giving it to the American of color who would serve and took a seat in the center chair. The shoe-shine boy, who was well in to his sixties, slightly stooped with very distinguished graying temples and balding plate, set about his work. He was resplendent in black slacks, gleaming leather brogues and a waistcoat of green velvet which covered most of his dark brown button down shirt that was noticeably frayed at the cuffs.

Oscar listened to very little of what was said as the man engaged his verbalized auto pilot, but did hear the joke about the pill bottle and the cotton wool; Namely that the reason for the cotton wool was to remind the Americans of color that before they were drug dealers they were cotton picking slaves. He thought the content quite surprising, but the shoe-shiner laughed aloud as he went hard about his work. Perhaps prophetic that soon one of their own would rise to the very highest office? The shine served as a foot massage and was very soothing to Oscar. The boy rubbed hard and skillfully.

Outside, through the cathedral windows to his immediate right, he saw the large bellowing cloud of steam as it floated down and across, steadily enveloping the building. He had grown used to seeing these steam clouds and vents all over the city, almost all of the time. To seeing steam vapor escaping out of a manhole. It epitomized the North American attitude. The cultural landscape. These steam outlets, whether building vent or man-hole released, perfectly exemplified big city America and made Oscar feel very at home.

After the first coat of polish, the boy offered Oscar a newspaper, which was accepted. *The Buffalo News*.

"Rx for lower healthcare costs" was the banner headline…

Oscar set down on the chair next to him the main news section along with the City & Region and Sports sections which comprised the four section paper. He concentrated on the Life & Arts section.

He turned to the page under C3; Life Columns. Dear Abby…an agony aunt feature addressed by Abigail Van Buren. He read a couple of exchanges and found them boring. He then looked to the feature immediately to the left of the inside broadsheet by Judith Martin headed MISS MANNERS…which detailed a profile of a sociopath.

It offered a profile of what she commonly referred to as a sociopath and listed character traits to watch out for. To identify. Oscar read the characteristics with interest.

* Glibness and Superficial Charm, Manipulative and Conning.

* They never recognize the rights of others and see their self-serving behaviors as permissible. They appear to be charming, yet are covertly hostile and domineering, seeing their victim as merely an instrument to be used. They may dominate and humiliate their victims.

* Grandiose Sense of Self.

* Feels entitled to certain things as "their right."

* Pathological Lying.

* Has no problem lying coolly and easily and it is almost impossible for them to be truthful on a consistent basis. Can create, and get caught up in, a complex belief about their own powers and abilities.

* Extremely convincing and even able to pass lie detector tests.
Lack of Remorse, Shame or Guilt.

* A deep seated rage, which is split off and repressed, is at their core. Does not see others around them as people, but only as targets and opportunities. Instead of friends, they have victims and accomplices who end up as victims. The end always justifies the means and they let nothing stand in their way.

* Shallow Emotions.

* When they show what seems to be warmth, joy, love and compassion it is more feigned than experienced and serves an ulterior motive.

* Outraged by insignificant matters, yet remaining unmoved and cold by what would upset a normal person.

* Since they are not genuine, neither are their promises.

* Need for Stimulation.

* Living on the edge. Verbal outbursts and physical punishments are normal. Promiscuity and gambling are common.

* Callousness/Lack of Empathy.

* Unable to empathize with the pain of their victims, having only contempt for others' feelings of distress and readily taking advantage of them.

* Incapacity for Love?

Only this latter trait seemed out of place with Oscar. The rest were very familiar. Almost disturbingly so.

Oscar had realized that he had faults. He had also realized that 'America dislikes complexity'; it was his over-riding thought and one which served to provide an uneasy degree of assuaging comfort.

Oscar then paid the boy, tipping heavily. $20 for an $8 shine and grabbing his overcoat, he made haste toward the Seattle's Best coffee lounge where he ordered a strong black coffee and a bear claw and then took a seat at a high round table to relax. Adjacent to him on the next table were two uniformed gentlemen engaged in deep conversation. One was a policeman from Cheektowaga police and the other an immigration officer, no doubt from the Peace Bridge station which linked the US to Canada. Oscar did not eavesdrop, casting his attention over to his right at the Dunn Tire Baseball Park, which looked deserted. He ate the bear claw which only made him hungrier. It was a nervous hunger pang. But nonetheless it needed satisfying.

A *Bob Evans* lunch of cheddar & potato soup with saltine crackers and a biscuit, followed by a pulled pork sandwich would do the trick, was his thought and with that in mind, he made his way back out in to the cold day, passing the FBI building and the state trooper's black & white car which was parked at an entrance to one of the many Buffalo city roundabouts. He then began a walk down Delaware Avenue. It was cold.

His thoughts as he walked down the big city street ignoring the general populous were focused on the fact that though he had never had a chiseled jaw, a distinctive hairline, a seemingly permanent pompadour in the style of Jack Lord's *Steven McGarrett* or Roger Moore's *Simon Templar*, a gleaming Californian smile nor an athletes physique, he did however have other redeeming characteristics. If they were sociopathic in nature…then sobeit.

Oscar looked over the street at a massive old building which dominated the corner of the block. Etched in to the stone building above the very decaying entrance way was the name; The Hotel Statler. Oscar crossed the road. Jay walking. He peered inquisitively through the thick glass green shaded window built into the bank of doors, not sure if he should enter. He saw above a stairway a long row of quite captivating antique chandelier lights. Without going in, Oscar realized that it had probably seen much better days. Like himself in that respect.

He continued on up Delaware. Crossed the street near to the Walk-in clinic. At number 274 Delaware he came across a dilapidated old hotel which had been converted to apartments. It was called the Touraine apartments and 'it had also seen better days'. The ideal motto for Buffalo perhaps? The hotel was directly across the street from the Channel 2 – NEWS WGRZ –TV NBC affiliate offices.

Oscar went up the ten or so steps to the entrance and pushed the heavy door open. Inside was another stairway of concrete presenting six larger and wider steps which Oscar managed. The building was then a lock-down. On either side were closed 'dirty brown' entry doors or doors that were dead bolted from the inside and had wired windows. Aesthetically challenging but nonetheless effective. Oscar was unsure whether the purpose was to keep people out or in? Directly in front of him at eye level was a listing of tenants. It was old and showed signs of decay. Oscar traced down with his finger to apartment number #712. It was difficult to make out because of the aging of the board and the fact that it did not have a glass or Perspex cover to protect it, which left the print exposed, but Oscar thought he could just about distinguish the name printed on to the sheet.

It said; Mr. & Mrs B. Keelan...

Taking this information in, the gravity of which was not insignificant,

Oscar had been clearly stunned. Flabbergasted!

Chapter Eighteen

Then, abruptly the mensroom door was pushed open with a jolt, which served to have Oscar instantly re-engage in the moment. The sweat beads had dried. He began to swallow hard and with rapidity. His thoughts were of; exposure, capture, shame, embarrassment… the game was up! Not like before though. On this occasion he was not prepared.

Walking through the door with purpose, was a familiar face, followed swiftly by another, though this one more surprising. Oscar's close associates and friends, Wendell the Texan and Sylvain the Parisian had arrived on cue and in full laundry room garb. Their faces were only partly obscured by feature concealing white terry cloth netted hats, with a fine gauze visor which they had lifted up high at the front upon entry. The head-gear was sanitation approved and quite transparent and they had heavy seamed duty gloves, with a large whicker basket on wheels being pulled behind them in tow.

In seconds they had taken responsibility from their colleague and friend. They whisked the body of the Russian and her belongings first into a sack cloth laundry bag which they then pulled tight at one end with a rope cord and then placed her body, which was quite lightweight into the basket. They secured the lid shut with a large peg which fitted neatly into a loop at the side. Oscar looked on in stark disbelief which quickly became relief, casual wonderment and gratitude as he arose to his feet in redundancy, senses gradually re-engaging and locking-in.

The two 'laundry men' then proceeded to push the basket out into the narrow hall, sinking with the weight slightly in to the shag pile and up and out most inconspicuously through the kitchen area before loading up in to a large blue Holden SV6 Ute parked at the loading bay underneath the QVB. There had been an unseasonable shower of rain evidenced on the ground, but it had passed. It had served to make the air taste sweeter and quite thick. It was Business as usual. Efficient.

Wearing the wounds from ghosts of both triumphs and calamities past... Oscar felt a little bit like Churchill must have done in September 1945, after being voted out of office...it was written in the wind. Gratus.

Chapter Nineteen

Later, later on in the evening, Oscar had had time to assess and evaluate the situation. To step back and look at it for what it was. His performance had been below par. Weak even. It was good to have friends upon whom he could rely. There was an element of payback and for that Oscar was thankful. But there would be questions and repercussions. No doubt.

The three of them, Oscar and his guests; Wendell and Sylvain, had a dinner reservation at the Pyrmont Steak & Seafood restaurant in the Star Casino at level #1; Lyric Theatre.

Oscar ordered a co-mingled mess of seafood, delivered lavishly on a wide silver platter garnished with Italian plum sliced tomato, onions, capers, lettuce, scallions, cress, lemon rind and a rub of parmesan cheese. He also ordered an accompaniment of long and crisp golden french fries and several small white pots of plain mayonnaise (neither garlic nor truffled), cracked black pepper, dispensed from a very pretentious looking mill of gargantuan proportion and copious amounts of malt vinegar. He encouraged his friends to 'dig-in'.

They did. Reluctantly at first but with increasing gusto as the culinary delights began to work their charm.

Wendell's eyes narrowed at first in prevarication, then widened in anticipation. Sylvain the Frenchman was somewhat more reserved and ever so slightly repelled by the prospect which at best he found daunting and at worst, quite repulsive.

Oscar had first cultivated this flavourful hybrid dish while engaged on a short sortie in Northern California with Lori Kasabian at a restaurant nearby the cannery in Monterey. They had then repeated the experience at Bistro Giovanni in Carmel.

The "Rocks" oysters had looked promising with their distinctive blue, white and silver pallor and had proved to be quite superb!

...As the sumptuous meal came to a conclusion with the quaffing of the oysters and South Australian blue mussels, Sylvain casually gifted Oscar with an envelope that he tossed languidly on to the table which had been cleared for coffee and liqueurs.

Calvados was Oscar's choice, more out of reminiscence than taste.

It was a long legal-size envelope in plain white and of good quality which was sealed at its end. Oscar opened the envelope and took out a bank statement. The financial institution represented was the Camden National Bank in Maine. Upon scanning the content, Oscar's glance held at the bottom line... The balance was for $77,232,012.11 USD and it was largely made up from a single transactional credit dated about one month earlier, received by wire transfer in favour of one of Oscar's designated holding companies, activated by an unlisted originator. There was however an alpha-numeric reference number beginning in *mcc* and ending in a 111 and 222 sequences, which Oscar recognized. 'Nelson and Double Nelson' in Cricketing parlance.

"For our friends...the Brethren of Acadia", Sylvain whispered.

"Just so." said Oscar.

He mused further and sighed audibly. He looked across at Wendell the Texan, who was devoid of his usual Sunday smile.

"They won't take kindly to this." was the Phelps somewhat resigned and considered retort.

A moment passed and not a happy one.

"They'll come after us won't they." said the Frenchman with a hint of Gallic remorse. It wasn't a question.

"Yes they will" said Oscar. "Loaded for bear."

Distracted; Oscar bid his farewells and paid the bill at the bar, where he also took a swift double *Remy Martin* cognac. It was time once more for matters of business.

Oscar dismissed the travelator going down to the street which lay across from Cockle Bay and instead walked out to the side of the main bank of Casino doors and down the expansive and narrow steps before exiting down to the main concourse where the taxi's waited in an orderly line.

It had been an interesting though slightly daunting meeting, though the meal had been a delight. He was now however feeling a little discomfort in his abdomen, which he did not attribute to the food.

That evening he sat alone in his apartment, looking out from his balcony on to the Chinese gardens. He had arrived at an important decision. He had to kill someone else, perhaps more than one sole and these particular someone's were very significant figures. A difficult target they would make in fact. One which would challenge his ingenuity and guile. It would be a worthy challenge.

The constantly hectoring *Morag Glendenning* & the fastidious beyond reason *Farren Granier*. They represented the portal to the *Brethren of Acadia*.

Oscar had to navigate the way through...and carefully.

It was time to take the white gloves off!

Chapter Twenty

It was the darkness of the search that bothered Oscar the most. Like an interrogation without any real purpose other than that it be conducted. Going through the motions. The inevitable being just that, despite protestations and attempted diversion to the contrary.

Oscar recognized this as soon as he awoke from the in and out slumber that he had gotten used to on Virgin Blue short haul and inter-state flights around Australia. Oscar felt like the whole stark picture in front of him was becoming depressingly bleak.

He would only give them the very minimum he decided, nothing more.

He had been through this kind of machination before, albeit many moons ago when a similar mission had gone badly. Something to do with the good doctor in Boston he recalled. He had at that time found himself at the mercy of people who had little class and had found himself a captive in a place where no self respecting Englishman would ever feel comfort or find solace.

Oscar found his glance wondering across the aisle to the other passengers in his section at the front of the plane. The nearest chap was a mouse of a man sporting a very unsuccessful comb-over which consisted of no more than half a dozen strands of hair, thickened with gel in an attempt to mask the expanse of very wide parting that was tucked beneath the elaborate follicular construction. Underneath his scalp looked very flaky and there was evidence of dandruff collected behind his ears and nestled in the graying hair that was smoothed around his temples. The man had very narrow shoulders and was pigeon chested by the look of his torso which was heaving tight up against his shirt. His legs where thin, but his belly was bulging and hanging unappealingly over his belt line. This was a man in waiting for a heart attack.

Though still in his forties, the days when achieving a climax in anything more than a sweaty exhaustive 40 seconds or more where long past.

This gave Oscar encouragement. Though the years appeared to pass quicker than ever before, he had looked after himself. He considered it his duty. After all, he was a professional. People tended to rely upon him.

Hillary was having a splendid and productive time in North America and Trent was en route a very hot and arid, Javelina infested Arizona. Oscar missed his friends. He looked forward to meeting with them again in the Big Easy. He could almost taste the order of 3 beignets that would be served up at the Café Du Monde... interestingly enough, brought to Louisiana by the Acadians...

He was visualizing the square piece of fried dough with a fine powdered sugar coating. The taste for coffee and chicory that had been developed by the French during their civil war and for which Oscar had nurtured a liking. Coffee had been scarce during those times, and the French had found that chicory added both body and flavor to the brew. Oscar wondered if Sylvain would approve? He hoped that he would be afforded the chance.

Oscar's thoughts were that he could not fail to enjoy the bitter edge of the dark roasted coffee once imbibed. How could he? The French were supposedly so discerning. Something that served to annoy the average Englishman. Oscar's belief was that it added an almost chocolate flavor to the Cafe Au Lait served at Cafe Du Monde.

Oscar was lost for a few more moments in a tide of reminiscence. It was a pleasurable daydream held in Jackson Square and Decatur Street.

The day couldn't come fast enough.

Interlude at the Iolani Palace, Honolulu, Hawaii

Interlude at the Iolani Palace, Honolulu

"Out of darkness, through fire, into light".

It had been for Oscar a cold and lonely Christmas, spent in Boston with only trusted henchman, friend and confidante Trent Alexis for company.

The New Year had ushered in a mood of cynicism and with it the realization that Oscar had things to contend with that just could not be ignored. The news from down-under had also served to both annoy and depress. The Australian cricket team had defeated the England tourists 5-0 in the series and retaken the Ashes. Oscar was deflated by this and knew that his friend the Rt.Honourable would have been singularly unimpressed. This series lost, only a slew of quite meaningless one day internationals and the ODI World Cup in the Caribbean held any future interest, but not any more for a purely sporting reason.

Oscar's interests in the sport had grown beyond those of the supportive patriot. Unfortunately so.

With Bean town almost three January weeks in his wake, Oscar was holed up in a corner suite high at the top of the Princess Kaiulani Hotel in Honolulu overlooking the Waikiki beach and in his bed was a very attractive and voluptuous lady in her mid thirties, who had long since passed into a liquor induced new dimension. She had given her name as ***Mishka***, which Oscar had found endearing. She had been wearing a little black dress and expensive perfume when he picked her up in the Pikake Terrace bar the previous evening. The real attraction however had been that she had been extremely willing and proven very able especially with her tongue.

She made Oscar think of matters 'Cold War'. Of the concept of the 'Honey trap'...but he did not mind. She had been worth the risk...

She was naked, sprawled across the bed in post coital slumber and clearly a natural blond. She was a *dead ringer* for Melissa Doyle, the Aussie Seven Network SUNRISE breakfast news anchor and this had been the main initial attraction. Oscar had a well developed 'predilection' for news women. She did not look as though she would surface from her dreams anytime soon, so Oscar after his mandatory ablutions, decided to go out and honour his appointment.

It was a very humid 40 degrees Celsius on the wide flat street and the high mid morning sun was beginning to take its toll on the amiable tourist.

Hawaii or at least Oahu was forever to Oscar the land of Steve McGarrett and 5-O, Chin Ho Kelly, Kono Kalakaua and Danno Williams.

Where the local version of the 'Miranda Warning' was liberally interpreted as not to empty the whole magazine of bullets into the bad guy before availing him of his rights.

Oscar remembered with fondness that the only time McGarrett appeared to smile was when he was digging his shoe heel into a fresh bullet wound while interrogating a suspect.

Happy days...a reminder of events from a much more socially innocent time.

Oscar took a Honolulu Advertiser from the hotel newsstand and looked at the personal section.

After scouring it for a few moments, it was there.

He took a cab, destination; 364 S. King St.

In ten minutes the building was in front of him to his left. It was as he remembered it and very impressive.

Perhaps best recognized as detective Steve McGarrett's headquarters in Hawaii 5-0, the Iolani Palace had gone through several reincarnations since it was built by King David Kalakaua as a royal residence in 1882.

When Hawaii's last queen, Liliuokalani, was deposed and the monarchy overthrown in 1893, a room in the palace temporarily functioned as her prison cell. The building was converted to the territorial seat of government and became the state's first capitol in 1959.

Finally, it was painstakingly restored and opened to the public as a museum, according to the taxi driver who was used to acting as unsolicited tour guide. Oscar didn't care much and had not been listening. He had business inside.

It was the hour of the Mojito, which Oscar didn't care for.

The man sat across from him, dressed in a dark grey business suit, white shirt and solid grey tie was happy with his second Scotch.

Though there was an empty chair, Oscar chose not to sit.

In stark contrast, Oscar was seasonably attired in a very lightweight off-white single breasted lounge suit, an elegantly crafted shirt of purest white cotton, leather moccasins and his MCC bacon & eggs tie. A gift from a dear friend, now lost.

He looked what he was. Cool and collected.

The Baldessarini fragrance completed the ensemble.

The large ceiling fan continued its work in relative silence high above their heads. The effect was welcome and complimented the conditioning.

"You are worrying, aren't you?" said the man.

"Yes, I am worrying." said Oscar.

"Is it still the blonde women?"

"They keep on appearing you see and I keep on losing them, which wouldn't normally disturb but..."

Oscar looked past the man and out through the window.

The man drained his Scotch and poured himself another. Not offering a libation to Oscar which he saw as rude but which he had decided not to challenge.

The man was comfortable with himself. Oscar had witnessed this kind of bearing before in a man. It was slightly off-putting without a hint of pretense. Oscar did not know the man's name and did note care to enquire. Inconsequential.

"Phelps" he said with a certain disrespectful ambivalence.

"Have you always had the need for money?"

Oscar considered the question.

"Yes" he said and the comfort of the statement was as warm as he imagined the man's Scotch would have been.

"Information is always easy to give." said the man.

...."One just needs to know where to ask."

Oscar was growing tired but decided to wait it out.

The man finished his drink which he had taken without ice (not a polar bear in sight) and tossed over onto the flat empty desk a fax sheet for Oscar to consider. It said:-

KINGSTON, Jamaica - A pathology report indicated that Pakistani cricket coach Rob Bulmer died of "manual strangulation" according to a statement from Jamaican police commissioner Lucien Thomason.

"In these circumstances, the matter of Mr. Bulmer's death is now being treated by the police as a case of murder." the statement said Thursday night.

The potential Whistleblower it would appear, had been blown!

Oscar went on to read that Bulmer had been found unconscious in his room at the Pegasus hotel the day following a humiliating defeat to a relative minnow in the world cup qualifying stages which had put his side out of the tournament. There had been blood, vomit and diarrhea splattered on the walls of the hotel bathroom.

Oscar knew of Bulmer's relationship with Rt. Honourable which went way back to Bulmer's England playing days. He also knew that Eric had before his death been involved with Bulmer in matters of business in the sub-continent. He had only recently found however, that this business involved betting syndicates, Ukrainian investment and the quota risk share participation of a

Louisiana based organized crime unit. It was a mess and only Oscar had the ability to clear it up.

In the next 20 minutes Oscar had received the information that he sought. The denouement of which was;-

Bulmer had been killed to prevent him from exposing the personalities who had taken the bribes to influence matches. The Louisiana people had had him terminated to avoid complications with their friends in Pakistan & India and even more so suffer the possible wrath of the Ukrainians, who were not reputedly, very nice people.

The inference from this information was that Oscar was himself open to similar measures if he did not cut off any further potential leak.

Ordinarily, the task at hand and the rationale as to why would not normally bother him, but this involved the noble game, which cut Oscar to the quick. Above all else he had learned much since the demise in Nice of the clandestine dealings of the Rt.Honourable which he had contended with quite efficiently and admirably with the help of his friends, but sullying the name of cricket was quite beyond the pale. Oscar considered it very poor form from Eric, even if it was post mortem.

Oscar had been the recipient of a series of subtle messages in this connection, which each time had become more and more succinct and troublesome. They had culminated in a direct threat to his person, which in itself was not a concern as he had learned to live with this kind of specter over the years. But these people seemed insistent upon demonstrating their capability to catch up with him by playing a game, to keep him on his watch. They were systematically culling Oscar's female liaisons, just to prove that they could. Capability through demonstration.

This tactic was fast becoming abhorrent to Oscar as it made him uncomfortable and dangerous to be around. So far, three ladies had met with their maker soon after being involved with Phelps and the threat to Hillary was obvious. Oscar had a problem to be expunged.

After the man in grey had completed his task, he drained the remnants from the bottle of Johnny Walker Blue and took his leave of the Lolani.

Oscar had said not another word and had sought nothing more from the meeting. He was consumed by thought.

David B. Green

The consequence of this new information was fast becoming obvious. That Trent would have to brave another Canadian winter and experience similar in Arizona. *Chalk and cheese.* Hillary would face a Scandinavian sortie, mainly to get her out of the way and keep her occupied, and that Oscar himself now appeared, against his better judgment, destined to visit the old country and also faced another trip alone to the land down-under.

As he hailed down a cab he considered his position. He still had the problem of the illness which was not going to go away. It was chronic and could only be contained through care. He had the people in the Big Easy to deal with along with the problem of the threat to his person and his female acquaintances. But because he was needed as a solution provider, he considered that he still had time on his side. He could however do with a little more, if it could be so engineered. In this he took a measure of comfort.

Ten minutes later, outside the hotel main entrance, as he alighted the taxi, he was met by a scene of sheer pandemonium. The police were in evidence, as was an ambulance with paramedics and a black SUV marked 'Coroner's office'. Something on the concourse was being cordoned off. A blue coloured tent was being hastily erected by officials to cover the crime scene.

Oscar, like the rest of the congregating crowd was straining to find what the commotion was about. As he struggled to see over the melee, he met with the realization that the bloodied and jellied mess spread and seemingly clinging to the ground, which had clearly impacted from several stories above, was by consensus a lady and it appeared that she had been naked.

Oscar looked up high, squinting into the sun, toward his balcony.

Poor **Mishka**.

February was just around the corner and Oscar was destined for Blighty. Devon bound. To Capstone Hill.

Those who run cricket in this country, especially at the domestic level, are for the most part a self-serving, pusillanimous and self-important bunch of myopic dinosaurs unable to take any but the shortest-term view of everything.

- Henry Calthorpe Blofeld

One-day cricket is an exhibition. Test cricket is an examination.

- Henry Calthorpe Blofeld

The aim of English cricket is, in fact, mainly to beat Australia.

- Jim Laker

Well bowled Harold!

- Douglas Jardine *after Larwood fells Woodfull with a ball in the chest.*

I have on occasion taken a quite reasonable dislike to the Australians.

- (Lord) Ted Dexter

Part 2
Anatomy of the Underground

Chapter One

Oscar had always viewed society, convention and people with indifference. He hated the thought of getting caught up in the minutia of people's lives.

People always looked to teach other people a lesson…it was nearly always resentment based. Payback based. Getting one's comeuppance! Families were the best at this practice, Oscar had come to realize.

Nothing worse than someone stepping away from convention. From expectation. It was the ultimate insult.

Murder and theft were actually more acceptable.

Being English, Oscar understood the true value of failure.

He had long since accepted that pursuing dreams, winning and losing, seeking and gambling were traits that were simply alien to the general psyche of the typical pommie. The English love losers, simply because it places less expectation and creates fewer burdens upon themselves to actually seek and achieve. To take risk.

A nation of supplicants had evolved. Grateful just in survival as long as those surviving more comfortably eventually got what was coming to them in a form of admonishment.

Deep down, the people closest to Oscar always wanted to see him struggle. In just recompense for his coasting through life with flagrant disregard for the natural order.

Just desserts and all that…

David B. Green

Schadenfreude

At every street corner there were men who called out "Taxi" at him as though he were a tourist. Similarly the pimps and charlatans who ran the whores in Melbourne accosted him without any real hope of success, such was Oscar's bearing. Oscar was off to another appointment. This time with a new Doctor. A specialist in tropical diseases.

The sky outside was a very deep darkening blue, there was a haze and the rooftops of the buildings on Collins Street were barely visible against it. Oscar could hear from down below the distinct and oh so familiar *buzz* of the aperitif hour which had degenerated over the years to something crassly termed as merely 'happy'. Something of the like was about to take place at his chosen hotel the 'Rialto', just around the corner from his current destination.

Oscar had dealt with many people of dubious quality over the years and he had always been careful to give them suitable respect and occasionally had allowed his curiosity to get the better of him. This new lady medic would be a challenge.

Oscar did not underestimate her and expected to be afforded the same consideration...

It was a slanted consideration, pertaining more especially to the looser of moralistic women, who though the thought was quite repellent to him, had always held a kind of sordid attraction. It was as if they belonged somehow to a different creed. In point of fact to a quite different species altogether, from the quality of the type with which Oscar had become comfortable. Still he considered; the sex, irrespective, had always been carnal and satisfying.

It had been Hillaryesque!

People like this, of this ilk, were often found in Oscar's observations, frequenting casino ships in Scandinavia, or purporting to be executives operating from behind a wholly respectable facade as hospital directors and medically trained vagabonds in Latin America.

It was long Oscar's considered view that Doctors were usually one of three things; thieves, liars or rogues. He was rarely proven wrong in this assessment, which was in itself a source of disappointment. In some instances their attitude and demeanour would border on that of fringe theatrical in

Continental Europe, or traders in Singapore and even the tiresome and loathsome wholesalers in Africa.

Now they were even cropping up in the former Eastern bloc, in the Caribbean corners of St.Martin and in Habana and in the ABC islands of iniquity; Aruba, Belize and Curacao. They were even to be found in Axarquia; in Nerja even, which one would have taken some years ago, for the most remote place conceivable, and galvanized, insulated even, from all of the terrors, the sordidness and despicable human tragedies that the involvements of these types often delivered…

Charlatans, masquerading being the congenial façade of respectability and trust, afforded by the medical profession. The world was indeed on a fast track to degeneration.

It made Oscar think of the old adage; 'What's the good of happiness…you can't buy money with it!' Something from his younger, more innocent days.

As he waited in the small and sterile, clinically white holding room…he cast his mind back to the days when he had been encouraged and cajoled, on the basis of good common sense and planning for the future, by all and sundry to invest in a series of petty life insurance policies hawked by people from the Wesleyan General, the Refuge and the Pru, which at maturity would pay out enough combined to cover the cost of a bulk standard coffin for when you died, and for penny shares and all manner of ridiculous financial and assurance savings and investment schemes, established by tired old rich manipulative individuals in smoke filled and fluorescent tubular lit offices, who toiled long into the night in the design of programs aimed at exploiting the gullibility and naïveté of the young, oppressed and poor working class masses.

It had been the respectable, sensible, practical way and most everyone had got caught in the trap.

He remembered how he had been ostracized for not buying in to the endowment mortgage caper, the contributory pension and the single term life policy, all of which proved to be worth either very little or completely worthless, thirty years later at supposed fruition.

Oscar had once calculated that if he had purchased an endowment and stayed in a house typical to his income level at that time for 30 years, his short-fall at the end of the policy term would have left him with a GBP short-fall of 75,000 and still no deed as property owner. Just the prospect of another loan and extended repayments, or even more attractive, a sell off to a scheme which returned a discounted per centage of the value of your home now and then when you died, they owned it! 30 years of toil and worry for Zero!

Oscar also loved the idea of all of the people contributing religiously to pensions only to find at retirement that the sum paid in each month had lagged way behind inflation, so as to become so derisory in value, that it needed a new post retirement job just to survive. Moreover, then the ultimate insult would be faced, in the stark realization that in order to recoup the whole of the sum invested at great personal sacrifice over the years, one had to live to be at least 117 years of age! Wonderful!

Oscar considered his lifestyle justifiable, vindicated and fully, as he stepped into the main consulting room of the clinic.

No fool he.

The Doctor in front of him wore designer eye glasses with what seemed outmoded heavy prescription lenses, behind which lay darting rheumy eyes of a sharp Azorean color with slight grey flecks. His sports jacket was well worn but not dirty. His shirt collar was pristine, starched and white. The kind of shirt which always looked brand new due to it being professionally dry cleaned and re-packaged every morning. His necktie was too long, just a trifle, and was of woven silk by Burberry. However, he had one betrayal. A rancid smell emanating from his body and which filled the whole room.

His name tag announced him as Dr. Pinkus Minot. It did not say that he was quite unappealingly ugly.

Two minutes later the lady Doctor who Oscar feared, came into the consulting room and sat. Crossing her legs. She had been the one he had visited with in Sydney.

"We have found a substance in your blood -- a highly toxic dioxin of the type 2,3,7,8-TCDD (Tetrachlorodibenzo-p-dioxin)" she said blandly, almost a monotone delivery, not looking at Oscar, but studying the report in front of her.

Oscar said nothing but adjusted his legs to gain more comfort.

Swallowing hard.

She continued;

"As to how it entered your system. The nature of the poisons themselves sometimes determines the delivery system. For example a ricin pellet in a sharp-tipped umbrella, a spray vented from a tube hidden in a rolled newspaper, a poison-carrying bullet shot from a very short range pistol concealed in a cigarette packet etc.etc."

Oscar didn't like the etceteras.

A moment passed in silence as everyone considered what had been said.

"It is an atypical case," said Dr. Minot, interjecting enthusiastically.

"One seldom observes complex acute disease combined with neurological signs." He continued.

Oscar was pleased that he could provide them with such intrigue.

Chapter Two

I

It was a day he was never likely to forget.

It took all the strength he could muster to walk back out on to the main drag of Collins from the clinic on Little Collins. This was a time when he had to show his true mettle. Important to withstand the blows and ravages of time. Though still alive, Oscar felt that he was already turning in his grave.

He took a left at the street corner and determined to just walk for the strength that it may bring him. He carefully crossed the road.

The news had not been great. He was aware that the symptoms and effects of the toxins could be controlled if he managed the necessary daily sugar intake prescribed, took the capsules to hold down his blood pressure to an acceptable level and kept himself reasonably fit. The shaking could also be tempered, as could the effects on his skin and hair and the reduced libido. However, the attack had done its job. It had succeeded in destabilizing him and for that, Oscar had a task of revenge to exact. One which had begun weeks earlier in Devon, surfaced again in Niagara on the Lake and continued relentlessly on into regions antipodean.

For the first time in his life, Oscar Phelps felt completely debilitated. Like an invalid. Like an old man. He felt mortality tugging at his soul. He even thought that he might be developing a slight stoop and checked his image in shop front windows periodically for evidence of such.

He felt himself drifting with this handicap toward invisibility and even worse he felt himself cleaving without the ability to achieve any grip at all at the loss of presence, which he knew would be disastrous. He had to find something to hang on to. His mind wandered to how he imagined *Francesca Luciani* must have felt immediately before she relented in the fight and fell into the chamber at the caves in Maro. Instinctively, he thought of *Jose*. Poor *Jose*.

He decided that he would take the advice given and visit the herbalist in Hahndorf, South Australia and take the battery of tests at the Private clinic in Brisbane. What was there to lose...?

He was trying to restore a semblance of order.

His stride began to assume more purpose, becoming more steadfast as he reached the corner of Collins and William Streets.

He called in to a Lucky 7 News & Lotto shop and purchased a Cherry Ripe. He ate it. He took an AUD$200.00 cash advance from the convenient WestPac ATM machine and then after exiting the door, he returned immediately to the shop and bought and consumed another bar. This time the larger size, along with a cherry *slurpee* type drink.

A hundred yards further on, across the street he saw the impressive tall heavy wooden paneled doors of the *Treasury* bar and restaurant at number 394.

He just about made it into the toilets before giving up to the nausea. He lost his breakfast, lunch and the two Cherry Ripe confections in two wrenching episodes which served to quickly clear the mensroom of patrons. The *slurpee* was most likely the cause.

Several arduous dry heaves that produced stomach lining followed, as he clung for dear life onto the toilet basin with both arms wrapped around the porcelain *Caroma Dorf* 'Dunny'. He did not even have the strength or resolve to close the cubicle door behind him.

The sweat had risen to form lines of beads on his forehead and his hair was matted with sweat. His vision became obscured as the perspiration ran into his eyes. The last image that he could visualize clearly, was of a red beret of distinction and the little Spaniard upon whose head it was perched.

Oscar sank to the floor alongside the toilet seat. Not at all dignified.

His eyes closed in relief.

II

Thirty minutes later, Oscar was back on Collins Street, feeling a little the worse for the experience but with a clearing head.

It was fast becoming dark outside and he needed somewhere to relax and could not bring himself to turn back for the *Rialto* in this state.

His clothing was soiled and he was aware of a smell.

The people in the *Treasury* who had offered him assistance had been very kind and realized that Phelps was ill and not intoxicated.

They concluded it perhaps to be from heatstroke. Effects of the sun. After all, Oscar was a pom.

A few sips of water later, a cooling wet towel on his brow and a personal hand fan with spray and he assured them that he was fit to go on his way.

Oscar crossed the road at Elizabeth street and carried on passing by the large square and tall AXA Australia building elevated up a concourse of steps high to his right. In minutes he was approaching the Collins Place shopping complex and he made for the lower ground floor level and the Dendy KINO Cinema at number 45.

The theatre was small and fitted out like an art-house with plush seats, new carpets, 4 state-of-the-art cinemas, wall-to-wall screens, stadium seating, digital sound and most importantly very few patrons. In minutes, Oscar was seated in the third row. He undid his shirt at the collar and cuffs and released the button on his trousers to free himself of all encumbrances. He kicked off with a little difficulty his shoes, which had grown tight from swelling, as had the gold rings on his fingers and the TAG on his wrist.

The movie about to commence was "SCOOP" starring Woody Allen, Hugh Jackman, Ian McShane and Scarlett Johansson.

'The perfect man, the perfect story, the perfect murder' was the banner headline on the flyer which he was given at the door.

The house lights dimmed.

Oscar Phelps was asleep long before he could witness Miss Johansson's more than ample breasts housed snuggly in the red bathing suit during the pool scene.

This however would not be one of the biggest regrets of this particular day.

Chapter Three

Hillary Robinson knew what to do next and she intended to do it.

After locating the article from the well, she had made haste her exit from Mississauga Street and sped her way with conviction to the Irish Tea Room on Queen Street.

The room which was located at the very rear of the high-end *Irish Design* store, catered for the discerning, disorientated and often just plain tired tourist, seeking home cooked Irish favorites including Fish & Dill cakes, Boxty pancakes, Shepherd's pie, Guinness Steak Pie, scones, Bark Brack, soups, salads, quiches, accompanied by fresh and inventive salads. Hillary chose the fishcakes and the beetroot salad which was sublime. She also took a pot of Barry's Tea and a slab of BushMills whiskey cake. She would need it for her strength. The errant deer had sapped her resolve somewhat.

After replenishment, Hillary turned right outside the Irish Design and passed by the Royal George Theatre. It was Monday, they were dark.

She strolled down Queen Street in her country casuals feeling elegant and quite revered. After a short diversion in the Angie Strauss gallery where she sought out and engaged the artist in inconsequential chit-chat she continued her stroll and came upon the Charles Inn. One of Niagara's finest apparently. She continued on. At the end of the street where Queen met Mississauga she found the Golf Course to her right. As instructed by Oscar, she walked onto the pedestrian trail winding around the green of the second hole and made her way in the direction of the Niagara River. Lake Ontario was way over to her left but as she trod the serpentining pathway she came to a natural fork and took a left away from the direction of the clubhouse and across the top of the ninth hole green.

In just over a minute she was waved on by a trio of enthusiastic and admiring male golf aficionados who had noticed her waiting for a signal to proceed. They were posing, posturing and preparing to tee-off at the second as she cut through a narrow pass. In seconds she then saw emerging to her right the quite dour looking Fort Mississauga structure, stood erect and naturally fortified in the near distance, close by the shoreline.

At the entrance to the Fort she crossed a deep moat and then walked through a cutting into the main expanse which held the principal building, erected in the winter of 1813-14 by British and Canadian soldiers. The stone and masonry had been retrieved and used in the construction, salvaged from materials rescued from the demolished Mississauga Point Lighthouse and remnants from the fire ravaged town of Newark. The Fort had earthen walls that were four feet thick and twelve feet high. Substantial.

The fort consisted of a box–shaped brick tower and historic star–shaped earthworks. This was of little consequence to Hillary, as was the war of 1812 from where its origin so derived. Hillary just saw it as more evidence of disrespectful foreigners who sought independence from Britain when in truth, they could not handle it. It was a contentious point, but Hillary tended only to make this kind.

Behind the building to the left was a small arched tunnel. A "Sally Port", which lead to the dock at the water side. Hillary, after moments of initial hesitancy, carefully moved forward and went inside.

It was a short and low tunnel and had a heavy iron gate at its end which was partially open. The ground under foot was softening and the walls smeared with graffiti. It was horrid but Hillary soldiered on.

Once at the gate, she pulled it open and it squeaked its seeming disapproval. She walked through and down the narrow rocky pathway toward the shoreline.

Lake Ontario was at her level, with the Niagara River flowing in from her right. Across the river was Old Fort Niagara, clearly in view at the very edge of Youngstown, New York state. She felt very secluded and alone. Vulnerable... which she was.

All of a sudden her usual confidence and ambivalence deserted her as she heard the sound of someone coming from behind her. She turned and was ready to fight.

Then came a familiar face.

"Gerald!" she said, slightly startled.

"At your service and happy to be of assistance." replied the venerable and permanently non-plussed Bostonian Doctor.

Hillary studied his face and then hugged him tightly in relief.

As she did so she could feel, quite surprisingly, the hardness of his growing erection pushing up against her belly as she held him close.

Gerald was as embarrassed by his unexpected rigidity as Hillary was pleasantly surprised.

Hillary was never one to miss out on an opportunity.

Chapter Four

Oscar awoke to find Woody Allen meeting with his demise as his *Smart* car careened into a tree. The movie was reaching its climax and he had lost about an hour and a half to sleep.

He looked around the small theatre quite sheepishly and found that he was the sole patron excepting a woman occupying the very middle seat of the back row.

She was wearing what appeared to be a white mackintosh of the type that

Burberry manufacture and she had long platinum blond whispish hair which was unkempt.

He could not tell, but she looked to have an attractive bearing, quite buxom and nubile and though he couldn't be sure, he thought that she had purposefully cast him a hint of a 'Sunday' smile in recognition.

She appeared now to be looking directly at the movie and had become oblivious to Oscar's presence.

Oscar slowly returned his attention to the screen and started to lose his lucidity again. His head began to feel light and the room began to spin. He had lost the ability to swallow and in seconds he was away, lost to another void. Back to the land of dreams.

The 'Shanghai Kafaro Club' was located in a very narrow Manila street in the Makati City financial district. The entrance to the club was surrounded by deep bars. An advertising hoarding promised delights at the 'live-sex' club for the discerning gentleman. The entry tickets for some reason where being sold outside on the pavement.

Perhaps because there wasn't room for a formal box office as the foyer inside was occupied by bookshelves of pornographic materials, instruments and hand-held DVD's and players for the benefit of those patrons who had a developed penchant for entertainment, self-gratification or abuse during the entr'acte.

Oscar was now in the club at the bar-side. Looking across at the scene unfolding in front of him but seemingly unable to interact.

The beautified Pilipino girls who were small, brown, firm, lithe, painted and lovely where flagrantly exposing themselves to the elderly Western gentleman who was perched on a stool with a Bud and a stogie for company. His black and grey hair was heavily gelled and covered a balding area at the back of his head. His complexion was heavily pockmarked and he had a drinker's eyes and nose which where red and bulbous. Not appealing. His fingers were nicotine stained, hands calloused and his finger nails blackened by manual labour.

He wore a garish polyester Hawaiian shirt in predominantly yellow and black and Wrangler jeans with open toed sandals in brown. No socks. He was the worse for wear, but clearly open to a little debauchery as the taller of the two girls, both of whom where early to mid teens pulled open her blouse to reveal a small but firm rounded breast with the brownest of hard nipples.

She invited the man to take a suck, which he duly did before she pulled away with feigned, exaggerated and shrill laughter.

The other girl who looked considerably more mature than her years then moved herself toward the man and went down to his crotch with her mouth and licked with exaggeration at where his penis was now straining against the material. She had clearly learned at an early age the virtue and reward of being capable of 'blowing' a Westerner.

The Westerner looked down and laughed as he pulled her head closer to his crotch and rubbed her face into the protruding area.

He held onto her, roughly by the hair with his free hand, manipulating her head as if it were a cadava and not attached to a real human body.

The taller girl then turned her attention to Oscar. She moved toward him provocatively and placed her face and lips close to Oscar's without quite making contact.

Her breath was sweet.

He then felt her hands reach in to his trousers, cupping his genital mass and he could not resist. The girl fondled him with a harsh and sustained squeeze of his balls and dick until he became fully aroused. She then withdrew without warning, laughing as she moved away and back to her girlfriend. Oscar saw them exchange some words and laugh.

Oscar knew that he should have been repulsed, but strangely he wasn't.

He had found the advance quite impossible to repel. Impossible to resist.

Then from nowhere a little, fragile looking, elderly Pilipino man appeared in a dark suit and started to remonstrate with the Western man. The argument became aggressive and the girls stood back, still laughing as they elected to take a drink at the bar. Their job done. Sipping very red *Mai Tai* cocktails through a straw.

The drinks resplendent in decoration with a sprig of mint, a slice of lemon and to complete the ensemble, a small blue cocktail umbrella.

Oscar then witnessed a fast exchange of money between the two men.

US Dollars and not many of them.

He then saw a photograph of a small refrigerator emerge partially folded from the Westerners wallet, of the kind found often as a hotel mini-bar and which was clearly being offered by the Westerner to the Pilipino as part exchange... it would appear, for the girls.

The trade completed. The Westerner called the taller girl over and attempted to kiss her hard on the mouth. She recoiled in disgust at first but at the encouragement of her 'master' gave way and allowed the Westerner to place his tongue inside her mouth and attempt his drunken stinking, slobbering version of a French kiss.

The two men then took a drink together and the two girls where told to wait at the door for their new master. They had been rented out.

Oscar then felt the tug on his shoulder and instinctively looked sharply to his left. The young lady from the Dendy KINO concession counter was enquiring as to his welfare.

Asking him if he was alright?

Telling him that the movie had ended and that it was time to go.

Oscar looked around to see if the woman in the white mackintosh was still there.

She wasn't.

Pulling himself together he rubbed at his heavy eyes and hauled himself to his feet. It was all he could do to make his legs move. As his senses began to fully engage, he could feel the wetness at his crotch and on his left upper thigh, which was not appealing.

He had suffered an embarrassment and needed to make his exit quickly.

In a few extended and numbed seconds he found himself stood uncomfortably on the short escalator headed to the Collins Street level and then attempting to move quickly through the revolving entrance doors which did not want to let him through… resisting his every frustrated attempt to liberate until he found the end door in the row, which relented.

His angst and ardor was nearing a peak as he pushed the heavy door outwards and emerged into the now dark and thick night air.

Oscar, at the reaching the street side then hailed a cab. He was struggling to breathe; such was the staleness of the air. He started to perspire. The humidity was heavy and unrelenting.

In a matter of minutes, Oscar with a combination of quiet relief and desperation was entering the main entrance of the Rialto hotel realizing that there are times in life when reality can be a little dull.

The Rialto had become Oscar's primary hotel of choice in Melbourne, in the same way as the Scribe had become a favourite in Paris, the New Otani in Tokyo, the Kras in Amsterdam and the Grand Bretagne in Athens. The hotel entrance opened up to a high cavernous atrium of dark neo-gothic elegance which served as the centerpiece as the rooms and suites circulated up and around the sides of the principle structure. The architectural style was awe inspiring and defied the condition of its main entrance which was masked by scaffolding and largely obscured from view.

The Rialto had a nine-storey atrium and featured a Juliette balcony, each room having its own, that opened out and overlooked the restaurant and bar lay down deep on the ground floor, resplendent with piano forte grand. The hotel was a classic and contemporary hybrid, located quite fittingly at the PARIS END of Collins Street.

The lobby was busied and noisy with incoming international and inter-state businessmen and touring international swim teams in town for the eighth FINA World Championships.

There appeared to be a large contingent of statuesque Croatians in their red and blue checked track-suits.

Oscar was pleased by the scene in the lobby and keen to merge in with the milling crowd in his current condition and needed to make haste to his room and take a shower.

As he rode with one of the Croatian contingent the elegant old world iron latticed elevator to the immediate left of the main lobby aside the concierge desk, Oscar Phelps understood that this had not been one of his better days. Not a 'Flagship' by any means.

His hope was that Trent and Mrs. Robinson had been faring rather better in their respective quests.

At the top of his ascent to the eighth floor the doors opened out onto the corridor which leads to his room. Phelps hurried himself along, Croatian managerial delegate in his wake, feeling in his pocket for his room key-card.

Almost there.

He looked anxiously at each room number, each door looking the same and the corridor ever extending, willing his number to appear.

As he arrived at the designated door to his room he met with yet another in a day of surprises.

Stood at the entrance in wait was a woman.

David B. Green

She wore a lightweight white mackintosh-half trench coat, pulled together stylishly at the waist with a distinctive Burberry patterned belt and she had whispish platinum blond hair.

Oscar, using his key-card switched on the lights, adjusting the dimmer and closed the door behind them. The woman walked without hesitation toward the bed, which had been turned down by housekeeping. The curtains on the doors to the Juliette balcony were closed together.

She turned to face him and started to undo her coat.

It fell open to reveal the body of a woman who was ready for sex. She was mature and looked very good for her years. She carefully took off her shoes, tossing them aside next to the bed.

She was quite white but beautifully sculpted with the firm body of a female Russian Tennis player. She had high shoulders and a wide upper torso which extended down into a very full and attractive rack. She did not need a bra, she was fully loaded and her nipples were clearly visible pushing hard at the fabric of her thin deep burgundy-red silk dress. She looked a very slinky and capable minx.

He saw now in the half light that her hair was a little more strawberry blond than platinum as it cascaded in lengthy curls down and over her shoulders. Not quite so unkempt anymore.

She had golden drop ear-rings. Eyes of Hazel. Exquisite. Her cheekbones were high, her jaw line tight and beautifully smooth. Not a blemish. She had a light dusting of pinkish blusher on her cheekbones, but not too much. She had a highish wide classical forehead and a quite long snub-pointed but pretty nose. Her mouth was full, wide and with lips painted the same colour as her dress. Her teeth were white, even and attractive.

As she pulled the dress up and over her head, he saw that she had pastel blue silk panties.

Her body was formidable as she stood in front of him, smiling, awaiting his approval. Her breasts were bigger than he had first imagined and the nipples were brown and had quite large circles featured in support of her protuberance. She had a very firm and flat tummy and as she removed her panties a deep dark bush.

Her legs were long and beautifully developed with lengthy and shapely calves. She had a way of tilting her head down and to the left, showcasing what she probably saw as her best side.

She portrayed a stylish almost *forties - English Rose* bearing and grace but with a slight but noticeable *Latin* quality, that was not at all diminished by her nakedness.

She licked from side to side the underside of her full top lip with her pink, narrow, wet pointed tongue.

Oscar went to the bathroom, washed his face and mouth with cold water and then turned off all of the main lights.

Just the ambient light remained as he moved towards her...

He was destined for a night that he would not forget.

He owed himself that, after the day he had just survived.

Chapter Five

All things considered, Trent Alexis had believed the brief meeting at the Beacon Hill Park Cricket pavilion to have been nothing other than a triumph!

The discourse had been cordial as Oscar had predicted and Trent had not felt out of his depth. In fact, he thought a role in the diplomatic corps was no longer beyond him, allowing for his tendencies toward the darker, less spiritual side of life. The fellow he had met had been specific and to the point with a slightly condescending attitude initially, but had listened intently to the message Trent had been delegated to deliver. There had been no room for either compromise or misunderstanding. They had parted on equal terms and without acrimony.

Victoria BC had proven a nice little diversion for the Boston equalizer.

Trent was on yet another plane. This one Air Canada, bound for the Phoenix Sky Harbour international airport, terminal four.

After claiming his luggage at the baggage claim on level one he took the elevator to level three and took a seat at the *12th Fairway Bar & Grill*. He was hungry and needed pulled pork and a beer. The waiter had proven slow to attend and as was his right, Trent decided to vote with his feat. He was hungry and could not wait.

At the Great Steak & Potato Company concession in the expansive food court he got what he was looking for. A little while later he was at the Dollar car rental office located within its own building at 1805 East Sky Harbor Circle South and waiting for his vehicle to be delivered at the parking garage. He had insisted on a GPS system.

Ever prepared for his virgin assault on Arizona roads. The car issued to him was a full size white 4-door Dodge Charger. Trent approved.

As the rental formalities were completed he read the day's version of the *Daily Star* newspaper purchased from the terminal's CNBC newsstand.

The three stories that he focused upon were not at all promising. Not promising at all.

The three banner headlines in the Star read;-

Four arrested in £420m fraud case

Spanish police have arrested four people on suspicion of perpetrating a £420m ($600m) fraud relating to a London-listed company, it has been confirmed.
The arrests relate to the fraud committed at an AIM-listed company between 2003 and 2005 according to Spanish authorities.
Reports suggest that the main suspect involved is among those arrested.
The arrests were made in Madrid, Barcelona and the town of Nerja in the south of Spain.
The Serious Fraud Office began an investigation in 2005.

False advertising
"The suspects are accused of using false advertising to boost the value of shares without making any deposits.
"They entered the London share market with a value of $300m. Police say the suspects created enough public interest in the company to fraudulently resell shares to a value of $600m."
He added that the police said they had searched six premises where they confiscated computers and documents.
"Through complex commercial and stock market operations, as well as falsifications, the arrested managed to make the value of the shares increase, without deposits to back it up, and profited from the subsequent sale of the shares," said a statement from the Spanish police.

ᛋ

US fraud charge tycoon disappears

The US financial authorities say they do not know the whereabouts of Sir Barrington Sanford, the Nevada billionaire accused of an $8bn (£5.6bn) fraud.

He has not been seen since Tuesday, when the Securities and Exchange Commission filed a civil case in court.

The SEC said Sir Barrington and two other executives promised clients unrealistic returns on certificates of deposit.

Depositors in the US, the Caribbean and South America have queued to withdraw money from banks associated with him.

No criminal charges have yet been made.

The 55-year-old, who holds joint US-Barbadian citizenship, is a flamboyant figure who has links with prominent US & UK politicians and sports stars, particularly within cricketing circles.

ξ

Iran jails journalist as US spy

An Iranian-American journalist branded a US spy has been jailed for eight years by Iran, her lawyer says.
Roxana Saberi, 31, was arrested in January and went on trial this week.
She worked briefly for the BBC three years ago, and has also worked for the American public radio network NPR and the TV network Fox News.
Ms Saberi originally faced the less serious accusation of buying alcohol, then of working as a journalist without a valid press card.
Her trial was held behind closed doors in front of Iran's Revolutionary Court.
"She has been sentenced to eight years ... I will appeal," Ms Saberi's lawyer Abdolsamad Khorramshahi told the Reuters news agency.

US unease
The US has previously expressed its concern at Ms Saberi's detention, dismissing allegations against her as "baseless".
US Secretary of State Hillary Clinton has demanded her release.
However, public awareness of Ms Saberi's situation is low in Iran, where local media do not seem to have reported her arrest or trial in any way, our correspondent says.
A US-Iranian national, Ms Saberi has spent six years in Iran studying and writing a book.
The daughter of an Iranian father and a Japanese mother, she was once crowned Miss North Dakota and was among the top 10 finalists in Miss America 1998.

Trent re-read the three stories just to make sure. Growing increasingly uneasy as he took in and processed the information.

The photograph of this man 'Barrington' bore an eerie resemblance to the man he had just met with at the cricket basin. After careful study Trent concluded that this was indeed the man he had met with - shit!

The Nerja arrests were also a concern and he would be sure to include this news in his next discourse with Oscar and as to the *Roxana* woman. While having no direct connection or concern she was, Trent concluded, a FOX. Even if she was an Iranian..!

Trent programmed the GPS and put his foot on the gas.

The destination was the Rancho Manana Golf Club at 5734 E RANCHO MANANA BLVD. CAVE CREEK, AZ 85331.

Trent was accomplished at many things, but none of them Golf!

Chapter Six

The last time Oscar Phelps had enjoyed anything as much as he had enjoyed the woman with the unkempt platinum hair, he had been dining at the Smith & Wollensky steak house in Las Vegas and his appetite at that time also, had been ravenous.

Much like the prime rib that evening, this woman had fully satisfied.

She was a woman of few words but who more than made up for it in deed.

There was something about her that was intoxicating. She had a Latin bearing and strong inflection in her voice. English was not her first language. She was not young. She was however in great shape and very experienced sexually. She asked few questions, offered few explanations and Oscar had little idea of what her objectives were. He would however take the time to find out later.

Much later.

Trent Alexis had emerged in Cave Creek, Arizona. It was a small hamlet, a little off the beaten track and he had somehow confounded the GPS and made an involuntary detour via Scottsdale and an unscheduled excursion to Carefree. He was early for the proposed rendezvous at the Golf Club and pulled a hard left in from the dusty western road to a restaurant and bar called HAROLD'S CORRAL. He was pleased the Charger had aircon as the temperature outside would prove stiflingly hot. The air oppressive.

The large broadsheet press marketing advertorial from the *Arizona Republic* newspaper fastened on the door said that *Harold's is THE place in Cave Creek, Arizona for good food, great music and a dang' good time. Hitch yer hat, hang yer hoss and kick back to enjoy some good times eatin', drinkin' and dancin'.*

Harold's serves up the best durned cooking in these here parts (or any other parts, for that matter).

It looked right up Trent Alexis' particular street. He wondered fleetingly if they would be ready to receive cordially, a Bostonian sophisticate and world traveler such as himself.

He decided to take his new leather (British police issue) 'cosh', with him, just in case, secreted about his person. Unobtrusive.

The main dining room was big like a saloon and roomy and the bar was long and old looking in dark wood; very in keeping with the western theme, except this was no theme. This was natural. Very real. Thoughts of spittoons, sawdust and pistol whipping sprang to Trent's mind.

Trent was not the only patron, as the restaurant was occupied by several families loudly taking brunch. The main bar however was empty except for a youngish very buxom brunette lady who was quite pretty in a desperate kind of way. She was dressed in a tight red bra (showing lots of cup and breast which appeared to be spilling out) framed within a white frilly open silk blouse with a black thigh length skirt and black ornately tooled leather cowboy boots. She was seated and sipping a virgin Bloody Mary and she appeared to take a casual interest in him from her sideways glance and half smile.

Buoyed by this, Trent ordered a Bud light and sat at the nearest table in silence as his natural austere face broke out into the beginnings of a smirk.

The young woman went over to the jukebox, strutting her stuff in open display and made her selection before retaking her seat and casually staring at her reflection held in the full length mirror behind the bar. She touched in casual rearrangement of her hair and retouched her make-up using a clear lip gloss and a compact before making her way confidently in the direction of Trent.

Trent waited patiently for the music to start.

A *Sunday Smile* began to play...

Chapter Seven

Buenos Aires is a city famous for its elegance. A place where business meetings were often a competition as to who can smell the best and like many of his contemporaries the average Argentine Doctor would first forget a tie for the office or consulting room before forgetting his cologne.

Oscar listened intently to the woman as she lay flat on his bed wearing only Oscar's slightly vomit soiled shirt and looking square at the ceiling. She had begun to open up in a measured and calculated way.

She was espousing the style and elegance of her country, which Oscar found a little ostentatious, a little repulsive, but he would tolerate it...for now.

The woman, though not encouraged by Oscar who was feigning an exaggerated casual indifference, continued on with her rhetoric unabated.

Oscar, wearing a white *Rialto* flannel dressing gown with motif, went out towards the window and opened the paneled glass door which opened out on to the Juliette balcony. He took a seat and looked over at the atrium. It was busy across in the lobby and the succulent smells emanating from the restaurant bar way down below were wafting north, which caused Oscar to feel very hungry for breakfast.

The Aussies cultivated a distinctly British attitude toward breakfast and bacon, eggs, pork sausages, mushrooms, fried bread and baked beans were much in evidence. A veritable elixir.

The platinum blond began to speak of the aptitude of her countrymen following the Second World War. It was almost gushing and completely unsolicited. Oscar realized that she was on a quest and he started to be more attentive.

He did not need or indeed appreciate a history lesson. But having spent most of the night studying the topography of her curvaceous and supple body, he decided to listen to her utterances and pay lip service.

He owed her that.

She was offering information as a form of validation and explanation and he came to understand that she was a mere messenger, just like the grey suited man in Hawaii.

Her qualification of the reasons correct and just for providing refuge to the Nazi regime and salting away funds and treasures in the late 1940's as Nazi sympathizers, fell on interested but largely deaf ears. Oscar's own private concerns about the origin of monies in the Argentine associated with Nazi Third Reich descendants from WW2 which had been secreted away via Switzerland into Latin America through assorted insurance debentures, bearer bonds and gilts, was less gallant. He detested the insurance companies in Scandinavia who continued to provide health insurance for this population and saw collaboration with certain parties as a way to gain some degree of reparation for his friends and associates in Paris and Amsterdam.

Oscar had developed into a man of principle in his middle years. A renaissance man!

Mission accomplished, veiled message delivered, the woman headed into the bathroom, closing the door behind her. Turning the lock.

Unconcerned, Oscar turned his attention back to the atrium and the events unfolding down in the lobby and he knew instinctively that his carefully engineered demise in Boston had in all probability been exposed for what it was... a hoax.

Gerald the venerable Doctor, had helped buy him some time.

That time bought, had now been spent...

His Bostonian friend indeed, had always proven a useful and valuable ally, but over recent years he had developed a tendency to begin winding down for the weekend... usually sometime during the late Tuesday afternoon. His time spent in the Consulting and operating rooms had diminished greatly in favour of his time spent at the Marina, on the Golf Course and enjoying very extended lunches at the Union Oyster House, where he had become something of an eccentric fixture.

The experience at the Royal George Theatre in Canada and at Niagara Falls, some years earlier, had served to quell his ambition somewhat. He had grown contented. All in all, Oscar didn't have a problem with that.

As the platinum blond began the business of replenishing herself in readiness for the day, Oscar decided that if she was willing, then he would take her with him to Adelaide and to Brisbane. Keeping her close would be a gamble, but some times better to keep the unknown close by. See what develops. Fate would no doubt play its hand.

He checked her Burberry coat and in the pocket there was a watch and a golden locket. Both of good quality. The locket was inscribed.

Oscar Phelps had spent the night with *Ariana Danielli.*

Chapter Eight

Trent's *brunch-sex* episode up against the wall in the disabled cubicle in the mensroom of *Harold's Corral* would not have made his personal highlight reel. It had been rough, fast, liberating, pipe cleansing and had cost him fifty bucks. Refined.

The buxom brunette returned to her seat at bar-side, smoothing her panty-line and firing up a cigarette. She had particularly enjoyed the 'cosh' which had been used with no high degree of subtle imagination.

Trent paid his bar bill and wandered back out to the Charger. Cobwebs cleared. *Otis Spunkmeyer* Banana Nut Muffin in hand. Ready for the day.

The commotion down in the lobby at the Rialto, viewed from Oscar's distant vantage point on the Juliette balcony, was intensifying.

The neo-gothic interior was illuminated to almost gaslight candescence and created a very surreal atmosphere.

If mist or freezing fog had appeared, then Oscar would not have thought it out of character.

The atrium was characterized by huge, high interior spaces and filigree stonework; the French Gothic cathedral style seemingly reached to the heavens and let in the outside light through stained-glass windows at the roof level. Oscar was impressed.

There was at ground level evidence of several television news crews representing Channel 7, CNN, SKY and Foxtel and also a large contingent of what were clearly reporters jockeying for position near the concierge desk, as the activity headed toward the elevator bank, and the Rialto Guest Services staff struggled to maintain order.

Something was clearly amiss as according to his TAG, the hour was only five before 6am.

The telephone rang out, breaking his concentration on events down below just as the TV arc lighting illuminated the section of the crowd under scrutiny. Oscar spoke quite tersely with the operator.

"A gentleman from the police for you Mr. Phelps..." she said, offering no apology for the hour.

Oscar instinctively and without any obvious concern told her he would be down in a moment and that he would meet the gentleman at the entrance to the bar. As he replaced the phone onto its cradle, Oscar heard the shower start up and calculated that he had time to visit with the officer and return most probably before the Argentine had finished in the bathroom. He quickly dressed. Black chino trousers and Ralph Lauren cotton button-down shirt, short sleeves in white with a black polo player motif. Dapper.

As the doors to the elevator opened, Oscar was exposed to the brightest of lights as it shone directly in to his face.

This attention was quickly diverted away from him as the TV crews realized that Oscar was not the preferred target.

His few seconds of attention escaped, (he didn't even get the legendary Warhol 15 minutes), saw Oscar make his way quickly through the crowd and toward the bar.

The officer's name was *Stanton Roverini* and he was in plane clothes. Shorts in fact. He did not look very senior or for that matter very much interested in his task. Clearly a job of routine administration for the record, of the type that served to make police work mundane.

Oscar had greeted him with a warm handshake, studied the offered credentials in identification, *Roverini* was a sergeant, and they then sat on one of the many brown leather Chesterfield couches arranged stylishly to compliment the heavy teak and glass coffee tables which were the centerpiece of each of the many seating patterns in the bar. It was the kind of seating arrangement that would quite easily suit *32-Red* Oscar noted mentally. Something to mention to Alberto during his next visit to Hernando de Carabeo. Oscar had a developed eye for these things.

Roverini apologized for the time of his call, the noise and fracas coming from the lobby and explained that it was related to the father-coach of one of the Serbian girl swimmers who had been caught on a cell phone camera admonishing his daughter for her poor performance in the heats and beating her with his fists. The media were understandably keen to pursue this story and the father and daughter were guests of the hotel and soon to reappear for the new day's events.

Roverini dismissed this as something and nothing, Inconsequential.

Tabloid fluff. Tomorrow's fish and chip paper.

He moved on to matters more pertinent to his being there, which was appreciated by Oscar.

Roverini was all business and said that there had been a report from Boston in the US that one *Oscar Phelps* had been discovered dead on the Boston Common and that physical official documentation found on the body had proven that it was him. Clearly this was not the case and the officer sought an explanation or at least clarification of sorts.

He looked hard at Oscar. "Do you believe in fate?" he added.

Oscar hesitated.

"Oh, I'd very much like to." He replied glibly.

The officer screwed up his face, not quite knowing how now to respond.

Oscar protested mildly that obviously this was a case of mistaken identity and even more concerning, possibly a case of identity theft to square the question of the Louisiana drivers permit away. He then produced at the request of *Roverini* his British passport and Canadian permanent resident card both of which bore his image and signature to verify his identification. This seemed to satisfy Roverini who made notes and asked if he could copy the documents for the sake of good order. Oscar duly agreed.

Apparently the police had received a *tip-off* from a telephone number traced as belonging to room 1014 at the Radisson on Flagstaff Gardens hotel on William

Street, indicating that Oscar was at the Rialto and alive and well. Oscar naturally assumed that the Radisson would prove to be Ariana's hotel.

When he returned and gave Oscar back his documents, *Roverini* enquired as to the reason for Oscar's visit to Australia.

"I have a medical condition which needs attending to by specialists in tropical diseases." volunteered Oscar.

He went on to explain his visits for tests to clinics in Sydney and on Little Collins Street, he detailed the prognosis and also his intended visits to the *Santa Evangelina* clinic in the Adelaide Hills and then up to the Brisbane Private Hospital.

Roverini appeared genuinely concerned and wished Oscar well, which was comforting. He also made a parting quip about taking care of his personal documents and to ensure to check in with the *Back Bay* police department the moment he was next back in Boston to verify his situation.

Oscar said that he would do so.

Chapter Nine

It was during the descent into Adelaide, after checking the miles on his *Virgin Blue* Velocity Rewards program which were mounting up, that Oscar's thoughts drifted back to the Rt.Honourable and matters of the Quildeberg group and the probable connections to the Brethren of Acadia and the cricketing imbroglio.

Oscar was recalling the names of Eric's influential friends and learned gentry who included Julian Vawser, the late and much lauded Hartley Smith and the revered and heralded but very secretive Peter de Savary who he remembered kept his pile in Hungerford. The Earl of Connaught and Lords Avebury and Marlberry respectively were part of the set. He remembered the chaps from Harlaxton Manor, Caversham House, Tavershall Castle and Tuxford Hall and how they had been so influential with Eric and helpful when called upon to be so. How many of them would still be alive and liquid, Oscar wondered?

He considered that he may be able to pull in some favours and exact some degree of pressure if he traded upon his late friend's influence, such that it was?

Eric also had close chums and boyhood friends, Syd Caine and Monty Sarto from Uppingham School in Rutland, Marlborough School, Reading Blue Coat and Malvern College. Expulsion from all the best schools had its benefits in later life, when it came to network building.

The old boy's network.

These old boy's all shared similar distinctive characteristics and habits. Marshalls of the Communities of Self-Interest. Clandestine meetings at *The*

Bear at Woodstock and Weston Manor at Weston-on-the-Green in Bicester. Ritualistic gatherings up in small hostelries in Scotland he recalled, at Kirkcudbright, Newton Stewart and the Isle of Whithorn in Dumfries and Galloway.

Eric had taken Oscar to Weston Manor for luncheon on occasion. Part of the educational process. The induction. The proverbial *showing of the ropes.*

It had all been with the benefit of hindsight, just a joke in doubtful taste. Eric had not been without humour.

The jet circled the new efficient South Australian airport and appeared to be in a holding pattern.

Oscar remembered Weston Manor to be a beautiful 11th century country house set in acres of tranquil gardens and close by the M4. It had great roast beef, terrific ambiance and an excellent claret wine cellar.

Possibilities existed and were being cultivated in Oscar's mind.

He considered that these people also shared other useful common traits and business profiles. Oxbridge men usually. Utterly corrupt. Absolute old school and second and third generation old money class and concomitant arrogance.

Most were dressed by Douglas Hayward in the sixties, seventies and eighties. Sharing style, elegance and cultured image with the clientele of Britain's most celebrated bespoke tailor of forty years. The dresser of Britain's *Jet-Set. Michael Caine, David Niven, Peter Sellers, Rex Harrison, Roger Moore, Terrence Stamp, Bryan Forbes, Oliver Reed, John Mills and Lord Patrick Lichfield.*

Hayward, was the inspiration for The Tailor of Panama... How very apt.

Oscar concluded rather enviously that he had been born just too late. Not the first time he had arrived at that conclusion.

The jet was leveling to touch down. Landing gear down and locked in place.

It was a shame, but the lovely and informative Ariana had both showered and taken her leave by the time Oscar had made his way back up to his room at the Rialto. Her job was done no doubt, Oscar supposed. It would have been good to have kept her near. But no matter.

As he deplaned in Adelaide he walked a little heavily through to the Arrivals concourse and was buoyed only slightly by the large full colour mural of the Adelaide Oval cricket ground which met each traveler as they made their way through the lengthy and meandering staircase and out into the car parking area.

Waiting outside the multi company Car Rental office looking a little the worse for wear was an old friend bearing gifts from the Avenue Montaigne and the Galleries Lafayette. He also had a supply of Cherry Ripe bars.

A considerate Frenchman.

Oscar and Sylvain drove to the Stamford Plaza hotel at downtown Adelaide's North Terrace and Oscar was debriefed on events over the house specialty SQUARE MEAL lunch at the Swish on Terrace restaurant. The Saffron, Potato and Leek soup was a stand-out as was the yearling sirloin.

The news and revelation from Trent in Western Canada was of most interest. The new and very expensive BOSS tie from Paris, given to Sylvain to deliver to Oscar by Emmanuelle David was a nice reminder of days past.

Though it may appear an amazing coincidence...a man can smile and still be a villain.

In the afternoon they motored up into the Adelaide hills to visit the German town of Hahndorf and consult with the referred herbalist as planned at *Santa Evangelina* and then had an early evening drink or three of Tooheys Extra Dry and Hahn Premium Light at the German Arms pub on the Main Street.

There was a lot to do before jetting off to Queensland and Sylvain would be doing most of it.

Chapter Ten

The Frenchman appeared ever so slightly trepidatious at the prospect of watching *In Bruges*.

He was a little bit of a culture vulture and this was not exactly high brow fare...

Oscar had taken Sylvain to one of his favourite and most comfortable places in the whole of Australia. The multiplex 8-theatre cinema in the Myer Centre at Elizabeth and Albert in downtown Brisbane.

Oscar was relaxed as Monsieur Honore-Panet struggled to reconcile with the concept of tilt-back seating. On the point of an apology every time he leaned back to an angle he considered perhaps a little too far and impinged upon the leg room of a fellow patron.

Sylvain found watching Oscar as entertaining as the movie.

Ken: Coming up?
Ray: What's up there?
Ken: The view.
Ray: The view of what? The view of down here? I can see that down here.
Ken: Ray, you are about the worst tourist in the whole world.
Ray: Ken, I grew up in Dublin. I love Dublin. If I grew up on a farm, and was retarded, Bruges might impress me but I didn't, so it doesn't.

The Frenchman looked at Oscar as he was falling into a fit of raucous laughter. He was quite mystified.

Ken: Harry, let's face it. And I'm not being funny. I mean no disrespect, but you're a cunt. You're a cunt now, and you've always been a cunt. And the only thing that's going to change is that you're going to be an even bigger cunt. Maybe have some more cunt kids.

Harry: [*furious*] Leave my kids fucking out of it! What have they done? You fucking retract that bit about my cunt fucking kids!

Ken: I retract that bit about your cunt fucking kids.

Harry: Insult my fucking kids? That's going overboard, mate!

Ken: I retracted it, didn't I?

Oscar was quite literally in tears and doubled up with laughter in his seat. Monsieur Honore-Panet thought this surprising behavior, manic at worst and eccentric at best.

Ray: One gay beer for my gay friend, one normal beer for me because I am normal.

Ray: Maybe that's what hell is, the entire rest of eternity spent in fucking Bruges.

Ray: [*beating a tourist that he believes to be American*] That's for John Lennon, you Yankee fuckin' cunt!

Oscar's eyes were squeezed tight shut with mirth, as he reacted to the delivery of the line, which Sylvain did not quite, being a Frenchman, fully understand.

Ray: A lot of midgets tend to kill themselves. A disproportionate amount, actually. Hervé Villechaize off of Fantasy Island. I think somebody from the Time Bandits did. I suppose they must get really sad about like... being really little and that... people looking at them, laughing at them, calling them names. You know, "short arse". There's another famous midget. I miss him but I can't remember. It's not the R2D2 man; no, he's still going. I hope your midget doesn't kill himself. Your dream sequence will be fucked.

Chlo: He doesn't like being called a midget. He prefers dwarf.

Ray: This is exactly my point! People going around calling you a midget when you want to be called a dwarf. Of course you're going to blow your head off.

Oscar laughed out loud along with the remainder of the audience, whose funny bone this discourse clearly tickled...

Chlo: There's never been a classic movie made in Bruges until now.

Ray: Of course there hasn't. It's a shithole.

Chlo: Bruges is my home town, Ray.

Ray: Well, it's still a shithole.

Chlo: It's not a shithole!

Ray: What? Even midgets have to take drugs to stick it.

Chlo: Okay. So, you've insulted my home town. You were doing really well, Raymond. Why don't you tell me some Belgium jokes while you're at it?
Ray: Don't know any Belgium jokes, and if I did I think I'd have the good sense not to... hang on. Is Belgium with all those child abuse murders lately? I do know a Belgium joke. What's Belgium famous for? Chocolates and child abuse, and they only invented the chocolates to get to the kids.

[*Ray sees Chloe's shocked expression*]

Ray: What?
Chlo: One of the girls they murdered was a friend of mine.
Ray: [*after a long pause, feeling bad*] I'm sorry, Chloe.
Chlo: One of the girls they murdered wasn't a friend of mine. I just wanted to make you feel bad. And it worked! Quite well.
Ken: [*Ray walks into the bar high on cocaine*] How'd your date go?
Ray: My date involved two instances of extreme violence, one instance of her hand on my cock and my finger up her thing which lasted all too briefly - and then I was away - , one instance of me stealing five grams of very high-quality cocaine and one instance of me blinding a poofy little skinhead: so all in all... my evening pretty much balanced out, fine.
Ray: After I killed him, I dropped the gun in the Thames, washed the residue off me hands in the bathroom of a Burger King, and walked home to await instructions. Shortly thereafter the instructions came through - "Get the fuck out of London, you dumb fucks. Get to Bruges." I didn't even know where Bruges fucking was.

[*pause*]
Ray: It's in Belgium.

Ray: Bruges is a shithole.
Ken: Bruges is not a shithole.
Ray: Bruges is a shithole.
Ken: Ray, we only just got off the fucking train! Could we reserve judgment on Bruges until we've seen the fucking place?

*Sylvain had found the **In Bruges** experience quite a challenge. However, he was pleased to see his friend relax. It had been therapeutic and in a way prophetic...*

They had visited the Brisbane Private Hospital up on Wickham Terrace, which overlooked the tiered parklands and the city skyline earlier in the day and learned very little. Just more tests. More concern and consternation. Oscar had appreciated Sylvain's presence though. Comforting and distracting as they jabbed and took yet more blood and urine.

Oscar had also decided to take the time to reward the Frenchman for his friendship, discretion and reserve and had introduced him to the R.M. Williams clothing store - The Bush Outfitter - in the Wintergarden Centre. Not exactly *Old England* in the 9th arrondisement, but an acceptable diversion. Oscar purchased a red R.M.Williams signature tie in silk and bought a similar one in blue for his friend. Sylvain had been delighted.

The mutual debrief in the Hahndorf pub had proven of interest while lacking inspiration. The Lutheran barkeep had been a little too inquisitive, politically correct and vocal and as a result the conversation had meandered along without much colour, delivered in hushed tones and leaving just the basic needed points to consider. Sylvain, who had risen through the ranks very creditably since taking over the responsibilities of the late Enrique, had offered steadfast support to his associates whenever and wherever called upon and he possessed both fortitude and resilience in matters that often lacked the proper level of decorum and necessary deportment. Impressively so for a Frenchman.

Indeed, his value had fast extended beyond that of Hillary who saw her position as elevated following Eric's death to that of a non-executive, almost honorary director. A kind of President in Emeritus or Minister without Portfolio in her own mind. This self delusion held few concerns for Oscar or others with interest.

Oscar had come to see Sylvain's elevation in status and trust within their group and general operations as a logical progression for such a gifted individual. Staving off Hillary's advances had not been a worry as for some inexplicable reason she had not made any toward Sylvain? This in itself was as remarkable as it was welcomed by Oscar. Hillary could be a virus.

In the German Arms, Oscar decided that teaching the intricate points of the noble game of cricket, which Sylvain had never even seen played, would have been a desultory exercise, so Oscar talked win, lose, margin and quirk and put these aspects in to a gaming perspective. In minutes, Sylvain came to understand the value of insider information in this scenario and the risk from the sub-continent protagonists. He was a very quick study.

After *In Bruges*, which Sylvain had found profoundly disturbing though bitingly dark and humorous in part, they moved out into the Brisbane night and took a cab to the popular South Brisbane restaurant area, Oscar resisting the pull of the Treasury Casino which was just around the corner. When they arrived at Melbourne Street at the corner of Merivale, they decided upon the *era* bistro, which was beginning to crowd. Oscar was relaxed and ready for whatever was to come next.

Deep down however he yearned to be back at his home on the Mar Mediterraneo.

Nerja was a very long way away and had become too distant both in time and geography. It was something which after the current troubles were resolved; he steadfastly intended to do something about.

Solo Hay Uno.

Chapter Eleven

Sylvain had learned much during the meal at *era* relative to the *Brethren of Acadia* and their relevance to *Quildeberg* and the impact upon Oscar and his associates and they had taken the discussion back to their hotel, the *Watermark* at Spring Hill, which was modest, discreet and had good proximity to the Private Hospital and overlooked the Roma Street Parklands.

They continued their briefing during the early evening out on the patio which stood alongside the modest bar and narrow breakfast/restaurant area. They were seated beneath a large yellow Castlemaine XXXX parasol drinking small glasses of cold Victoria Bitter to counter the humidity. The vantage point looking down on to the distant Brisbane city vista was impressive at night (more so than day) and to the far right of the panoramic view could be seen the glow of an array of floodlights raised from the GABBA cricket ground that was hosting a largely inconsequential One Day International between Australia and the touring England side. This backdrop was particularly apt as Oscar set aside the days editions of the Herald Sun, the Australian, the Age and the Sydney Morning Herald which he had been reviewing and studied the content of the 4-page dossier faxed over to him by Trent from the Scottsdale Resort & Conference Center in Arizona, that had been provided for Oscar's attention following Trent's appointment with the forensic accountant at the Rancho Manana Golf Club, a matter of a few hours earlier.

Oscar shared the information with Sylvain and suddenly matters started to fall into place and with it the inherent danger.

The gist of the detail related to an International Cricket Test Match recently played at the end of the previous 2006 year during the week between Christmas and the New Year.

The revered Boxing Day Test Match is a cricket tradition in Melbourne played at the MCG and it had become evident that the Australian team management has filed a report with the ICC's Anti-Corruption and Security Unit after one of their players had been approached by a man suspected of links to an illegal bookmaking syndicate.

The approach was apparently made in the bar of the team's hotel and the man was of Asian-American origin.

Senior ACB officials had expressed concerns that illegal bookmakers, emboldened by the new betting possibilities opened up by the shorter Twenty20 game, were becoming increasingly prevalent around match venues and team hotels. In direct response to the match-fixing scandals involving disgraced international captains; (the late) Hansie Cronje, Mohammed Azharuddin and Salim Malik - barriers had been established to block bookmakers and their intermediaries from direct contact with players. But the approach to an Australian player during an Ashes series, coupled with those allegedly made to other international cricketers at the World Twenty20, have raised concerns that a new wave of corrupting influences is attempting to infiltrate the game.

An anonymous source it went on to say, warned that cricket was under renewed threat from illegal sub-continental bookmakers.

"Those in charge in the ICC understand that Twenty20 cricket has the danger of going back to the bad old days and that the outcome of the most recent Boxing Day Test had fallen under suspicion and scrutiny as unusually high volume betting patterns had been suspected and large amounts of cash had been shifted offshore following the outcome of the Test and had been found to be destined for North America.," the source said.

Oscar understood the ramifications. He believed that the focus on the shorter game and all of the commercial spin-off's had deflected attention from the traditional Test series and that Eric's associates at Quildeberg had used the diversion to bilk the Boxing Day Test by placing bets on state of play situations concerning the number of LBW decisions given in a sessions play. The target had been shifted away from the players who could influence play, directly to the arbiters. To the Umpires who gave the decisions. It was an interesting switch of emphasis and one which was well beneath the radar of those powers keeping vigilant watch.

Oscar knew, as did the late *Rob Bulmer*, the identity of the umpires concerned, their countries of origin and also where the $77 Million dollars had come from and moreover where it was destined and why. Oscar had been used as an unwitting mule and he didn't take kindly to that. A final insult from his deceased former friend.

Oscar also realized that he was in the box seat. Though there was pressure to bear. He controlled the flow of the money. It was time to exercise this control.

The following day, after a sumptuous lunch at the *Café San Marco* on the waterfront of the Stanley Street Plaza at South Bank, where a Bridal Expo had been in full force; Sylvain was dispatched First Class back to Paris via Sydney and Auckland, with a promise of a new rendezvous in Europe and a vacation in reward for his Antipodean efforts, down South in Axarquia, at the end of the month.

He first had another series of important errands to run.

Oscar made ready for the Big Easy.

Chapter Twelve

Dr. Gerald Mercer in his advancing years had become reserved to the point of achieving tenure. His associations with Oscar had taken a toll. He had become a slightly withdrawn and introspective figure living with a constant fear that exposure was always just around the corner. He had morphed into a caricature, an eccentric. A persona almost approaching invisibility without any discernable semblance of either wit or humour. He was boorish, ego-centric, cheap and arrogant. Displaying characteristics of the intellectual, though not quite. He was an absolute snob of the highest New England order, extremely wealthy and with few friends. He was extremely rich. Frequented the right gentlemen's clubs and attended the right social events, often as patron. He was a property owner in Back Bay and Beacon Hill and had also taken a lodge in Greenwich, CT. Moxley Country. He had a cottage and a cruiser berthed near Hyannisport and had taken with a degree of success to the game of golf. He had developed a creditable 10 handicap. The Fertility & Cosmetic surgical clinic that had been renamed in his honour along with the road on which it was sited was thriving due to the concept of destination healthcare. Flocks of rich Arabs had descended, seeking a cure for their affliction. They had also expanded services to include prostate procedures which were minimally invasive, highly topical and very profitable. They were doing very well. He still however disliked people, but would tolerate them. He had evolved into everything to which he had ever aspired. Achieved his life's ambitions. A man truly happy with himself. For this he reluctantly was indebted to one Oscar Phelps.

Returning to the Niagara region of Canada for Gerald would prove a trial. His previous visit had not been exactly pleasant. He had bad memories of Niagara-on-the-Lake which involved a theatre, a tarpaulin and a body.

As Hillary and Gerald walked back from the Fort, across the golf course and down toward the "Dead Zone" movie production company donated Gazebo erected at Queen's Royal Park, they stopped momentarily to view Fort Niagara which stood at the tip of the most western point of New York State, across the river on the US side. As a huge Greyhound bus number 1299 destined for Chicago belched its way behind them to King Street, Hillary looked long and hard at Gerald and wondered. The Doctor rather embarrassed, looked away, distinctly agitated and his face blushed markedly. Hillary took his hand and to his surprise he did not pull it away. It occurred to him that the tarpaulin and the body experience may soon to be surpassed in his nightmares. As they carried on their walk to the Harbour House Hotel on Melville Street, Hillary could sense a thaw in the good Doctor's demeanor. Perhaps he was a candidate for a quick rumble after all? The rigidity had been very real and perhaps she could muster it up again? It would be a challenge, but Hillary would try. She was nothing if not a trier and she was also very much on heat. A young female personal assistant and a vibrator could satisfy only so much.

As they rounded the corner at the junction of Ricardo and Melville, opposite the main Harbour and across from the Queen's Landing hotel where Gerald was staying, they entered the Harbour House. The lobby was small, understated but comfortable and quite sartorially elegant looking such was the appropriateness of the decor. Everything worked. Quality. Tastefully furnished and with an obvious eye to detail and duty of care to guests whom Hillary saw as being quite discerning and attracted by a style and quality of service that encouraged frequent repeat visits. The Harbour House was a little out of the way from the main commercial Queen Street area and the theatres, but provided privacy and discretion for those seeking it. It was perfect for Hillary Robinson who had her nubile and highly sexed PA Nikki ensconced in her room #302 on the third floor and who saw an opportunity with Gerald. To their immediate left on entering the hotel was positioned a bureau with laptop for guests usage, a leather Chesterfield couch and coffee table located opposite a large open fireplace which was the centerpiece of the room and flanked either side by French windows which gave access to a small external patio area. They had a good selection of books and DVD's on hand in the modest bookshelves and displayed the most delicious home made cookies housed under a clear glass GALA cake plate and dome, which Hillary had sampled at every possible occasion and had in all of her honesty, felt quite guilty about doing so. Hillary was very conscious of the need to maintain what still remained a remarkably full, sexy and alluring figure.

They both sat on the couch and Hillary told Gerald to relax. It was more of an instruction than a request and it did not help Gerald that Hillary's blouse had appeared to come unbuttoned revealing significant cleavage and her skirt had risen up slightly as she sat, providing a wonderful view of her shapely stocking clad legs and thighs. Though there was no fire in evidence and the conditioning was on, Gerald began to perspire

Hillary looked down at the newspapers and magazines available on the coffee table which were set down between the various assorted quirky table games and a large wooden bowl of fruit. She discarded the National Post in favour of the HELLO magazine as Gerald became a little more relaxed and tried to stop his gaze from landing too obviously at Hillary's legs and breasts. He made a decision to make himself look at her directly in the eye and this was even worse as he realized just how attractive Hillary Robinson was as she smiled seductively and licked at her lips, rounding with the tip of her tongue, which had the effect of striking Gerald dumb as he returned his attention quickly to the fireplace.

Hillary smiled inwardly and opened the magazine, stopping at the feature article that compared Princess Diana, Princess Grace and both Queen Noor and her successor Queen Rania of Jordan. They were all veritable beauties of their respective day. Hillary studied the article intently for a few minutes before asking Gerald which Royal he preferred from a purely sexual attraction point of view? Gerald, seeing the question as being in very poor taste took the magazine away from Hillary and replaced it on the coffee table. Petulant. He looked at her again, this time with clear irritation and annoyance which took her aback just a little. She returned the stare. Inquisitive.

A few silent moments lapsed during which Gerald became resigned to the inevitable.

"Hillary, are you sure?" he said in voice of very low timbre.

"I'd like you to meet my friend Nikki." she retorted, ignoring his question as she launched herself up with enthusiasm from the couch.

They made their way through the doorway which leads to the elevator, depressed the level 3 button and Gerald knew as the lift ascended, that he would have to be strong.

The following day in the early afternoon, Hillary, Nikki and Gerald were in a stretched limousine on the QEW headed in the direction of Fort Erie just passing the Sodom Road exit and bound for the Peace Bridge border crossing and Buffalo International airport. Hillary was busying herself with Nikki on the back seat in a deep and mutually gratifying embrace, petting heavily. Lots of deep wet probing tongue. Lipstick would need a significant reapplication, when they reached the border.

The good Doctor was now relegated to a bit part watcher in brief. He looked out at the window, not really surprised and sipped at his decanted Crown Royal Special Reserve Scotch whiskey and realized that the previous night had been a huge mistake.

He reminisced and not entirely happily to a very liquid late summer evening in Nerja at *32-Red*, when Oscar had been a touch refreshed and had confided in him that sometimes Hillary had needed the occasional severe talking to. That these occasions had sometimes left her with bruises on her upper arms, which she had relished, and that it had all been for the general good. Oscar had mentioned that Mrs. Robinson had a developed a mild sadistic streak and that she took pleasure in Oscar holding and shaking her heavily in admonishment. Oscar had taken the view that Hillary needed to know when a man cared for her and that she felt it the most through passive aggression. She liked to know that Oscar cared about what she did. Her achievements. Her failings. If this called for a man to beat the hell out of her occasionally when she got out of line, then she liked that too. It did her good. It was a disturbing philosophy, but one in which Hillary appeared to revel and enjoy and which Oscar, her friend, would pander to, if and when needed.

Meanwhile, two time zones back in Arizona, Trent Alexis was preparing to leave the Scottsdale area after what had been a very interesting meeting with the forensic accountant that Oscar had arranged at the golf club, located in the high Sonoran Desert. The accountant had been most forthcoming as she nibbled at her cobb salad, the like of which Trent had never before witnessed, such was its magnitude. She had supplied both narrative and detail of monetary movements, diversions, concealments, forex transactions and deferred electronic transfers and had covered everything off in a very well written summary document. Even Trent understood it. The man he had met in BC was greatly implicated, as was Oscar Phelps.

Trent then took the Charger down into the Carefree area and stopped off at a general mercantile to look at the deals on Cowboy boots. He found a pair which met closely with his personality and decided he would wear them at his next destination. They were of heavy duty looking light tan leather and devoid of any ornate tooling as he wanted a boot and not an accessory. They were basic, strong looking and cheap at $139 dollars. Trent made his purchase.

His time in Phoenix was nearing an end. He had one more scheduled meeting in Scottsdale and then he was happy to be destined for New Orleans. The next day he would be there and soon once again with his friend who at this very moment was crossing the International Date Line over the Pacific Ocean.

Worlds were about to collide.

Chapter Thirteen

I

Mrs. Robinson and the good Doctor had made it into downtown Manhattan, just in time. Nikki had been let loose in Macy's for the evening to look for a parting gift for herself and Hillary had taken the key she had retrieved from the well (secreted there by Oscar soon after the impromptu encounter with the girl in the white coat on Queen Street) in Niagara on the Lake to the appropriate bank. The Wachovia Bank, a Wells Fargo company at the ROCKEFELLER PLAZA FINANCIAL CENTER, 49 ROCKEFELLER PLAZA. In 45 minutes Hillary had been able to provide the appropriate documents for purposes of identification, as had Gerald. The fax from Oscar in Melbourne had validated them as his legal representatives. They had been shown to the assigned safety deposit box, opened it up and collected the contents. Apart from the non-negotiable bearer bonds, there had been two elaborate cases gift wrapped by OMEGA in New York of 711 Fifth Avenue and marked individually for Hillary and Gerald with Oscar's appreciation for their efforts.

To kill time, they took drinks at the NAPLES ristorante in the METLIFE Building at 200 Park Avenue on East 45th street. This was followed by more liquid refreshment of a lighter caffeinated variety at the Rock Center Café at Rockefeller Plaza at number 20, West 50th Street.

At 7.30pm they were on their way around the corner to Brasserie Ruhlmann, located at number 45 Rockefeller Plaza, which was a meticulously-crafted restaurant that pays homage to the great Art Deco designer Émile-Jacques Ruhlmann. None of which meant anything to Gerald. He just wanted to make the exchange safely and quickly and get out of town. Gerald looked nervously out of the showcase window out at the complex's center and the sunken Lower Plaza, site of the world's most famous ice-skating rink.

Gerald could imagine skaters swooping and stumbling across the ice while crowds gather above on the Esplanade to watch the spins and spills. Hovering directly above was the gold-leaf statue of the fire-stealing Greek hero Prometheus — Rockefeller Center's most famous sculpture. Carved into the wall behind it, was a quotation from Aeschylus which read; *prometheus, teacher in every art, brought the fire that hath proved to mortals a means to mighty ends.* Gerald still did not care. He was growing nervous.

On the stroke of 8pm, they were seated and taking drinks in wait for their guest who would not be ordering. Hillary had a *Beefeater* Gin martini in a glass with an odd number of olives, while Gerald took a large cognac.

At 8.04pm the waiter pulled out the empty chair at their table and in it sat a radiant and expectant *Babet Dublecet.*

Right on time.

Hillary and Gerald had succeeded in their quest. They had safely passed over the bonds with a US$10million dollar value to a very excited Babet.

New OMEGA watches and all confidence intact. Their next stop would be New Orleans.

II

Trent's final Arizona meeting was with Wendell Madison at the Scottsdale resorts - *Sangria's* bar.

They met at the appointed time and Wendell had long looked forward to meeting again with Trent, who he very much admired. The admiration was mutual. They stepped through the glass and wrought iron doors into the welcoming ambiance of the main bar and billiards room. It was the hour for a pre-dinner cocktail, but both went for several draft beers followed each time by a shot of the special house tequila. Sangria's also served up appetizers and light fare with a Southwestern flavor which they gladly accepted. These were not men for a candlelit dinner in the Palm Court restaurant.

The antique pool tables were of rich red baize cloth and they shot a couple of games. Each winning a frame. Inconsequential.

Sangria's wall mounted plasma TV screens fired up on CNN and ESPN. The billiards room was flanked by a wall of French doors that opened out to shady patios bordering on the neighboring rattle snake and javelina populated golf courses. The attractive red-head bar-keep told Wendell that on cool Arizona evenings, he could curl up with his beverage in the glow of the patio fireplace, under a brilliant canopy of stars. Wendell asked her if she would like to join? They made a date. Trent was impressed as the Texan flashed his trademark smile.

In the hour that followed they had agreed upon the planning and execution for the anticipated *Brethren of Acadia* meetings. They agreed that at best there were only two kills to me made and that they would be best managed indoors. As Wendell was familiar with New Orleans his suggestion was that they stay at a different hotel to Oscar. Trent concurred and reservations would be made at *the Monteleone* hotel.

The meeting was professional, cordial and specific. Above all it was friendly. At its conclusion Trent and Wendell embraced in a warm manly bear-hug which could not at all be open to misinterpretation. These were men's men. Kindred spirits.

After a final draft they toasted a private toast and went their separate ways. Trent to the check-out desk in the entrance hall and Wendell to the bar-keep, where he took a stool. She looked pleased to see him.

As Trent waited for the print-out of his bill he read over a leaflet he had picked up in Cave Creek. It said;-

"Experience the True Arizona in Cave Creek - eclectic shopping, art galleries and the unrivaled beauty. More than 30 restaurants to choose from, everything from fine dining to cowboy cook-outs. Horseback riding, rodeos, country and western dancing, museums, parks and nature preserves, hiking and biking and old mining tours."

"It's not often you can find a town like Cave Creek, Arizona that has preserved its wild west character so well after more than 100 years especially when its located so close to rapidly growing cities like Scottsdale and Phoenix. But Cave Creek, established as a gold mining town and stopping point for the U.S. Calvary in the mid 1870's, is not like most other towns. While most of the buildings built in the 1800's are probably gone, many that are standing have been there longer than anyone can remember and are reminiscent of what things looked like in the Wild West so long ago."

"Located high above Phoenix in the foothills of Black Mountain, Skull Mesa and Elephant Butte, Cave Creek has accomplished the nearly impossible task of maintaining its old west character and charm in an era of exponential growth within the metropolitan Phoenix area. While Scottsdale has now become most deservedly known for its world class resorts, spas, and golf, and Phoenix for the Suns, Coyotes, Cardinals and Diamondbacks, and Tempe for ASU, Tempe Town Lake, and great Block Parties, their smaller friendly neighbor to the North, Cave Creek, has become one of the most recognized Western towns in the U.S. featuring several saloons, western shops, Rodeo Events, Galleries and live music. Throw in some championship golf, several unique southwest jewelry shops and numerous other specialty stores and you have a must visit location just minutes *but a time warp away* from nearby Phoenix and Scottsdale, Arizona."

Trent thought inwardly..."Amen to that."

Chapter Fourteen

Oscar had arrived too late for the daily *Continental Airlines* direct flight from Heathrow to New Orleans which had departed just after noon. So he had to content himself with a night at the *Sheraton Skyline* hotel on Bath Road, where he had stayed many times previous, before taking the next day's flight.

London Heathrow   New Orleans   Dep:12:05 Arr:19.24   Continental Airlines   CO 5

Flight CO 5 arrived on time and Oscar was checking in at Le Pavillon - *the belle of New Orleans* - at just before 9.45pm local time. He was exhausted.

"Please take a seat." said the Guest Services Manager, offering a chair.

"I prefer to stand." said Oscar, feeling a strange sense of déjà vu and who was sure that this was a famous quotation of some sort. He could not place it, which served to peeve and build upon his tiredness.

He had several messages waiting for him at reception, which was not busy. One from Trent, one from Hillary and another from *Granier*. He decided that he would shake off the jet-lag before attending to them and that they could be deferred until the morrow. As he waited for his credit card to be authorized at check-in he took the time to look around. This really was a very elegant and grand hotel, worthy of its *leading hotels of the world* designation. Located at 833, Poydras Street, with a history stretching back to the Gilded Age and with impeccable décor throughout, Le Pavillon piqued his imagination. Located in the heart of downtown New Orleans, the hotel is seated adjacent the historic *French Quarter* but not quite in it. Just five blocks to the celebrated music clubs of Bourbon Street and the famous restaurants and antique shops of Royal Street and with an ambience that was earned through the passage of time and not created in a designer's office.

The oblong lobby was comprised in rich royal gold, with a row of five statuesque central pillars stood tall and erect with a strength of purpose and chandeliers which shone down on to the immaculate floors of cream and gold. The seating areas were occupied by real and substantial antique furniture and a host of ornate figurines and cut glass bowls were tastefully littered about the place interspersed with decorative flowers and centerpiece arrangements on the grandest of scale. The artwork on display was authentic, the hearth clocks of quality and that actually told time and all of the table tops were of thick polished marble. Then came the one faux pas.

As Oscar completed the check-in procedure for suite #608 and the bell-hop took hold of his luggage he could hear coming from the piano bar located in the Gallery Lounge to his left, a sound so objectionable as to make him wish to cover his ears.

She was the resident classical vocalist and she was dire! Oscar hurried toward the small elevator and the bell-hop followed in quick pursuit with his cases on the trolley, his face almost screwed tight in agony, as if he were chewing upon a wasp, as the singer went for the highest of unachievable notes. The relief as the elevator doors closed was palpable.

The next morning, Oscar, batteries recharged, took a lavish *Sunrise* breakfast buffet of Strawberries, waffles and copious amounts of fresh cream, followed by a large and bulbous dish of *Bananas Foster* that was so good as to have no real comparison, in the relaxed ambience of the lobby level *Crystal Room*.

As he ate the breakfast in a slow and deliberate manner he delighted in the surroundings of the Crystal Room and the Gallery Lounge which offered an extremely rare Sienna marble balustrade with green onyx balusters and bronze ormolu. This really was the highest of class. His deceased friend the Rt.Honorable would have approved.

Oscar decided that Trent Alexis deserved a reward for his endeavours, as he read his note. He would buy him a watch of rare quality and distinction to replace the old one that he remembered he had given him to *hold for safe keeping* these many years ago. It would be very expensive. Trent was loyal, trusted and deserved the very best. Perhaps his only true friend remaining from all of his associations.

He considered for a moment the issues at hand and the probable dangers. He also contemplated his position in life now and the reason he was in New Orleans, the possible effects. Ramifications. He considered;-

...to the English, success is measured not by how you have lived your life, but by how much money you have still got at the end of it. It is ironic that the man who has lived life and made money, who has fulfilled all of his dreams and ambitions and spent money freely throughout his life in pursuit of a better quality for himself and those all around him, is so derided. Much more so than the man who has survived on the basic minimum all of his life, given nothing, achieved little, long abandoned and forgotten all of his dreams but at least when dead, has money to show for the sacrifice!

What Oscar sought now was to be beyond reproach from both perspectives.

Oscar read the other two notes. He signed the check, tipped the large pretty African-American hostess lady in waiting appropriately and left. Satisfied like never before.

The valet called him a cab. Destination *Lafayette Cemetery No. 1. 1400 Washington Ave.*

Thirty minutes later in relatively warm weather the cab driver dropped him directly outside of the main high, black, wrought iron arched gateway to the famed cemetery in the Garden District of the city.

The rows of tombs inside looked very white and well looked after. Oscar checked his TAG. It was the appointed time. *Granier* was usually very precise.

Oscar opened the gate and walked in, stopping only for a moment at the side of the first caretaker's building to take a drink of water from the external standpipe tap which was used for the connecting hose system. As he lifted his head up from the tap he caught a glimpse of two people in the distance, stood next to one of the smaller tombs. They were a good one hundred and fifty yards away and the sun's glint prevented Oscar from identifying them, but he did think one was a colored man and the other a more slight figure of a woman.

She displayed what looked like an awkward and painful looking gait as she stood next to the man, looking it now appeared as if she were struggling to break free of the grip he had on her upper arm. Oscar stood tall and approached them with a degree of caution. He had no weapon and the man looked larger with every step Oscar made.

As Oscar instinctively looked again at his TAG, the man pulled a long knife from behind his back.

Without hesitation, he pulled the girl hard towards his left side and slid the blade from left to right, pulling deep and hard across her throat. Dark blood appeared immediately as she squealed with shock. The man let her fall to the ground and he turned immediately and ran.

Oscar, stood dead in his tracks quickly calculated the situation he faced. He waited a moment until he was assured that the man had fled the scene. He looked behind him for any signs of other people. There were none in evidence.

He could see the girl squirming in the distance. She writhed on the ground, slowly bleeding out in what was fast becoming a large pool of blood.

As he arrived at her side he witnessed the final shuddering of her body as it accepted defeat and became prone. Her arms which had been clutched at her neck had grown relaxed and her legs which had assumed the fetal position had begun to straighten. She was gone.

Her eyes were stark wide open and her chin and lower mouth slightly obscured and bloodied by her soaked fingers. Her face was frozen in terror and shock. She looked young.

The girl was (Oscar observed) wearing a white coat which had opened out slightly revealing a naked body. She appeared curvaceous and quite buxom. Heavy white breasts. She had blue eyes and was wearing a knitted lime green toque which had bunched up and was now almost falling from her head. Her head appeared bald. Shaven. Oscar realized that he had seen her before.

It was the girl from Queen Street who he had last seen going off in the direction of Simcoe Park.

Chapter Fifteen

It was during a very arid evening in Nerja in the late summer of 2005 that *Oscar Phelps;* sporting white knee length cotton shorts by Alex Cordon, Nike ankle socks, Skechers casual loafers and a very loud orange, yellow and blue *Tommy Bahama* shirt in silk, first happened upon the idea. It was more evidence of the work of a very sardonic, mordant, straight forward and prompt intelligence.

He was sipping a Lanjaron water *con gas* at a courtside table of the bar at the Tenis Club Andaluz de Nerja, located on the side of the main carretera Malaga/Almeria N-340 which services to the south the Hotel Nerja Club and to the north the Capistrano conurbation.

Oscar had just witnessed on satellite TV at *32-Red* the English cricket team beat the touring Australian's to regain the Ashes virtue of a drawn match in the final test of the series at the Oval cricket ground in SE11 South London. He was elated.

On the show court playing a game of mixed doubles were the unlikely pairing of Horace Boylan and Hillary Robinson who were engaged in a frantic two-setter, littered with inappropriate expletives and cursing and very unsubtle gamesmanship played against Babet Dublecet and Dr.Tagliapietra who were vacationing in Andalucía from the Argentine.

Horace and Hillary looked resplendent in matching predominantly white NIKE attire and had Wilson top of the range equipment at their disposal. However, their actual performance bordered between the point of embarrassment and mirth. Something that did not quite escape the on looking Oscar who did well to repress his natural disposition toward mocking the afflicted. He was suppressing a guffaw, but only just. The aging northern

Europeans were on the way to a very flattering 1-6, 2-6 defeat and not gallantly. They were the very model of consistency, insofar as each set started off abject to poorly, leveled out during the middle games in mediocrity, during which they accepted a few charitable points and claimed some highly dubious line calls, before completely petering away, quite lamentably, toward the inevitable conclusion of the set.

Horace displayed very little hand to eye coordination and hardly any appreciation at all for the subtleties and nuances of the game. He had neither speed nor stamina and very little positional sense. He did however know the rules, something with which his playing partner was only vaguely acquainted. Hillary's athletic attributes were entirely cosmetic. She was a complete liability. No discernable aptitude at all for matters sporting which did little to detract from the fact that she thought Horace to be the weak link in the team. Something which Horace did his level best not to dwell upon as he encouraged her and praised her every effort because he genuinely believed that if he remained loyal and supportive, then perhaps it would be rewarded with a post match blow-job in the locker room.

With Hillary, who had shaken off the spectre of Nerja and long since reconciled with the Ghost of *Francesca Luciana*, this would be a fair bet.

Interlude at Caxton Street, St. James, London

Interlude at Caxton Street, St.James, London

"Drink to me, drink to my health, you know I can't drink any more."
- **Pablo** Diego José Francisco de Paula Juan Nepomuceno María de los
Remedios Cipriano de la Santísima Trinidad Ruiz y **Picasso**

Following on from Sylvain's departure from Queensland, Oscar had himself traveled down to Sydney with Qantas from where he boarded a direct Cathay Pacific Business Class flight to San Francisco and from there another conveniently connecting Virgin Atlantic Jumbo on to London Heathrow. It was not the most conventional way back to the old country from Australia, but Oscar wanted to satisfy his medical needs with Ghirardelli chocolate. So he saw it as the most logical route. He also wanted to savour the time in thought and preparation for New Orleans.

His first day back in Blighty was met with an additional battery of tests at the Number One Health clinic located at Number 1 Harley Street, W1, where all of the practitioners had similar designations; MBBS MRCP MSc Public Health DTM&H DoccMed DFPH. The tests were not arduous but were to Oscar's mind, more extensive than those carried out in Australia.

In the afternoon after a sumptuous lunch at the Crosse Keys public house on Gracechurch Street, he checked in at the St Ermin's hotel in St. James, a favored location from his distant past and an old dame of a hotel which had clearly and sadly observed better days. No longer part of the STAKIS group, the old girl had not weathered particularly well and Oscar believed she had come down distinctly in class.

Renamed the Jolly St Ermin's, the main characteristics that so resonated in Oscar's mind, still remained. Still part of the fabric of his life. Testimony to more innocent times. Times of lavish dinners followed by Brandy and cigars and fellowship. Of Taylor's vintage port. All on the Yankee dime. But somehow this place had been sullied and cheapened by time. Perhaps it was just perception and a dilution by the elements? Perhaps it was just reality kicking in?

In 1887 The St. Ermin's was opened as a block of mansion flats. In the early 1900's it became a hotel and it enjoys close proximity to the Houses of Parliament. It has always been popular with MP's as well as Lords, both spiritual and temporal.

However, this was of little import to Oscar. This was the St. Ermin's that had played host to Sir Michael Caine and Bob Hoskins during the making of the film *Mona Lisa*. The baroque staircase in the main reception lounge, the extensive curving balcony that overlooks and surrounds the main Victorian lobby still remained and so did the now slightly yellowing chandeliers, but the breakfast hall had been relocated and had been replaced with something much less elaborate. Less Grand.

This was a metaphor for London, Oscar reluctantly observed. Perhaps even for England. Nothing it appeared, could escape the savagery of time, the immigrant ravaged attack on identity and nationalistic sense of self and drudgery that prevailed under a socialist ruled Britain.

Everything socially and aesthetically had become so much cheaper.

Oscar was getting old. Perhaps he had been an expatriate too long?

After check-in which required pre-payment now, another sign of civility decayed, Oscar retired to the Caxton Bar and lounge area which was ornately patterned in dark grays and with a long brown bar, neatly hemmed in by dark reddish purple material laden walls and brown wooden coving with a deep red ceilings with embedded crass spot lights and a crowd of neo-Georgian furniture crafted to look antique, but which wasn't. The carpeting was of small same patterned squares in black and grey which made the head ache and the eyes blur and the couches and wing backed chairs were all comfortable, but of dubious quality. Factory produced en masse. Disappointing but functional. Again, a possible metaphor for England.

Suitably depressed, Oscar turned his attention to the reading of the day's Times. They did not have a Trib.

His attention, as yet another batch of flustered Japanese tourists took their seats opposite him, was drawn immediately to the banner story on page four:-

Five dead, skating champ missing
Olympic skater's leg partially amputated
Rescuers dive into 'bloodied water'
Two inquiries into cause of crash
Second fatal ferry crash this year

...was the gist of the report.

"Australian ice skating champion Sean Carpow saved the life of his mother, Olympian Liz Coin, when she blacked out after her leg was severed in last night's Sydney Harbour ferry crash."

"Australia's tight-knit ice skating community is reeling from the disaster, which killed and maimed some of its leading lights and devastated "dynasties of families".

Among the dead were international skating judges, a young champion skater and a female tourist, traveling alone.

"Ms Coin lost part of her left leg and was flung into the harbour when her husband's 10-metre motor cruiser and a Sydney Ferries HarbourCat collided under Sydney Harbour Bridge just before 11pm (AEST) yesterday."

Leg severed in impact

A family friend, said Ms Coin passed out when she saw her injured leg and would have drowned had it not been for her quick-acting son.

"It appears that her left foot from about half way down the shin was severed from the impact ... and lost - it went down with the boat," he said.

"She saw that her left leg was severed half way down that shin and she blacked out and was floating in the harbour."

Oscar recoiled inwardly at the thought. It was indeed a tragedy.

There were seven other passengers on the boat at the time of the incident, most of whom were linked to the ice skating fraternity.

Came right out of the blue

"They were going up the harbour and right without any warning this ferry came up behind them. The first thing they heard was the crash - then it was physically on top of them. It appears to have hit them amidships going towards the stern (rear)."

Police are investigating eye-witness reports that the smaller vessel's lights were not working in the lead-up to the collision.

Rear Admiral Jeff Smithie, chief executive of Sydney Ferries, which operates the *Pam Burbidge*, said: "It was a catastrophic impact because this wooden cruiser appears to have just disintegrated and the people were flung into the water."

Two ferries and police and naval boats arrived on the scene almost immediately and helped pluck survivors from the water.

Cliff Marshall, a passenger on one of the ferries which helped in the rescue, said it was a chaotic scene. "There were people in the water. There was a lot of wreckage, lots of shouting, mayhem, a terrible sight," he told ABC radio.

The accident was the second this year and the 14th since 2004 involving the 28 state-owned ferries that ply Sydney Harbour. The catamarans carry more than 13 million passengers a year, including commuters and tourists seeking a waterside view of attractions such as the Sydney Opera House and Luna Park.

Oscar looked away from his newspaper. He thought for a moment. He then looked over at the marble surround hearth and open grated fire which was now blazing dispiritingly at mark 4 and then cast his stare directly above it, landing at the illuminated Scottish landscape monstrosity of a painting, thankfully unsigned, out of shame, which sat above the tastefully obtrusive cardboard *No Smoking* sign.

Oscar put down his newspaper, called the valet for a black cab and in fifteen minutes was checked out and traveling quickly on the M4 West, destined for the Continental Airlines desk at London Heathrow.

Part 3

Anatomy of the Game

Chapter One

Farren Granier was a man who was used to winning.

A Franco-American Harvard graduate and sometime Princeton NJ Professor of Anthropology, he was a product of the American dream. With provenance declaring that his ancestors came to the US on the *Mayflower*, he had a history which was both as interesting as it was embellished and fabricated. A man with an often garrulous manner but authoritative air, Farren could command a room and retain interest despite his relatively frail frame and un-athletic build. He had presence. He had a stentorian voice when it suited, which was both demanding and assuring, and which was also a little like his pigeon chest. In that he could inflate either at will.

His manner was confident and brisk with a pretention toward arrogance.

(Deep seated of course.) He was circumspect, careful and an ultimate charmer.

His appearance was that of a middle aged sophisticate, (he was near to sixty), with graying hair slicked back, a cleanly shaven face with prominent nose (almost classical profile) and large teeth which were his own. Something of which he was proud. He wore bland round framed spectacles, but more for use in illustration rather than the act of seeing, though this point could be observed as contentious. The spectacles often hung around his neck from a cheap black cord.

His dress was that of a conservative and wealthy businessman who went his own way. His shirts were not tailored, nor his suits, but they still bore a certain sober elegance. His only vanity appeared to be his club tie, which he wore religiously every day. He had a modest timepiece on his wrist and almost no jewelry save for a thin wedding band of gold and his Harvard graduation ring which was pre-eminent.

A sickly child with remarkable intellect, he had often been the subject of bullying. Something he had never forgotten. He was methodical and efficient in his work and clear of purpose. Neither over elaborate nor over confident.

He had been introduced to one Oscar Phelps by the late Rt.Hon. Eric Armstrong-Jones at a function in the City of London – Mayfair drinks party - these many years ago. They had exchanged pleasantries but little else initially.

When eating and drinking his favoured red wine, Farren gave a performance worthy of an Oscar. He was slow, deliberate and believed that a meal was an event to be savoured. A meal with himself and Dr. Gerald Mercer would have been an intolerable cruelty. Oscar never made the mistake of getting those two together at the same table.

Granier would use cheap pens and legal pads during meetings. He would take copious meticulously detailed notes and had a tendency to go off subject at a sharp tangent, waxing lyrical about personal foibles and experiences.

Married twice and with two lots of children separated by both a generation and a continent, he was a wonderful and caring family man. His prodigies had all been and were privately and expensively educated at the best schools in New England and France. He was also a devoted husband and doted on his younger wife, who adored him.

They kept apartments in the opera district of Paris, in New York, a chalet in Switzerland near Annemasse and a small cottage in Piraeus, Greece. He also maintained a largely dormant commercial office in Glyfada. The most cosmopolitan suburb of Athens, conveniently located 25 km away from the Athens airport; "Eleftherios Venizelos"

He was fiercely loyal to friends and always helpful. He did not however suffer fools, though liked eccentrics. He was also intolerant of disloyalty and betrayal. Many could attest to that, though not in life.

Granier had always displayed a gregarious and magnanimous nature and a genuinely happy disposition. He could be very funny. His laugh was whimsical, tending toward being a little overdone. Often displaying theatrical and sharp exaggerate movements. Though not over exuberant, he always sought to maintain a practical façade.

He was past president of the *Americans in Paris Association* and kept business away from his private life, which was guarded. In commerce he was laboured, organized but slow, which could serve to frustrate the opponent and ally alike into submission. He was also ruthless and capable of a double-cross. He could not use a PC, distrusted email and transcribed all of his memorandum longhand.

He was always prepared to go the extra mile and hated to be indebted to anyone. A case of High Corporate mentality, though cottage industry skilled.

His only short-fall until now, was that he tended to over estimate his own import and underestimated his vulnerability. He was sensitive to change and not open to criticism.

Farren Granier was a truly wonderful character...who Oscar hated to have disposed of. There were too few with his demonstrated whimsy left in the world.

But Oscar had simply been left with no other choice.

Farren was sat on a bench at the southerly perimeter of Jackson Square watching a street performer engaged in a magic show. It involved balloons.

He had chosen to miss his earlier appointment at the cemetery with Oscar Phelps.

It would be folly to miss the next one at the Rue Royal.

Chapter Two

Oscar was not amused.

He arrived at just before 2pm, accompanied by Trent Alexis and Wendell Madison, at the main entrance to the *Court of Two Sisters* restaurant on Rue Royal. The daily Jazz Brunch Buffet was featured. The music was in full flow and force and looked as though it had been so for quite some time. Winding down. It was a shame, as Oscar very much appreciated this kind of entertainment. He liked to bask in the atmosphere. But this was not the day for it.

As they first walked in, Trent took the lead and the hostess who initially appeared *super hoity toity* in asking if they had made reservations, decided quickly upon sizing up Trent, that this was not the time for the niceties. No smile. Not even real eye contact.

Oscar and his companions walked with purpose through what looked like the "service" area of the kitchen - plates being scraped into the trash, bain maries of... things wrapped up in plastic wrap, and just organized disarray. Not an attractive area to see before (or even after) brunch. Yet somehow, it added to the appeal. The restaurant held so much gastronomic delight and generated such an appealing ambience that these small imperfections, simply did not matter.

Oscar had changed and was now dressed in a single breasted 2-piece lightweight suit in off-white. He wore a white shirt of distinctive quality with lightly starched collar and his MCC bacon & eggs tie.

He wore burgundy brogues. Bostonian. Anywhere else in the world he would have been a stand-out. Not in New Orleans.

Wendell was replete in a Cutter & Shark shirt also in white and open at the neck, blue lightweight slacks, black Oxford brogues and a rather dapper Harris Tweed jacket with distinctive brown leather patches at each elbow. Trent was his habitual self. Dressed for business. He looked what he was. Formidable. Black suit, white shirt, thin black solid tie. His pants rode a little short but not so much as to matter. His collar a little soiled but more so from character than dirt. He had on his new boots. He was not a slave to fashion.

They took their seats at a long wooden table set for eight and with a good view of the entrance. It was busy and noisy. Though in a good way. Joy masking out the despair.

The designated server was very eager which was cute but gave up early on the normal conversational gambit of asking the same old tourist questions (where are you from? what are you here for?). Trent asked for a club soda, but the server cleverly upsold him to a *Perrier* saying that the club soda was "too flat" and that the sparkling water was better. Trent snapped; "of course it's better, it increases the check!" He was not in a happy mood. The server did not stay around long enough for his views to be educational.

Each started on a first course from the various buffet carts. They went up together to make their selections. Oscar took the classic eggs benedict, Trent the veal grillades with gravy and corn grits and Wendell went for the boiled shrimp and crawfish with remoulade. Oscar also asked for a pot of coffee.

The picturesque old-world courtyard with original gas lights and flowing fountains was clearly visible, just by where the entrance was hidden away to the narrow doored bathrooms. Wendell checked the bathrooms out - Men's and Women's - there was only one way in and out. He then settled down to his shrimp, pawing at it but never taking his eyes away from the main entrance.

Oscar had earlier dispatched Hillary and the Doctor, who had certain sensibilities incongruous to this kind of ordeal, on a tour of the area. Out of harms way. Hillary opted for the **Katrina** tour of the lower ninth ward. She was excited at the prospect. Gerald was just relieved.

At 2.20pm Farren Granier walked in. He was alone. He was smiling and offering an outstretched confident hand in Welcome to Oscar. As he reached the table Oscar declined the gesture and urged Granier to sit by kicking out a chair next to Trent. Granier looked sheepishly at Trent, took off with slowness and deliberacy his mole-skin jacket and sat, still smiling. Not saying a word.

A few uncomfortable moments passed by before Granier opened with;

"It was here that I first learned to suck head and eat tail."

It was an interesting rejoinder, if a somewhat inappropriate start?

"Let me try that again..." he said in a lower tone.

Oscar, Trent & Wendell were not moved and remained silent.

"This place is lovely isn't it? (he enthused gushingly)...with the open courtyard and the blessed air-conditioning and the glassed-in terrace area with live jazz", he continued, struggling to make an impression.

"It is also the place where I discovered crawfish. And, oh lord, how I discovered crawfish, indeed!" was his assertion, soon after which he stopped short with the performance, realizing that his bravado was dying a death. A very painful death.

Granier made one last plaintive attempt.

"I did snap those tails off, sucked head, and peeled shell to feast my eyes on succulent and meaty flesh, before giddily devouring said flesh. Mmmm..." he concluded.

Trent looked at Oscar, to gauge his reaction to this diatribe. He had witnessed Oscar's brutal side, but had never gotten to the point of judging him.

Wendell nudged at Trent's leg under the table.

"This is going to be interesting." he whispered.

Chapter Three

NERJA

The venerable and impressionable Sylvain, the highly debauched and irrepressible Horace and the omni-cultured and reserved Alberto were dining from a vast "smörgåsbord" of delights comprising; bread dipped in ham broth, a variety of fish (salmon, herring, sardine, whitefish, scrod and eel), Serrano ham, chorizo, small meatballs, head cheese and various sausages, potato, boiled and potato casserole, soft and crisp bread, melba toast, mantequilla and a host of different cheeses including Brie, English cheddar, Goat's cheese, Dutch Edam and Stilton, beetroot salad, cabbage (red, brown & green) and rice pudding, churros with crema chocolato, at the Tropicana restaurante in 32-Red on Hernando de Carabeo.

Johnny Cash was singing 'I saw the light' on the background loop and would be followed by *Katy Perry* with 'Waking Up in Vegas" and the *Magic Numbers* performing 'I See You See Me', an altogether eclectic, somewhat mystifying if not eccentric musical taste inspired by Alberto, the now well established director of operations and part owner of the restaurante. Oscar had shown the love and rewarded the loyalty. Alberto had also graduated to the stewardship of the *Dolores IV* cruiser, still moored but in a larger berth at the Marina del Este.

I saw the light, I saw the light
No more darkness, no more night
Now I'm so happy, no sorrow in sight
Praise the Lord, I saw the light

I've walked in darkness, clouds covered me
I had no idea where the way out could be

Then came the sunrise and rolled back the night
Praise the Lord, I saw the light

Just like a blind man, I wandered alone
Worries and fears I claimed for my own
Then like a blind man who God gave back his sight
Praise the Lord, I saw the light

Come on!

Both Sylvain and Alberto were noticeably succumbing to the beat as Horace observed and found mildly amusing.

Sylvain, upon seeing that Horace had caught him unawares, hurriedly began examining his recently manicured nails and then turned his attention to his travel itinerary provided by *Marie-Carmen*, (who Horace oft referred to with reverence as 'the fat-arsed dago girl who he would quite like to knobble') from *Viajes Verano Azul* on Calle Chaparil, in contemplation of his planned trip to Antwerpen and Amsterdam. Oscar had him scheduled to meet with Byron Tyler-Walker, a long time acquaintance and man with very specialist niche talents and provider services. He was a little bit of a *character*, but with his uses.

The Frenchman, at being caught off-guard, his usual Gallic reserve exposed, was somewhat embarrassed. Something upon which Horace thrived.

Alberto however, viewed Horace and all matters related to Horace with casual indifference. Only large problems ever irked him. He had, upon accepting the equity offered by Oscar in *32-Red*, decreed that he would accept with honour and deep gratitude with however, one proviso. That the 'volcano' mural be taken down and replaced with something altogether more colloquial. Oscar had agreed and where once was a dormant *Vesuvio*, there was now erected a tasteful and apt wall painting by a local artist, of the *Sierra Almijara*, complete with snowcap.

Horace took a drink from his *Dos Equis* beer and turned his attention to the study of the well formed ample rears of two young lithe olive skinned Spanish *'Penelope Cruz wannabee'* girls in their mid to late twenties stood chatting at the Rotunda bar drinking *Corona* and *Brava* beers and who were dressed for sex. Alluring. Alberto was leafing through a *Museo de Malaga* catalogue and his browse had stopped at *The Bay at Cannes* by Pablo Picasso. A work from his cubism period placed at between 1910 & 1919. The entry was headed by an explanation of Cubism as being a 20th century avant-garde art movement, pioneered by Pablo Picasso and Georges Braque.

Horace glanced over at the catalogue; "fucking pretentious crap!" was his candid and forthright unsolicited assessment.

Alberto ignored him as being altogether too frivolous to be serious, while the Frenchman attempted to rationise the value of the painting in the broader scheme of world art and European cultural evolution. He maintained to Horace that the "background and object planes interpenetrate one another to create the shallow ambiguous space".

Horace started to laugh and turned his attention back to the women at the bar.

"I'd like to see them interpenetrate one another..." he said crassly in his deep lilting Irish brogue, while smiling roguishly

Sylvain looked quizzically at Alberto, who rolled his eyes and shook his head slowly.

The musical genre had once again changed so that what could be heard in the background was the brass instrumental melody from *A Sunday Smile* by Beirut.

"That sounds like carousel music." Horace observed with a guffaw.

Chapter Four

The musical numbers being played out in the background by the Jazz band at the *Court of Two Sister's* were taken from the catalogue of *Riverside Blues* by King Oliver. Oscar and his associates listened, waiting for the next statement of the absurd as Farren Granier further observed;

"I wonder, is it a fair exchange do you think, four hundred years of horrendous slavery, murder and oppression for a culture of genius that produces music like this?", he said to no one in particular.

Though repulsed by the notion, Oscar thought that perhaps in this, Farren Granier did make a valid point. Would this wonderful music have been possible without the horrific history?

Probably not. It was after all, part of the very fabric.

Trent and Wendell seeing that there was no immediate cause for concern with Granier, decided to revert to the buffet carts for a second round.

Examining fully the board of fare on offer.

No one had offered a response to Granier's question.

This time Trent went for the Zesty Cajun Pasta, Sweet Potato with Andouille Sausage and two thick carved slices of tender roast beef and a pile of slow roasted turkey breast with natural au jus, apple and horseradish cream sauce. Wendell selected Duck à l' orange, Creole Jambalaya and a slew of Southern BBQ Pork Ribs. They both picked up Cornbread, & Homemade Buttermilk Biscuits.

At the table they ordered a pitcher of local *Abita Amber* beer and only three glasses. Granier did not appear at all slighted by the oversight.

"You know, I really am trying to be civil here and you all don't appear to be in the least receptive?" he said in a resigned southern intonated, exaggerated tone of voice that came out as a rather recalcitrant drawl.

A moment passed as Oscar considered Granier's latest pronouncement.

"Was that your idea of civility this morning in the cemetery?" said Oscar.

Granier found the comment churlish and did not react. He pushed his chair back and crossed his legs, blowing out air in the process.

"Outside I have a troupe of very nasty, very large, very partisan friends who would like nothing more than to rip off each of your heads and feed them to the alligators in the Bayou." he said.

Trent put a little more horseradish on his beef and Wendell started to show signs of actual interest. Oscar didn't blemish. The family on the next table on overhearing Farren's comment decided that it would be prudent to move and picked up their plates, flatware and glasses and walked over very quickly to a table which was not in earshot of the four men.

The volume on the jazz music playing and its tempo appeared to move up a notch. Subtle though distinct.

Oscar looked at his associates and then turned his attention back to Granier. Slow and deliberate.

He adjusted his bearing at the table and leaned forward, staring now directly at Granier. Giving him his full attention for the first time during the whole discourse.

"My dear Farren...we have been very poor hosts, perhaps you would care to dine? He offered.

Granier looked intently at Oscar, trying with little success, to weigh him up, and with more than a little trepidation as to the reason for the sudden change of mood and tac.

Granier smiled a forced smile. Neither pleasant nor appealing.

"I will indulge myself with a dessert." he replied.

Oscar stood and with a sweep of his hand directed Granier toward the Dessert Cart. The selection was extensive; Mardi Gras King Cake, Southern Pecan Pie, Bananas Foster, Bread Pudding with Whiskey Sauce, Home Churned French Vanilla Ice Cream with a choice of Praline or Chocolate Sauce.

Granier cut himself a small slice of the Pecan Pie. Oscar piled into a deep dish, a mess of *Bananas Foster* and Bread Pudding. He covered it with whipped cream and chocolate sauce. He was Not counting calories.

When they got back to the table, Trent had got a fourth glass for the *Abita* and a new bottle of *Perrier*, while Wendell was stood at the window looking out into the courtyard.

He counted seven very large African-American and two equally proportioned Caucasian men, dressed in what looked like fatigues. They were collected around an outdoor table which held duffle bags. The bags looked as though they held a very heavy and potentially destructive cargo. The table was of the wooden kind you often see at a barbeque or picnic. The men were looking directly back at him and not out of admiration. Wendell returned the stare and followed up with his usual flashing smile and then shot them each symbolically with his Index finger. Wendell had been reading a *SPENSER* novel by Robert B. Parker and he had always wanted to do this. This was his chance. Next, he would find a hydrant to park on.

The men paid no mind.

Chapter Five

An hour later as the musicians took a break and Mssrs. Alexis and Madison finished up at the dessert cart, Oscar had reluctantly made a deal under slight duress with Granier.

Conscious of the proximity of Hillary which with hindsight was a mistake, allied to the greater good of his associates for the longer term, he made an agreement reached under deliberated negotiation to discount (with specific operational trigger provisos being met along the way) on the $77M dollars held in his account for a gross settlement to Granier, the Knight accomplice and the *Brethren of Acadia group* of $50M dollars payable in the currency of diamonds. Oscar's suggestion.

Diamonds would be a much better proposition for trade and appreciation and much easier to move, evading the attention of the IRS or any other interested parties and government agencies.

Granier liked the sound of that.

All of the time that Farren Granier had been speaking, in his very contrived deep voiced methodical business tone, Oscar could not help but conjure up in his mind the image of the young girl in the lime green toque who he had seen fall to the ground helplessly and then lay prone, her body throbbing, jolting horrifically and quivering, bleeding out to her death next to the most elaborate tomb in the row. The tomb he now realized, that closely resembled the structure of Antonio Gaudi's; *Templo de la Sagrada Familia* in Barcelona, that he had first encountered in 1977 and which had so caught his imagination.

The final transaction it was decreed would be completed in Amsterdam.

Granier expressed his satisfaction with the compromise arrangement but also his sorrow and disappointment in that *Phelps* had not proven either as genuine an accomplice or as accommodating a conciliere as the late *Rt. Honourable Eric* had lead him to believe would be so. Oscar explained that the funds had prostituted and brought into disrepute a game, an institution close to his heart, and for this he could not forgive his former friend or him.

Granier dismissed this under his breath as maudlin sentiment. Oscar diplomatically ignored the comment and rung his hands out on his table napkin and then he enquired casually, with an understated, matter of fact, almost throwaway, afterthought line...

"Where is Morag? I am very sorry to have missed her."

Granier looked over Oscar's shoulder and then down at Oscar's dish which was cleaned and empty.

"Vacationing in Montreal with that man *Tagliapietra*." he said.

He clearly did not care for the Argentine Doctor.

With that, Granier rose from his seat, in truth, much more comfortable and assured than when he had arrived.

He looked at the table, surveying the leftovers and pointed at Oscar's dish and asked if he was *eating for his health?*

It was a calculated, petulant though telling parting quip, which Granier obviously could not resist delivering and that took Oscar by complete surprise.

It was also one which would ultimately seal Granier's fate.

Chapter Six

It had been one hell of an ordeal.

Twenty minutes into the bus tour with Hillary Robinson and Dr. Mercer had realized that 'putting himself in harm's way' would have been much the more palatable preference.

The Katrina tour had started off in the car park alongside the *Grey Line Lighthouse* and was scheduled for a three hour duration with a promise that they would;

Learn the history of the original city, the French Quarter, and why it was built at this particular location along the Mississippi River and they Would drive past an actual levee that "breached" and see the resulting devastation that displaced hundreds of thousands of U.S. residents and left so many dead...

Hillary Robinson could not have been more inappropriately dressed, for what was a somber and heart rendering, soul searching event.

Dr. Mercer wore a sober dark blue suit and solid blue tie out of respect and in keeping with the remainder of the bus passenger contingent. Whereas Hillary's garb was suited more to *'Ladies Day'* at Royal Ascot. She covered parts of her body in a very tight thigh-length pink leather skirt by *D&G* and a figure hugging silk white blouse with frills by *Chanel* which featured a huge pink bow. Black silk stockings and suspenders, pink silk panties and black high heel shoes rounded off the ensemble. Her blouse was so tight that her bosoms were heaving for a release. The pierce de resistance was a hat perched upon her silky blond locks which defied description, other than it was black, haute couture, vulgar and expensive.

Within minutes of the excursion leaving the French Quarter on its way to the St. Bernard and Ninth Ward parishes, Hillary had made new friends.

Donny and Leonard were from San Francisco and on honeymoon having recently received their nuptials following the change in the law. One was Dean of a reputable California University and the other the owner of a health food store in Sausalito. They were very open, very gauche and very hospitable and open to making Hillary a *bus buddy*. The tour had become superfluous.

Hillary learned about and was intrigued by their relationship. The age gap. The difference in ethnicity. In intellect. In size. In who put what were? Who was the more submissive? Hillary displayed no tact. No diplomacy. No element of political correctness. She was incapable. She learned how they had met at Venice Beach. Leonard pumping iron at the famous sidewalk gym facility and Donny rollerblading on the pedestrian way when they had first spotted one another. It had been love at first sight.

Mercer was feeling himself get more and more nauseated with every passing word as Hillary encouraged him, without success, to participate in the conversation. He rested his head upon and stared long and hard out of the window, not caring that he appeared both aloof and rude, positioning the aircon flute towards his face to get the full effect of the airflow and wished he were somewhere else. He turned his attention to the new OMEGA watch on his wrist and wondered what he would be doing now if he was back home in Boston.

To further exacerbate matters, when he eventually fully awoke from a series of catnaps, an hour and a half into the tour, the place next to him was no longer occupied. To his horror and consternation as he twisted around in search of Mrs. Robinson, he caught a glimpse of her, writhing on the back seat. She was in full heavy petting mode, engaged enthusiastically in a bout of sexual congress with a large nubile red headed woman of perhaps thirty who appeared to be a more than willing and enthusiastic partner. Hillary had absolutely no shame.

Gerald sank back into his seat, resigned. He closed his eyes and waited. Praying for the tour to come to an end.

Chapter Seven

Flanked by the dramatic *Sierra Almijara* mountain range to the east, Nerja had managed somehow to avoid being blighted by the concrete high-rise scenarios which had been the inevitable result of the tourist boom in a great many of *Espana's* coastal resorts. The old part of town was still virtually unchanged with its narrow winding arteries, a prominent shopping street in Calle Pintada and a host of whitewashed houses featuring wrought iron terraces overflowing with geraniums and assorted glorious flora on which a canary could sometimes be heard singing... It was a romantic setting.

The spectacular *Balcón de Europa* remained the centerpiece. Providing a magnificent promenade along the edge of a towering cliff that was once the site of the great Moorish castle. It provided sweeping panoramic views of the *Mar Mediterraneo* and the many small coves, inlets and beaches down below, set against an awe inspiring backdrop of hazy blue mountains.

However, Nerja had changed considerably from when Oscar was last in extended residence. Time had impinged and taken its captives.

Some fatally.

The 17th century Church of *El Salvador*, in a style combining baroque and moorish or mudéjar had become more commercial. There was no longer on Calle Granada a *DON COMER* tapas bar with Antonio serving up the delicious hamburgesitas con ensalada patatas. It had long since been turned to rubble and reinvented. Owner *Udo Heimer* had changed direction.

The *Nerja Bookshop* had been remodeled and had an owner change. It was now offering DVD's and video rental. The site of the *Sunday Market* had moved from Chaparil. The football team; *Club Deportivo Nerja* had moved to a new municipal stadium up in the hills off the N-340, away from their deeply confined backstreet surrounded open terraced long standing magical town center stadia location, which had now been abandoned to the developers.

Calle Cristo, better known by local expats as Post Office Street was no longer in a state of perpetual renovation. How the sound of the jack hammers and the wall of omni-present swirling dust would be missed.

W H Smiffs bookstore had new owners and *La Cocina* had closed its doors and with it the authentic and best *English Breakfast* on the coast had been lost.

The *Coastline Gazette* that Oscar had often read along with the SUR in English, Costa del Sol News and La Sentinella had revamped to become the Seaside Gazette and its editor, *George*, who had been a friend, had passed away. *Illy* Coffee and *Warsteiner* lager had evolved to become Global brands.

Sadly, there was no *Jose Rivero de Luque* marching proudly in his red beret of distinction, leading the *Semana Santa* parade, and the New Year's Eve fireworks extravaganza and musical celebrations held at the hastily constructed and *questionably safe* stage on the *Balcon*, no longer ended prematurely with an unscheduled explosion and an ambulance.

Still, Nerja remained and with it *32-Red* and all that it stood for.

Sylvain was looking down upon it all from the window seat of the airliner that was speeding him off to Belgium. Suitably it was *Tuesday*!

He was Antwerpen bound.

Chapter Eight

Hillary was nothing if not perceptive.

Oscar had been joined by his associates Trent, Wendell, Gerald and Hillary at the *Cafe du Monde* for breakfast. They were taking their respective orders of 3 beignets outside under the large blue canopy at a rear table facing *Jackson Square*. Street performers were once again in evidence, which made Hillary nervous. She had developed a deep mistrust, ever since an incident in *Nerja* with a character called *Kodiak Stone* several years earlier.

Oscar enquired as to the *Katrina* tour and met with a stony silence. Hillary smiled beguilingly, which Wendell did not miss and the Doctor just looked away in disgust.

Hillary then showed Trent her new OMEGA watch and gushed about how much she loved it.

She then, slightly out of character, looked over at Oscar and rested her hand upon his and asked why he had developed the habit of holding his left arm, bent at the elbow with fist clenched across his heart? She was truly concerned, which was touching to all.

They had *all* in fact noticed. Trent in a half jocular tone mentioned that he was also concerned by this new trait, as he dunked his beignet into his coffee cup, causing the light dust like caster sugar to sprinkle on the table and upon application to his mouth, cascade all over his shirt. He was trying to relieve the tension.

Oscar, slightly embarrassed, laughed the enquiry, which he knew was genuine, away, but was not entirely convincing. It was not his best performance and he was with friends. People who knew him well.

In the next hour, Oscar explained the imbroglio involving the Cricket betting syndicates, the tournament roll-overs, the sub-continental connection, the decision fixing, Rob Bulmer's involvement (a former associate of the late Eric from his days in the seventies as a member at the Kennington Oval cricket ground management, where he cultivated his friendship with officials) and his death, those responsible, the Brethren of Acadia, Quildeberg connections and ramifications and the money. The vast amount of money. The money that he controlled and that was sought for reclamation.

He explained the fate of those close to him, particularly a series of blond women who had met with their untimely demise because of their associations with *Phelps*. The fate of Ariana Danielli. News which clearly concerned Hillary for more reasons than one. Too many deaths in too short a time to be coincidental. This aspect alone made Hillary sit up.

Oscar said that they had been killed to intimidate him. As a warning that they could get to him at will. To demonstrate their power, capability and commitment. He also detailed the Agreement with Farren Granier. The reasons as to why and the loose ends to tie up. Hillary found it abhorrent, but was not sure why?

At the end of the breakfast, Oscar sped Wendell, Gerald and Hillary on their way. Wendell had to check out from the *Monteleone*, he had a plane to catch, as did Trent.

Hillary and Gerald would go to the Casino at *Harrah's* on Poydras Street for a flutter before they left Louisiana. *To calm one's nerves* was Hillary's rationalization...Gerald remained on guard. His job not yet complete.

They all had tasks to perform.

Oscar had thanked them all individually for their loyalty and support. It was moving and unprecedented.

Oscar had reserved a special word for Gerald Mercer. Pulling him aside from the group. Thanking him for minding Mrs. Robinson and all that that entailed while in Niagara-on-the-Lake and New York. He knew that it would have been a challenge and hence the watch. Gerald as always was appreciative and said that they must get together again in Boston. Who knew when that would happen? Oscar thanked him for overseeing the safe transfer of the bonds. A pay-off for *Dubuclet,* the daughter of an officiating cricket umpire from the Melbourne *Boxing Day Test* of West Indian origin, official affiliation and representation, who had assured future ICC World Cup participation and *help* for the *token,* and who had threatened exposure if the monies were not delivered...

Oscar had decided to settle now and revisit this situation at a later date. *Paying off* also meant the status quo with the Brethren of Acadia characters and the sub-continental wholla's would be maintained. He needed a moment of stability from which to operate and manage a longer term solution. The $10M was an acceptable price to pay and it was not really his money to lose.

As Oscar paid the check, tipping heavily, the resident sidewalk jazz band fittingly started up. He and Trent walked, comrades in arms, to the immediate right of the cafe as they exited and out toward the market. They then took a left up on to Decatur Street. At 1104, they entered *Jimmy Buffetts Margaritaville* and ordered a pitcher of beer.

Trent was waiting. He knew Oscar well enough to know that he had a favour to ask.

As the pitcher of beer and low ball glasses were delivered, Oscar seated on a stool, flexed out violently his left leg in agony as a cramp in his calf took hold. The muscle almost turned inside out as it delivered its excruciating message. He grabbed at the back of his leg and pulled it sharply upwards to alleviate the stress. Tears came to his eyes and perspiration matted on his forehead.

Trent wondered what to do. 'Nothing' was the only answer as Oscar assured he was okay. "Just a cramp." he said. "Not dying yet!"

It was not what Trent wanted to hear.

Moments later, crisis abated. Oscar returned to the stool and poured the beer. Trent clinked glasses and was clearly relieved. They drank. All was well.

Oscar reached into his outside jacket pocket and brought out a long box. It was not gift wrapped. It was bulky and had a FEDEX designation. He also pulled out a newspaper which had an article circled in red.

He passed both objects over to Trent.

Trent inspected the box first.

David B. Green

The label said;

Sydney Jewellers
Queen Victoria Building
Shop G37
Ground Floor Queen Victoria Building
455 George Street
Sydney NSW 2000
Regards, Peter S.

As he opened the packaging carefully with his huge ham fists, Trent found a brand new *Breitling A1935012-C667 Navitimer* Classic watch.

It was big and bulky, with diamonds, jewels, various dials and instrument controls with a black leather croco strap, clearly expensive and ostentatious. *Perfect!*

Oscar had purchased it in the QVB and had it inscribed on the inner casing;

'for Trent...from your good friend, Oscar.'

He had had it couriered to *Le Pavillon* and it had arrived just in time, that very morning.

Trent was lost for words. He looked at Oscar and did something very unusual. He smiled.

Oscar was humbled and a little embarrassed. He topped up the beers.

"Good Health my friend." he said.

"Good Health." said Trent Alexis. It was a poignant moment.

Trent then set the watch down on the table and turned his attention to the article circled in red. It was in the *Trib* and dated almost a year earlier.

It said; **Classic Euro Drama Review...**

Caught on a Train was a critically successful British television drama written by Stephen Poliakoff, based on an overnight train journey across Europe, and following the route of a journey Poliakoff had himself made from London to Vienna. It was originally shown on BBC1 on October 31, 1980.

It starred Dame Peggy Ashcroft and Michael Kitchen. The production had won a BAFTA Television Award and other plaudits in 1980.

Then followed a passage by an anonymous contributor:-

In 1975 thru 83 I was that man. My trains were from Barcelona to Paris, Paris to Venice - Zagreb, Hamburg to Kolding, Antwerpen to Bordeaux to Sevilla, London to Madrid (for the European Cup Final, Nottingham Forest defeating SV Hamburger) and several other origins and destinations across Central and Eastern Europe, before the wall came down...deepest cold war (Le Carre) times.

It was of the same time and bleak era, same kinds of people and same kinds of circumstances. Same deserted cities late at night and horrible European trains and Eurocentric stations devoid of sanitation, cold water or edible food. Hot, sweaty, grimy, stale, sweet and rancid air pushing to the point of losing consciousness and with a sense that while traveling, you never really went anywhere.

Behind every door a psychopath with a foreign language and a grudge. Each train leaving Gare de Lyon, Gare du Austerlitz and Gare Montparnasse at midnight so you could sleep through the night. Some hope, with all of the stops for border crossings and immigration checks pre-European Community unity. A convenient myth. I even met my own dowager on a SNCF train to Bordeaux who took me home with her, as a pet. Art so very often imitates life.

I saw *Caught on a Train* again recently. Brought the memories flooding back. Nostalgic for this...Not sure why. Yet in many ways, these were much more socially innocent times with an undercurrent of despair which masked the insecurity and futility and drudgery of life in Europe at that time for a young chap with a mission but little idea of how it would be achieved.

.... this drama exemplified just exactly what there was to live for... the alternative, wherever that was or whatever it may be.

After reading the passage, Trent asked Oscar if he knew the identity of the author? Though in fact he did actually know.

It was not in doubt.

David B. Green

Oscar thanked him again. Urged him to drink up as there was still work to be done. Places to go, people to see and deal with.

Trent Alexis duly did so. Never one to be asked a second time.

Chapter Nine

When Wendell Madison passed the Argentinians' compartment on the commuter *VIA* train traveling in from *Aéroport international Pierre-Elliott-Trudeau de Montréal*, (formerly Dorval) to Montreal Central station, not glancing in this time, he had seen out of the corner of his eye a confusion of figures. It was not the man but the woman pulling down a suitcase from the overhead compartment. She appeared a somewhat arresting androgynous beauty and clearly struggling. He had also heard laughter.

Fearing being spotted, Wendell moved on. He found that he had been holding his breath. Curious.

Wendell had tailed them down from *Mont Tremblant*. A resort better known for ski-ing than for early spring/summer pursuits, golf, hiking, trekking and such, but which provided a casual and comfortable atmosphere that the Doctor and his woman *Morag* obviously sought, after the cosmopolitanism of Montreal. The village and incorporated municipality sited in the Laurentian mountains of Quebec stood approximately 130 kilometers to the north-west of Montreal. Wendell and Trent had tracked down the couple to a small cottage in the village of Saint-Jovite.

Trent was in the restaurant car taking a beer. A bottle of *St-Ambroise* brewed at Quebec's foremost micro-brewery, Brasserie McAuslan.

"Still there?" he asked Wendell.

'Still there." was the reply.

Wendell sat opposite Trent and took a slug from the beer offered.

The train was due in at 2pm.

In Antwerpen, the Frenchman was extremely uncomfortable. It was drizzling with rain. He had not taken his Mac and he found umbrellas emasculating.

The cobblestone streets were playing havoc with his feet. Ruining his shoes.

He was in the Jewish quarter. Near Central Station. Antwerp had after the war become a major centre for Orthodox Jews.

About 15,000 Haredi Jews, mostly Hasidic, lived there.

Oscar had assured Sylvain that this was the perfect place to buy *sub-wholesale* diamonds and that Byron was the perfect intermediary.

Sylvain was a little early for his appointment and to escape the rain, looked in at *Van der Veken's* atelier where jewellery was being made by hand, using top-quality African diamonds, cut and polished to a pristine standard. He watched curiously as silent craftsmen, perched at chin-high benches, each peering intently through a loupe, plied their trade. He found it very impressive.

At the appointed hour Sylvain stepped into the Cafe *Günther Watté* at Steenhouwersvest 30, a charming chocolate shop and café, unique to Antwerp. Sat at the nearest table eating a chocolate bar and drinking coffee was a man who looked right. Dark grey pinstripe suit in heavy expensive material, red & grey broad striped tie, dark blue shirt and sporting a pink carnation in his left lapel, right next to the UNICEF/European Union pin, which he wore proudly.

Upon spotting Sylvain, the man bound over towards him, shaking his hand warmly.

"How are you my good man?" he enquired.

"and have you brought my money?.."

The Frenchman had met with Byron Tyler-Walker.

Chapter Ten

Byron was an interesting fellow indeed.

The discussion was protracted, disjointed and an exercise in patience for the Frenchman. Byron displayed a remarkable intellect, a distinct charm to which resistance was futile and a very short attention span. A master at going off at a tangent, not listening fully and only answering selected questions, he was quick-witted, a very quick study and absolutely corrupt. He was a shoe-in for political life. It was clear that he occupied his own personal *lebensraum* to which other people were just occasional visitors, subject to invitation. He was a happy kind of person, with Sylvain suspected, quite a ruthless and mean streak when crossed.

Byron was a *fence*. A lovable rogue of English descent, though a long time expatriate. He flew just below the wire and cultivated the ability to mix and ingratiate, within almost any social sphere. A very strong and accomplished salesman without a scruple in sight. He knew how to work a room.

The only son of a father who benefited from the vast privileges and rights of ownership gifted from being an hereditary peer, lost almost completely to alcohol and drug abuse. Byron had earned back the country pile in Norfolk, England, though chose to occupy it infrequently. He was not keen on contributing to Her Majesty's Inland Revenue so expatriate status suited him to the tee.

His wife of nearing thirty years was known as Lady Thetford, though Byron often chose not to use his full appellation, as in business it could often be seen as pretentious to do so. It could also serve to put people on guard. The aristocracy in the UK was not as revered as they once were. More reviled in fact.

Sylvain, for the first twenty minutes, couldn't decide what was really happening in their conversation. One moment Byron was drawing him in close as if they were soon to become the best of friends, the next he was beating a hasty retreat and seeking solace in the realms of the aloof. All this could have been tolerable, if it were not for the fact that the conversation was punctuated throughout, whenever an eligible female happened to either walk into the establishment or drift by the window. Byron never missed an opportunity to pass comment or to interact with them whenever and however possible. He was clearly a *ladies man* who took great pleasure in his interest. A very passionate interest.

Sylvain had arranged at the *Deutsche Bank* in Nerja, during a visit (with Alberto as co-signer) to the Playa Burriana branch, the issue of a series of gilts and bonds in favour of Byron's offshore account to the amount specified by Oscar.

These documents and instruments of monetary transfer were slid discreetly under the table to Byron in a large manila envelope, soon after Sylvain had satisfied himself as to the arrangements for delivery of the said items in question. Byron had prepared a dossier of instruction and letters of surety in guarantee of authenticity and value of the items involved. Which were numerous. This nominal amount would act as proof of deposit against the full amount, transfer of which could only be completed under Oscar's signature execution in Amsterdam within the next five business days.

Byron had just earned himself a 0.35% arrangement fee on the $50M and Sylvain unwittingly, had done similar. This was confirmed by an additional note provided by Sylvain, notarized as valid from the Deutsche Bank by a local **notaría sustantivo**, which confirmed transfer of this sum in favour of Byron's designated corporate account at his local *van Breda - Antwerpen* bank in respect of Consulting fees.

Byron asked the Frenchman if he needed a receipt?

Sylvain smiled. "But of course." he said.

Chapter Eleven

The church of *Notre Dame de Bonsecours* at 400 rue Saint-Paul E was positioned with its back wall facing the Old Port of Montreal.

The statue of the *Virgin as Star of the Sea*, sat high atop the building was its most impressive and haunting external feature, especially at night when illuminated and when it appeared to rise even higher and appear more intimidating and garishly sinister, resembling an elongated *gargoyle*, full of Gothic character, cleaving like a demented and refracted *obelisk* into the evening sky, like something from the *Exorcist*.

First established in 1657 by Marguerite Bourgeoys, the building dated back to 1771; its façade dated from 1890. The decor is simple but elegant, with a very nautical flair so derived from the chapel's longtime vocation as the *Sailors' Church*. The hanging lamps in the form of sailing ships are especially noteworthy.

It was to the inside of this highly impressive but small *Our Lady of Prompt Succor* church that Wendell and Trent had followed *Morag* and the Argentine medic. They were further observed kneeling at the front of the church in a pew near the main altar and directly beneath the high round multi layered chandelier, deep in prayer.

It was late afternoon.

The couple had lead them a dance all across *la belle* Montreal throughout the day. Starting off at the *Sheraton Centre* on Boulevard Rene-Levesque West, their hotel of choice, before breakfasting lavishly at *Rubens Deli* on St. Catharine's Street and then going on to a tour of the *Bell Centre;* home of the *Montreal Canadiens*, who were occupied in the midst of NHL play-off season.

Go Habs Go! From there they had taxied over to the Vieux Port and alighted at *Rue Berri*, opposite the main harbour. Their first port of call had been at the highly impressive *Marche Bonsecours* where they shopped before strolling around the corner and entering the church.

While busied with shopping, Wendell, whose turn it had been to shadow, had studied the inscription on the plaque at the main St.Paul east entrance. Built as the Parliament for United Canada in the mid-1800s, the building was now a mall for clique boutique shops and local galleries. The Bonsecours Market had also housed Montreal City Hall for more than twenty-five years. In 1852, the Municipal Council sat for the first time in a building that belonged to the municipality. It only left in 1878 to move into a brand new City Hall on the site of the present-day City Hall, located on Notre-Dame Street.

Wendell had found it boring and in truth did not find the shops and galleries much more inviting. He had made only one prolonged stop in a store while following *Morag* and that was in **La boutique de maroquinerie fine Serge Ricchi** where he had noticed some fine *Jean-Michel Cropsal* raincoats and bomber jackets by *Rosie Godbout*. However, he had decided that he would reserve a possible purchase for another time.

Outside, on the Rue de la Commune, Trent was exiting a cafe bar and ice cream parlour which was opposite the IMAX Science exhibit at Quai King Edward. He had a *Beaver Tail* and was struggling with the complex process of eating it. Conscious of the fact that he was due to relieve Wendell at the church, he hurried along, pausing only briefly to look up at the Marche and its imposing silver dome. Marché Bonsecours was indeed a new symbol of modernism in Old Montréal and it would have been wasted on Trent.

The 'tail', the "queue de caster" was much more impressive to him.

Trent rounded the corner on to St. Paul and saw in the distance on the cobbled streets the figures of the couple coming towards him. Wendell was perhaps thirty yards behind on the opposite side of the street. Trent kept on walking until they had passed him by, deep in conversation, happy with their purchases, designer-liveried shopping bags in hand, and content with the time spent praying, it would appear.

The next time he spotted them, he was at the bottom of *Place Jacques-Cartier*, looking in at the *Le Jardin Nelson* restaurant dining area at the apex of Cartier and St.Paul. They were eating supper, seated on the heated outdoor terrace, while Wendell was positioned at a table on the balcony eating crepes, looking down at them from above. Prophetic.

There was beautiful tree lined decor which created a casual yet cordial atmosphere and soft classical music was evidenced in the background. Perhaps **Rachmaninov**.

Close by, at the bottom end of the *Place Jacques-Cartier*, was a medley of many and various street performers, artists, painters and musicians, setting up for the evening. Trent decided to mingle with them.

He had to create a plan. Couldn't wait forever. Had to get on with it. Amsterdam awaited.

Chapter Twelve

You will feel that you have stepped back in time as you enter *Gibby's*, housed in a magnificent 200-year-old building in Old Montreal.

This charming restaurant boasts historic stone walls, original beamed ceilings, cozy fireplaces and romantic lighting that combine to make dining at Gibby's a not soon-to-be-forgotten experience. Gibby's is an institution. The ambiance, the atmosphere is so seductive.

Sitting by the hearth, marveling at the foot thick walls that have been there forever was one *Oscar Phelps*. He was wearing his lightest sports coat in gold by *Harry Rosen*. Distinguished.

He was dining alone. The entree always came with asparagus, which Oscar didn't care for and set aside on his side plate, a choice of potato, *Monte Carlo (double baked)* was Oscar's choice and a properly well cooked steak accented with a wonderful mix of garlic and Montreal steak spices. His main course came with a choice from two or three appetizers, but Oscar went with the "Gibby's" salad.

His choice of drink was a *Gordon's* London Dry Gin & Schweppes Tonic and a bottle of Kacaba *Meritage* 2004. He had rested next to his side plate in readiness for the end of the feast; a *Partagas* varnished Dalia (Lonsdale) Habana Cigar.

Oscar sometimes acted as if there was nothing that could be considered at all objectionable about his behavior. He was the veritable *poster boy for amorality.*

He was in reflective mood and making plans. Ready as ever to seize the day and help his associates whenever called upon.

Chapter Thirteen

Wendell agreed with Trent that it would be easier to manage if they could reach them while they were separated.

It was almost 7.15pm and the couples were still at the *Le Jardin Nelson* bar, taking early evening cocktails, a little the worse for wear and alcohol and listening to the live jazz band that had just started their first evening set. Trent and Wendell had taken a vantage point position on the balcony and had agreed that it was going to be now.

Trent asked Wendell if he had a gun?

"Always...I am a Texan." said Wendell...

Trent considered. You take the man and I'll take the woman.

It was agreed.

A few minutes later, Wendell was stood at the urinal of the Men's washroom, taking a piss.

Trent had moved himself downstairs and on to a bar stool. He ordered a Scotch and soda, which he would not drink. Morag, a relatively sturdy woman of around forty with a pale complexion, whispish auburn hair and thin lips smeared with pink gloss, was seated on the next stool. She noticed him and looked away, slightly intimidated by his attention and proximity. Trent unclipped his watch and placed it in his inside jacket pocket, carefully ensuring his handkerchief was wrapped around it for safe-keeping.

The door to the Men's room swung open and in walked the Argentine doctor.

He seemed in a happy mood. Wendell waited for him to complete his business and as soon as the shaking had been complete and the zip engaged, Wendell saw his chance. As the Doctor wetted his hands in the sink he caught first sight of the Texan in the mirror, as he came at him from behind with a nylon garrotte and pulled him backwards, dragging him hard into the end cubicle, garrotte applied, kicking the door closed behind them.

The struggle which was remarkably quiet and not particularly violent lasted perhaps three to four full minutes as the Latin gave a spirited but ultimately cumbersome and futile resistance. The alcohol had not helped his cause. It really wasn't a fair contest. His cologne did however smell quite nice; Wendell noticed.

The Latin's gurgle had stopped. His tongue had started to protrude from the awful wet mouth. His eyes were first closed in misery and then opened again in stark horror as his life was being squeezed away. It was a look of; "I have realized what is happening, but I am not quite sure why?"

When the job was done, Wendell checked for life signs. There weren't any. To make sure, Wendell positioned his hands on one side of the Argentine's head and snapped with a clean twist and jerk to sever the spinal cord. The series of fast cracks were somewhat disturbing.

Wendell positioned the Latin on the toilet seat and took care to double the body so that it held its own weight.

When the Texan returned to the bar, both Trent and Morag had gone. Though the shopping bags remained stacked up at a side table. The bar-keep had been called away and Wendell had witnessed as he approached, that he had left his station with some high degree of urgency.

He saw the Scotch and soda waiting on the Molson beer mat and took it down in one gulp. Pocketing the glass afterwards. He then adjusted his posture, standing tall and walked out casually. In the distance he could hear a commotion coming from the wash room area.

Morag Glendenning was not stupid. She had an idea about what this was about. She damned *Farren Granier* for his bumbling.

The Financial Director of the *Brethren of Acadia and Quildeberg* groups, she was knowledgeable as to the risks, dangers and personalities in her business.

Trent Alexis did not scare her, but he could maneuver her. They were headed back to the church on St. Paul.

As they made their way up the staircase at the rear of the church, Trent had the gun in the small of her back. At the top of the stair could be found the organ which was sited on a lengthy platform, an ornate loft in fact, which covered most of the back wall with pipes and such. A remarkable instrument which probably sounded as impressive as it looked. Trent wasn't there for music. Morag, now openly weeping, understood that her situation was quite hopeless. She was resigned to her fate.

Then down below, the sound of the large heavy door both opening and then closing could be heard. The lock could also be heard as it bolted shut. Trent stood rigid, holding her tight with his hand covering her mouth, in near silence. He looked down over the edge of the platform. A figure was approaching from beneath the covered main entrance walkway. Trent instinctively pulled back then he leaned over again, holding Morag even tighter. He was starting to sweat. Then he blinked and shook the sweat that had congealed at his temple away. The man coming towards them was *Oscar Phelps.*

Oscar headed up the same stairway and looked at his friend. Trent was somewhat surprised.

Morag began to twist and fight, but it was in vain. It had been her only sign of real defiance. Trent took his hand away from her mouth, still holding her securely by the arms. She stood upright, collecting herself and her thoughts and looking hard at Oscar. As he approached her she spat hard into his face. She missed and the gobbet landed on his shoulder. Oscar took out his Red *Cross of St. George* handkerchief and wiped away the offending substance.

"I'll take it from here Trent. This will be for Mishka and the others." Oscar said.

Chapter Fourteen

I

Take my hand
I'm a stranger in paradise
All lost in a wonderland
A stranger in paradise

If I stand starry-eyed
That's a danger in paradise
For mortals who stand beside
An angel like you

The Fleet Street Orchestra had disbanded, long before the time Mrs. Robinson had arrived on the scene. But the melody still lingered.

What was during the early part of the last century a thirty strong, classical ensemble of industrious, no holes barred, capturing the mood of the time, newspaper groups, had sadly diminished.

This Street had once been the street of Adventure.

If there was no news, then they made it,

Hillary had spent a good decade in and around Fleet Street; courting publicity and scandal for the benefit of her fledgling Publishing House. Years of roaming a veritable movie set of a workplace, stocked with larger than life characters and personalities, all eligible and willing to cater to Hillary's brand of **sex for favours** commerce.

The Street was one great big sexually charged watering hole to Hillary, which, if she could keep her legs together long enough and walked fast enough, could be traversed pub-to-pub, office desk-to-office floor, office wall-to-office cupboard, during a torrential downpour, without even getting very wet or very pregnant. An acceptable occupational hazard in those days. Pre AIDS and when London was still gripped in the aftermath of the *swing*.

The Thatcher Years when hard work, perseverance and a well targeted 'suck and fuck' could elicit the most valuable of rewards. The days of the yuppie. Of power lunches, red suspenders, thin blue and white pinstriped shirts, cufflinks, filofaxes, car phones, Cuban cigars, golden handshakes and golden hello's and the mandatory golfing umbrella, which no self respecting sophisticate of the day would be caught trawling the City streets without.

Hillary had been a player and in later life had consolidated and improved upon that position...

This is where the giants of the industry would gather at lunchtimes in legendary London pubs like *El Vino* to argue over matters of national importance and also spar as to whose turn it was to buy the next bottle of Margeaux. Whose turn it was to get a quality fucking by Hillary, who had a reputation that was as solid and reliable as any of the stalwart broadsheets and as sullied as the headlines that occupied the pages of the tabloids.

Insults and sometimes punches were exchanged and marriages were seen to crumble in the heady atmosphere of booze, news and nothing-to-lose relationships that she indulged in. Such was her ambition. Her capability.

Yet somehow this disparate, largely dissipated band of people had banded together not only to produce some of the most excellent journalism of the era. But also to build the legend that was soon inevitably to blossom into Hillary Robinson. Hillary had cultivated a DNA made up of the material, the cosmetic, the sexual and the financial. A formidable package indeed.

Hillary was in a Black Cab from Mayfair on her way to a rendezvous with a girlfriend at the *Cheshire Cheese*. Nikki Konopka who remained slightly "miffed" and dismissed by the fact that she had been taken to North America on a *beano* and had been treated as little more than a belly-warmer.

Hillary needed diversion. The horrid business in New Orleans had given her pause.

London in the new millennium had changed for Hillary. There was even more opportunity to quench her lust for matters sexual and monetary and less need now for her to go slumming than in the old days.

Hillary was as capable as anyone when it came to nostalgia and reminiscence, but at this point in her life, she had time only to look forward.

As the Cab drew up to let her out she looked over with annoyance at the building which once housed *The Stab in the Back* which is now a pizza restaurant. *The old Cock* had also made way for a bank. Ironic.

"Fleet Street is still my home," wrote Philip Gibbs in 1923, "and to its pavement my feet turn again from whatever part of the world I return."

It was a good and sentimental point. But the footsteps heard now are merely echoes from the past.

As Hillary closed the cab door and paid the driver through his side window, cocking him a cheeky wink, she heard coming from behind her the sound of heavy rushing approaching feet.

As the Cab pulled away from the curb in the direction of Holburn, they were upon her.

II

"Why make one woman hate you for the rest of your life, when you can have a lot of women loving you for moments of it?"

"What's the good of happiness...you can't buy money with it!"

"Girls are like pianos. When they're not upright, they're grand."

... Were three in a series of quite ridiculous statements made by the man in the next seat.

The man had been bumped up to Business Class by KLM because there had been a double allocation for his seat in 43B. He claimed to be the owner of a very lugubrious and mournful persona, which for some reason he had decided to abandon in favour of an alternative more frantic approach to life, debuting on the trip to Amsterdam.

He was seated next to Trent and just behind Oscar.

They had learned, in the hour or so into the flight from Montreal, that he was a Cambridge professor taking a sabbatical. A year off. His name was Peregrine Calthrop-Turner or 'Perry' for short. He was a part-time lecturer at a medical college for *buffoons* in Essex and his specialty was tropical and pandemic disease.

While this sparked some degree of interest in Oscar, the real igniter came when 'Perry' made mention of a dalliance he had entertained years earlier with a Lady Armstrong-Jones. A total non-sequitur, that made Oscar, not believing in coincidence, take note.

Perry was looking to be a man of the people. One of the great unwashed. But somehow, just could not manage to achieve it. He was what Oscar would have called in his youth; ***posh, but a prat.***

Perry had absolutely no inkling as to common sense, very little physical coordination or for that matter, verbal.

It was difficult to understand or even imagine how he could lecture anyone about anything. He appeared to have little or no attention span for incoming information or alternate views to his own and when a notion did get through his defenses, he failed to comprehend. He continually apologized for his obliqueness and his somewhat manic character. His mannerisms were, Oscar had decided, those of a charming and amiable nut! Most probably harmless.

As they crossed Godthab, he was however, beginning to endear. A halfwit who people would grow to like, someone who with time, could be tolerated and even liked.

Trent was asleep, KLM issue eye-patch deployed, woolen socks on, small pillow held tightly, IPod in full operational mode playing *A Sunday Smile*, and even if his condition changed, he had decided to feign slumber to avoid the possibility of Perry engaging him in further conversation. Oscar, was dozing, but remained open to amiable patter if and when it was offered.

Oscar adjusted his seat so that it was almost flat and as he closed his eyes, he began to take stock, secure in the fact that matters were coming to a head and that in Trent and Wendell, who had taken an earlier flight via London Gatwick, he had a high degree of security in support.

He considered the commercial empire under his stewardship. While it was still thriving, he had in recent years, since the death of *Lori Kasabian*, scaled back a little in his direct involvement. Sylvain had proven a very useful and capable recruit and Wendell was not devoid of ideas when it came to making money on both sides of the legitimacy border.

He had curtailed the 'Nigerian Scam' in 2006, simply because there had become too much competition! A case of better communications access to all, being counter productive to the few. It had simply become outdated, out-moded, along with hot water bottles, rickets, perforated ulcers and the consumption.

Oscar, never wishing to stand still, had diversified his business interests and prior to the current series of challenges had been attempting to influence and extend the corporate invoicing fraud within Central and South American markets.

He had also considered India. The *last great new empire*, as a suitable recipient for his creative initiatives. Few cities possess the chaos of Mumbai.

A place where rich houses and hovels stand next to each other and film stars and beggars jostle with each other. The expansion appeared endless. Immigrants are continuous. Hindu nationalism and Muslim fanaticism confront each other. There is always tension and excitement permeating. Oscar considered Mumbai the symbol of India's rise to power. The siege at the Taj Mahal Palace hotel had however, taken a little of the gloss off for him.

He had read of various schemes like the one's he had become familiar with in the Americas, which had been exposed as Ponzi's. Indeed, the Ponzi had become popular in recent years. Almost acceptable as a method by which to be swindled, such was the proliferation. The *Trib* had carried a story about *Bernie Madoff.* Who had been convicted and sentenced to 150 years in jail for running a $50bn scheme.

The Brethren of Acadia group had to his knowledge, prior to their recent sporting activities, always dabbled in schemes of this type. Reliant upon a strongly rising market when irrational euphoria takes over.

Oscar had concluded that the reason we are all easy to fool in the end, is because we are all so very good at fooling ourselves.

He had also concluded that it was perhaps better to *trust in the devil that you know.* In his associates, his friends, he had a strength. He just had to keep it all together. Do what has to be done. As always.

Oscar felt himself drifting off toward sleep. This process was further speeded as he opened his eyes for a brief second and saw Perry in the half-light, neck craned and looking across at him, waiting for an opportunity to launch into a new soliloquy.

In a little over four hours, *Schiphol* would bid a Welcome.

He knew in his mind that in Amsterdam at the *Rembrandtplein* at this time of year, the sunshine would be warm on his back as it cascaded across the square, drenching with multitudinous bright rays the numerous bar terraces. The air filled with the scent of bitterbrush and pine mixed with a generous helping of marijuana. The people would be gracious, their gorgeous surroundings imbuing them with that certain Dutch languidness.

And yet there would be an undercurrent of harsh bitterness.

Schiphol and A'Dam had always been good to *Oscar Phelps*.

Chapter Fifteen

Cuthbert Isaac Montgomery Dubuclet had first been elevated to the elite international cricket umpiring panel for the Test series in 2001. The Indian tour of the Caribbean between March & May.

Originally from Haiti, he had been an accomplished Caribbean cricketer but had never made the international grade. Over the years he had developed a reputation for solid decision making, absolute fairness and had established a sound rapport with the players of all cricket playing nations. He had a daughter with a questionable reputation upon whom he doted and who always appeared to need financial underwriting. He was the perfect *mark* for the creative thinkers of the Quildeberg and the Brethren of Acadia cabal for whom The Rt.Honourable Eric Armstrong-Jones appeared always well positioned to act as the willing and venerable conduit.

Indeed, the much learned and esteemed Rt. Honourable Eric had cultivated many relationships within the sub continent over the years and had been a very high level confidante of many of the highly dubious residents of the al Karama and Dubai creek districts of the UAE. He would have been genuinely shocked and saddened by the murder of his associate and fellow business magnate *Sharad Shetty,* who had controlled a vast cricket betting empire in India, before being shot to death by hired gunmen at the command of rival gang members upon entering the *India Club* in Oud Metha, a popular Indian expatriates' club in Dubai. This club had welcomed Eric, Enrique de Cesaris and one Oscar Phelps on occasion. Eric had also frequented along with several of his ICC cohorts, occupied in their collective efforts to promote First Class cricket in Sharjah through a series of India-Pakistan cricket matches which were widely followed by the Indian diaspora in the UAE. They had been moderately successful.

The trick was to take away the emphasis from the actual player, who historically had been the most likely protagonist for influencing and determining the outcome of cricket matches.

After much thought, though not much based in science, the orchestrators had decided not to bet on the actual outcome of matches, but to take the North American approach of *spread betting* and place many and various rollover wagers on the more difficult and less obvious variables to control. *A spread is a range of outcomes, and the bet is whether the outcome will be above or below the spread.* They had developed a liking for the LBW decision. The frequency that it would be invoked in a particular innings, game, session, test series etc. The LBW decision resided strictly in the bailiwick of the officiating umpire to whom the sub continental partners began to pander.

LBW, (short for Leg Before Wicket), is to cricket what offside rule is to football or soccer -- most people think they know it, but many can't explain it.

Many cricket aficionados do not understand the exact rules for judging an LBW dismissal. Casual viewers are badly confused. It is very common to hear shouts like "that was plumb!", or "why the hell didn't he give *that* out" and so on, while watching cricket matches. Many people *intuitively* decide whether or not a batsman was out, or whether or not umpire's call was a right one. Now with slow motion replays and a range of other high-tech audio and visual aids, a television viewer has a lot more at his disposal to determine a decision for themselves, provided that they know the basic rules.

However, the decision of the umpire is final and cannot be reversed.

A batsman is adjudicated out LBW, when the ball hits his *pads* and the umpire thinks that the delivery would have *gone on to hit the stumps.*

Of course, if it were that simple, there would have been no confusion or debate at all, about this form of dismissal.

In order to clarify just how the umpire decides whether the ball would have gone on to hit the stumps or not, there are two things to consider: the *line* of the ball, and the height of the ball when it hit the batsman. Umpires extend the perceived line in their mind (calculating any lateral swing/seam movement), until the ball hits the stumps. They also, consider the height at which it hit the pads, and decide whether the ball would have gone over the stumps or not. There is an unwritten rule -- if there is any doubt in the umpires mind, the *benefit of doubt* must go to the batsmen.

David B. Green

It was this *doubt* that was being manipulated. To huge financial effect and benefit.

Following the excitement of the 2005 Ashes series in England, there had been a very real doubt that the Australian based series that followed could ever live up to the expectations of media, supporters and players alike. England had struggled with injuries and form since the historic Ashes victory and Australia with the keenly anticipated swansong of heroes *Warne, Gilchrist and McGrath*, were desperate to avenge the defeat, which saw them hand back the famous urn after 18 years of supreme dominance.

None of this mattered to the Brethren. The result was academic. The frequency of LBW decisions at a given time was the all conquering matter of concern.

By the start of the Fourth Test in the series, scheduled for December 26-30 in Melbourne, The *Boxing Day* Test, the betting situation was at a critical stage. Australia had already regained the Ashes virtue of romping to a 3-0 unassailable series lead and were looking at a whitewash. A stunning reversal and humiliation for the English.

The Aussies had won at the Brisbane GABBA in November by 255 runs, had been victorious at the Adelaide Oval in early December by 8 wickets and secured the urn at the Third Test in Perth by a margin of 306 runs. The critical decision by Umpire Dubuclet came during England's second innings at the MCG in what was an innings defeat, when the number of LBW decisions at close of play had to be between 3 and 5 to activate the multiple betting patterns across the world and determine a colossal spread, generating a multi-million dollar *accumulator* bet win. The sequence of wagers laid had begun almost a year earlier during a Test series in New Zealand.

The crucial wicket was the eighth of the innings. A fast bowler controversially given out LBW by the West Indian umpire. The fourth LBW decision of the innings.

Within three business days, the *Brethren of Acadia* had collected on their bets and the spoils where destined for the corporate collection account owned and operated by one *Oscar Phelps*.

The plane was beginning its final descent into Schiphol. It was a bright sunshiny early morning. Oscar was not looking out of his window; he had other things on his mind. Trent was engaged with Perry in inconsequential chit-chat to which Trent's main contribution had been 'yeh' and 'really'. He was beginning to become peeved, but was controlling his natural urge to put this man to sleep.

Oscar had his brown leather SAQA document case next to him, it was unzipped and the contents lay strewn over the next seat.

Oscar was auditing the superficial residue collected from the last month or so of travel. There was in instruction and warranty/guarantee booklet for his recently acquired *3 mobile* cell phone which he had purchased on William Street in Sydney. Four Cherry Ripe bars. The labels from his Rodd & Gunn handkerchiefs and black socks from Auckland. An autobiography by Shane Warne and a Morecambe & Wise classic boxed DVD set both purchased from the ABC store in the QVB. Oscar liked *That Riviera Touch*.

There were also the remnants of a Cioccloato by La Perla di Torino con Zenzero Ginger bar also brought from a coffee stall which served breakfast and assorted rolls and pies and which stood in the centre aisle of the main ground floor of the QVB. Oscar put them to one side and looked at the balance. A receipt from DYMOCKS in Brisbane for a new *Spenser* novel which he had gifted to Wendell when in New Orleans. ATM receipts from the Commonwealth Bank, a beer coaster advertising Victoria Bitter. Several assorted business cards. His ticket stub from the Dendy Cinema in Melbourne. A tightly package personal wet wipe from Le Casino de Monte Carlo and a discount voucher for Sentineal Carriages in Niagara on the Lake.

Then, wrapped inside a bright orange **Next Wave** biennial festival XXL T-shirt that he had purchased in the POLITIX store again at the QVB on George Street, he saw something that he initially failed to either recognize or identify. It was an old small envelope in brown that had been torn open recklessly, causing it to rip. Inside was a note and a hotel key fob. Oscar had taken it from the Russian's purse at the Tearoom in Sydney and had quite forgotten it.

The fob was very old, almost antique looking in reddish brown hard leather with a resin hard finish. It was an actual fob that once had a key attached, before key cards and security coding. About three inches long and bulbous at one end, while sharp at the other, but with all edges rounded off. There was a blackened brass ring at the end and on one side, barely visible was the branding. It said;

Room Number 712 and Hotel Touraine, Buffalo. NY.

Oscar opened the folded note which was on legal paper. The note said.

"For Jolyon and friend. Best regards, Eric"

Curious.

Chapter Sixteen

Sylvain Honore-Panet was a tired man. He wasn't used to being a Global Traveler and in truth it was not a position to which he had ever aspired.

He was a Frenchman. The French are unbearably poor travelers.

He was resting up back in Nerja at Oscar's invitation and expense.

He was wondering where all this business might end? And When?

He was glad of a little time away from Horace who was wearing him out and beginning to bore him, just a little. Though Horace, as Sylvain would go to pains to admit whenever asked, possessed some very useful and splendid attributes. None of them however were tact, finesse or decorum. Sacrosanct to a proud Frenchman.

He was sat on the edge of the *Playa La Torrecilla* watching the calm Mediterranean Sea. So tranquil. There were few others on the beach because of the noon hour.

Mad Dogs and Englishmen and all that...

It was becoming very hot and Sylvain was naturally of pale complexion. Gaunt, in fact. Not a great combination. He was 'more likely to stroke than tan', had been Horace's acute and rather scathing sardonic observation.

At fifteen minutes ahead of the appointed hour, he wiped his rimless spectacles free of sweat with his monogrammed handkerchief, loosened his Windsor knotted tie, folded very carefully in preparation for carrying his jacket over his arm and placed the well dog-eared paperback novel that he was re-reading into the open side pocket. It slipped in nicely. It was a 1981 novel by Carey Schofield, which chronicled the life and times of infamous French outlaw; *Jacques Mesrine*. "French Public Enemy No. 1"

Sylvain started on his walk back into town.

He trudged through the Urbanizacion Puentes de Nerja, which was a series of avenue after avenue of new condominiums and town houses that he found aesthetically displeasing. He then took the *Avenida Castilla Perez*, passing by *Antonio Millon* to his left and *El Barrio* to his right. He could smell the enticing aroma of chicken wafting by, as it roasted on the outdoor spit, cooking slowly and succulently in the display window of the ZAZA concession, houses in a small inlet, next door to the LUAL office at edificio Casablanca. Just after passing the entrance to *Tutti Frutti* square on his left, he made a right onto *Calle Diputacion* which lead down a narrowing street, passing by the many small Spanish bars and the sole town dance studio, which was used mainly by the locals and store owners, into the Plaza Cavana.

Before he reached the end of the street he stopped at the doorway to the Centro Giner - Sala Patronata Social at *Calle Diputacion* 2.

The regular meeting room for ALCOHOLICS ANONYMOUS.

He was on time.

Chapter Seventeen

The report in the rushes of the *Trib* that was credited to a *Montreal Gazette* correspondent reported that Morag's death was a probable suicide.

She had been described as an industrialist on vacation from her native Louisiana.

There was no mention of the murder of the Argentinian.

Oscar and Trent were at Centraal Station in the heart of Amsterdam at a News and Magazine concession, nearby the main ticket hall.

"She was found hanging by the neck from a length of blue nylon rope fastened to the church organ and draped over the balustrade. Her wrists had also been cut. A small serrated knife had been found nearby. It was suspected that she had jumped and that her neck had broken upon the full extension of the rope being met." said the brief report.

Oscar gave the newspaper to Trent as they crossed Prins Hendrikkade and walked on Damrak down the side of the moorings with all of the Blue Boat Company canal buses.

At Beursplein they bought a couple of bottles of water. It was a hot day. Trent considered a cone of fries with mayonnaise, but then thought better of the idea.

To their immediate left was the Red Light district set between the Oude Kirk and the Nieuw Markt areas. This could wait for another day.

As they reached DAM Square the distinctive and highly familiar 21 metre tall white stoned obelisk erected in the centre was the focus of the congregating masses. The National Monument in memory of the victims of World War II both in the Netherlands and the Dutch East Indies. The monument was erected in 1956. In the 1960s it was a popular place for hippies who bundled up in sleeping bags, heads rested on rucksacks, hip flasks filled with liqueur, keeping them warm and who often spent the night and most of the day at Dam Square. In 1970 the marines chased them away forever and tourists adopted the place as a meeting point.

This vast square was buzzing with activity as Oscar and Trent got closer. The fun fair which runs at one side has become a traditional feature that attracts both locals and tourists alike, with its Ferris wheel a prized vantage point for sightseeing. Street entertainers and buskers of varying quality were mixing with horse-drawn carts looking for patrons and street vendors selling mostly what Trent would term; 'pure crap'. An army of marauding tour-guides with their mandatory umbrellas up thrust proudly to the sky were leading lines of Korean, Indian and South American tourists. In the background could be heard the Carillion of the Royal Palace as it peals out folk songs and popular music.

The Grand Hotel *Krasnapolsky* was prominent on Oscar's left hand side. For a moment they both stopped walking. Trent wondered what was happening but did not question.

"Just drinking in the atmosphere." Oscar said to Trent.

Oscar felt at home. Memories of his time here in the late 1970's and again more recently with the Rt. Honourable in the Winter Garden restaurant at the *Kras*.

"Look around you." Oscar urged Trent so to do. Trent duly did as he was asked and began to understand why.

At the corner of Dam Square and Damrak was *De Bijenkorf* a very up market department store which had often been a haunt of Oscar Phelps. Across from this building was *Nieuwe Kerk*, a Gothic building of distinction that had a name that betrayed. It now appeared to be an exhibition hall. Trent studied the posters on the hoardings outside. There was a *Corsini* exhibit in house. Attached to the building was a café. Again, Trent was becoming hungry.

A long queue had formed at the corner of Rokin at the entrance to the wax museum *Madam Tussaud* and just round the corner of Rokin and Dam was the *Amsterdam Diamond Center*, which caused Oscar's mind to re-engage and focus upon the purpose of their visit.

The square was getting even busier with students and tourists.

Almost overwhelmingly so.

Oscar flagged down a cab and in a little under ten minutes they were getting out at the main entrance to the Hotel Pulitzer on Prinsengracht.

The planned meeting with *Granier* in his rooftop lofted suite was five hours away. They had an appointment with Tyler-Walker near *Muntplein* in just over an hour. First they would take the time to reconnoiter.

As they walked through the lobby which was rich with a series of Oak paneled ornately carved reservation stations set upon black and white squared flooring, Trent touched Oscar gently on his arm and ushered him toward the concierge desk. Checking in at the station reserved for *Starwood Preferred Platinum Guests* was a face he recognized.

It was a woman. The last time he had seen her, she had been in the cricket pavilion at Beacon Hill Park in Victoria. She had been fondling genitalia and in the process of giving 'head'.

Following behind her was another familiar face. The venerable knight *Sir Barrington Sanford* himself in all of his pomp.

Oscar looked hard at the man as he arrived at the station, placing his arm around the back of his woman and laughing as he spoke with the front desk clerk. Exchanging pleasantries.

He had seen this face before and not just on an internet news report.

Then he remembered where. Before the breakfast meeting at the *Cafe du Monde* in New Orleans, Oscar, as was his want, had taken a short constitutional across the main riverwalk and had stopped for a breather and a *Cherry Ripe* in the *Plaza de Espana*. It was during this sortie that he had noticed a man leaning over the edge from the middle deck of the docked steamer the 'Cajun Queen', which was positioned next to its sister vessel the 'Algiers'. He had been taking photographs. Recognition was a wonderful thing.

Oscar and Trent beat a hasty retreat.

A new factor to consider.

Meanwhile, much further South in Andalucia, the Frenchman was paying his admission fee at the entrance to the Caves of Nerja in Maro. A destination that Oscar had encouraged him to visit while on his vacation. Sylvain joined on the end of a tour and put on the headset provided, setting the dial to select the French language version of the commentary. As he walked through the Caves, impressive for their stalactites and stalagmites he learned that they dated back to the Higher Palaeolithic Age. 30,000 years ago.

The first section traversed was the *Sala de Belen*, followed by the *Sala del Colmillo de Elefante*, before entering the highly impressive and cavernous thirty metre high *Sala de la Cascada*, famed for being the venue of the annual Festival of Dance and Music, which had approached legendary international status. Sylvain put on his jacket as it was getting distinctly colder. There was a chill in the air.

As the tape progressed in slow methodic detailed explanation they moved on into the Sala de los Fantasmas - *Room of Ghosts* - and the commentary mentioned that there had been many recent *sightings* claimed in the vicinity. Visions of a young and very beautiful *Anglo-Italian* woman leaning hard against a support rail, who had met with a particularly chilling death at the hands of a mute local war hero at the end of the last century.

It went on to say that the alleged 'murderer', the *asesino*, was never tried as he was determined a suicide soon after. It was claimed that his tortured spectre could also be sighted *by those with a guilty conscience*, scurrying in the silence and darkness of the *Cataclysm Chamber*, near to the central columned fusion of stalactites and stalagmites with a diameter of 18 metres.

It was said by many, that he was often observed *kneeling on the ground with bloodied legs, knees and hands*, scraping away at the surface in the darkness, rosary wrapped around his tight little fist, engaged in a frantic search for his *Red Beret of Distinction* which had apparently become dislodged during the fatal struggle.

Chapter Eighteen

Byron Tyler-Walker was as expected, right on time.

He was stood on the steps to the left of the impressive high towered entrance to the *PATHE* Tuschinski Theater on *Reguliersbreestraat,* just off the Muntplein. Leaning languidly next to the thin elongated billboard. He was reading a pink copy of the FT and wearing a Red Carnation.

The Tuschinski is a huge, Art Deco cinema located between the Munt Tower and the Rembrandtplein and Byron was nothing if not one with a flair for the dramatic. It was the perfect setting for a rendezvous with his old friend *Oscar Phelps.*

As Oscar and Trent approached from across the road, the crowds were gathering to pay and get into the main auditorium. Trent looked up to see standing tall in their full glory, two very striking towers flanking the front entrance, which in turn had two very gothic lamps pre-eminently positioned. The main foyer if they had bothered to go in, is executed in the Art Deco style in rich reds and golds - with paintings of paradise birds and peacocks. It has very plush and colourful carpets, hand-woven in Morocco. It also featured a bar made of bronze and marble.

The elaborate main auditorium was known locally as the 'dowager bonbon box'. The building boasted not only a great movie hall, but a cabaret-dinner club named "La Gaité", a Japanese tea room, a Moorish suite, and a series of elegant foyers. The Tuschinski was very often the venue of choice for Dutch movie premieres.

Byron was hugging Oscar and smiling graciously. He looked genuinely pleased to see his old friend. Perhaps the consulting fee per centage in the *van Breda* account had warmed his appreciation?

Oscar turned Byron to face an on looking Trent. Introductions were needed.

"My God...He's a big bugger isn't he." exclaimed Byron, quite flatteringly.

He did not immediately endear himself to Trent Alexis, but with his chasm of charm, reserve of smarm and general bearing...there was still time.

The two men followed Byron's lead as they continued up *Reguliersbreestraat*, destination *Rembrandtplein*.

"I don't suppose you've got time for a quick tug, have you gentlemen?" said Tyler-Walker, in a low, enquiring and hopeful voice.

"What?" said Trent to Oscar.

"He means do we want to visit the Red Light?" explained Oscar.

Trent considered the proposition for a moment. Then kept on walking. Taking more of a liking to Byron Tyler-Walker.

Oscar checked his TAG. He was conscious of time and its cruciality later on in the day.

"You don't look any older Oscar." said Byron, ingratiatingly.

"You are still a funny man." retorted Oscar.

"Yes...I retain that." Said Byron, quick as a flash.

They both laughed. It was a private joke and one in which all three shared.

They were both very clever fellows indeed...

As it was Amsterdam, in keeping with tradition, Oscar had a large glass of *Heineken,* head suitably leveled by a spatula. Byron had an *Amstel Beer* and Trent ordered a *Bud.* He was not a traditionalist.

They were seated at an outside terrace table at the *Amstel Taveerne.*

Pixie Lott could be heard singing on the bar system. Byron said that he liked her very much.

Trent was admiring the scenery. This was a hangout for the college girls from the Universiteit.

"By the way Oscar, while I remember, Thank You very much for the gift." said Byron, as he took the top off his beer in a long refreshing series of well practiced gulps.

Oscar thought for a moment, taking in another sip from his cold clear lager.

"Did you enjoy it?" he replied.

"Very much." said Byron.

"Please convey my very best regards to Mrs. Robinson when next you see her and tell her she is welcome back to Amsterdam, anytime..." he continued.

Oscar glanced at Trent, taking another drink. Trent understood what was being said and smiled inwardly to himself. Mrs Robinson was priceless.

"To business." said Byron as he got up and walked inside the bar restaurant for a moment.

Oscar looked at Trent and smiled. The time was approaching. Trent continued to survey the bar terrace and reveled in the pleasant and relaxed ambience. Two tables back were two quite delectable college girls. Taking in the afternoon. Happy. Lives ahead of them. Long blond hair, fresh pretty faces, sober white blouses and black slacks. Innocence personified. They were studying, comparing notes; they both had laptops or more conventionally notepads and iPhones. One was a *Storm*. The girl on the left who was a little more petite and with classically high cheekbones then produced a tightly wound reefer and lit it up. The single most effective way to relax and be at ease known to man. They shared it. Inhaling deeply. Then as they collapsed in a fit of girlish giggles, they wrapped themselves up in a passionate embrace and engaged in a long, deep, wet, open mouthed, sometime frantic, sometime gentle and loving kiss. Tongues probing, flickering and darting... hands all over each other.

Trent averted his gaze and switched his concentration back to Oscar, who was still smiling.

The sound of a large silver metal brief case, the kind used by photographers was the next thing heard as Byron placed it on top of the table.

David B. Green

"Is it all there?" said Oscar.

"It's all there." said Byron, "the balance can be arranged after we visit the ABN AMRO bank on Kalverstraat and they get your signature in release." he continued.

Oscar drained his Heineken and said,

"Let's go then."

Trent's gaze had wandered back to the girls sat behind him. There was as yet, no obvious sign of an imminent release. If anything the sexual interaction had become even more frantic.

He hoped that they would be alright!

A little over an hour later, Oscar and his associates were exiting the bank's upper floor executive office suite in the elevator. Documentation and identification duly produced and signature execution completed. The balance of the $50M dollars in stones had been paid for. Funds transfer and receipt by e-transfer had been confirmed by both originating and receiving banks.

The physical goods which were released as a result of the transfer were now transferred internally within the building and placed on deposit in the bank's vaults, secured by a security code known only to Oscar. The release to a third party would take Oscar's input and the presence and secondary code provided by a banking official.

They were ready to complete the deal. Just over two hours now to the meeting at the *Pulitzer*.

Not enough time to get nervous.

Back at *32-Red*, Sylvain was chatting in Spanish, which he was quite proficient at, with Alberto. Taking a long cold cool *Lanjaron water sin gas y zumo de naranja* and nibbling on an assorted platter of hors d'oeuvre's. He particularly was enjoying the *San Daniele Prosciutto, Asparagus y Grana Padano Gratin*. It had become a favourite.

Alberto was enjoying a *San Miguel* and eating some bread and brie, with red grapes and passion fruit.

"How was your tour?" asked Alberto, more out of courtesy than interest.

Sylvain considered the question.

He placed his fork alongside his plate after first taking a mouthful of gratin and then dabbed at his lips with his cloth napkin.

He looked over at the sea and then back at Alberto.

"What can you tell me about *Jose Rivero de Luque* and *Francesca Luciani?*" he said.

Alberto looked towards the terrace to ensure that there was no-one in earshot and then over at the Mar Mediteranneo. He then turned back toward the Frenchman and looked him directly in the eye.

"Ghosts." he said.

"Nothing more than ghosts..."

On the background musical loop which had just started up for the evening, could be heard the dulcet tones of *Francis Albert Sinatra*.

The summer wind came blowin' in
From across the sea
It lingered there to touch your hair
And walk with me

All summer long
we sang a song
And then we strolled that golden sand
Two sweethearts and the summer wind

Like painted kites, those days and nights
They went flying by
The world was new beneath the blue
Umbrella sky

Then softer than a piper man
One day, it called to you
I lost you I lost you to
The summer wind

The autumn wind
And the winter winds

David B. Green

They have come and gone
And still those days
Those lonely days
They go on and on
And guess who's sigh`s
His lullabies through nights that never end
My fickled friend,
The summer wind
The summer wind warm summer wind

Mmm the summer wind...

Chapter Nineteen

The WesterKerk is sited at Prinsengracht 281.

Built according to the design of Hendrick de Keyser in 1620. It has been said that *Rembrandt* found his final place of rest here, but his grave has never been discovered. Though he was aware of this because he was a man who engaged in meticulous research, none of it meant much to *Wendell Madison* as he scaled the spiral staircase on the inside of the main tower that lead to the spire. The clock made famous by *Anne Frank* was chiming. It had been such a source of comfort to her it was written. Right now it was deafening Wendell who had become stationary, covering his ears until the sounds relented.

Wendell was preparing.

Wendell Madison was in his mid forties. The slaying of his boss *Charles Harrison* and compadre *Tanner Schultz* in San Francisco had initially left a gaping hole in his world. That was until *Oscar Phelps* seeing an opportunity, made him an offer that he couldn't and wouldn't refuse. Since that time, his life had changed immeasurably and all for the most part, for the general good. He occasionally was called upon by his new found *associates* to 'help out' on matters often *Global* in nature and which very often required solutions of a radical nature. He was always pleased to provide a service. Taking pride in his work. He was an enforcer and protector. An accomplished one at that. He also liked the people who occupied Oscar's world and had endeared himself to them by being a relied upon source of assistance, whenever needed.

Wendell was a proud Texan with a chiseled, handsome and always tanned face, ever ready and winning smile and confident demeanor. He was a tall man, standing a little over 6 feet 5 inches. Just not tall enough to be considered a giant. His body was well conditioned with little fat and if he had a vanity, then it was that he was a little bit of a clothes horse. His wardrobe was varied, excessive, but of very high quality. Since allying with Oscar, he had benefited from a quarterly stipend (a retainer) paid directly into his bank account at the *Banque Espirito Santo et de la Venetie* located at 45, Ave Georges Mandel. 75116 Paris, originating from one of Oscar's corporate accounts. It was a sum significant enough to ensure his sole exclusivity and constant availability. A similar arrangement to those enjoyed by other *Phelps* associates.

It also paid for the upkeep of his lady friends and his daughters. He had one of each living in high-end properties that he was underwriting as prudent investments in both London, where he kept a flat in Strawberry Hill and in Paris, where he had a more than modest *pied-a-terre* in the Opera district. He also kept within his portfolio, small studio apartments in Henderson, Nevada, and on the Isle of Mann.

However, his principal residence was located in the very upscale neighborhood of Houston, Texas where he enjoyed a co-habitation with a professional lady in her mid-thirties, who was very polished, knew not to ask too many questions and was very discreet. They lived in the most prestigious part of town; *River Oaks*.

Oscar Phelps looked after him very well and he was a very careful and measured man who was very protective of the enhanced status that he now enjoyed. The relationship had developed to that of reciprocal close friend, confidante and ally.

The taxi pulled up at the apron of the entrance to the *Pulitzer*.

Trent Alexis got out first and was carrying the metal case. Oscar followed and over tipped the driver, which merited an extended use of the word 'bedankt'.

Byron had remained in the Mercedes car at the request of Oscar, though he had protested that he wanted to see it through.

Oscar had convinced him that his presence in Nerja later on in the month for a brief vacation was all that was needed and sincerely thanked him again for his efforts.

The Mercedes pulled away from the curb and Byron was destined for the Centraal Station and a lengthy rail journey back home to Antwerpen.

They entered the lobby which was far busier and much noisier than their earlier visit and which was receiving a group of British Airways flight crew. Checking in at their especially designated station.

They headed for the Red *house phone* which was mounted on a wall nearby the Concierge Desk and had a small transparent sound proof awning. Oscar asked the operator to put him through to Farren Granier's suite. The conversation was swift. Oscar doing most of the talking.

Before *Granier* could invite them up to his suite the conversation was abruptly curtailed by Oscar who refused to take the meeting in the hotel, his reasoning being because a hotel suite was too secluded and his movements would in all probability be caught on CCTV. Oscar said the transaction should take place nearby in a public place where cameras where less prevalent and that after the deposit was handed over they would then walk over together to the bank, to collect the balance of the materials. Granier, who was excited by the prospect and not wishing to piss *Phelps* off, agreed to the change of venue. There was logic in what *Phelps* said. Oscar closed the discussion by telling Granier that he should bring Sir Barrington and the lady with him.

It was not a request.

Granier was silent for a moment and then confirmed their agreement after consulting with his colleague. There was not really a choice.

`` Her name is Laura. `` said Granier.

``The WesterKerk in twenty minutes...`` replied Oscar, carefully replacing the telephone onto its cradle.

Oscar and Trent left the building. Outside it was starting to drizzle rain.

April showers...April Sunshine... (Love and Rainy weather...)

Chapter Twenty

I

At the appointed time, **Granier, Sir Barrington** and **Laura** were at the main entrance to the WesterKerk. They each had a **Pulitzer** umbrella from which they were in the process of shaking off the rain drops before entering the church. Granier opened the door and lead the way. They were conversing quietly and appeared to be engaged in frivolous laughter. It was almost banter. Discourteous, given the surrounds.

Farren Granier was perhaps two meters ahead of *Laura* and *Sir Barrington* when the first dulled `phut!` from Wendell's revolver, with specially adapted silencer, became audible.

Sir Barrington was still partially smiling as his body hit the ground face first. The top of his head, near where the crown once was, had been replaced by a deep cavernous hole of entry. The exit wound had been more severe and had served to take away most of the Knights lower mouth, jaw bone and chin. The second `phut!` plugged a dark hole in the middle of Laura's forehead and blew away the entire back of her skull. The ensuing mess that trailed was rather unfortunate. Both had been quite dead before hitting the ground.

The *Brethren of Acadia* had lost another member.

Time then appeared to distort as *Granier* flung himself to the blood spattered ground, waiting for his turn.

He started shouting; ``Not me!, Not me!, you'll be making a mistake if you take me. Fucking hell! Not me!`` he exclaimed in pleading desperation

He was rocking on the ground, holding his head with his forearms, crossing his forehead and face, almost curled up as if to reduce the target area.

The distinct smell of cordite was apparent; lingering in the air and it was strong as it funneled out then began dissipating, expanding and then diluting from the entrance of the church. Outside the rain was getting heavier. Beating down on the roof.

Wendell waited at Oscar's instruction.

Oscar, Trent and Wendell stood in silence and then each approached the prone *Granier* from a different part of the building.

As they arrived at where he was lay, almost simultaneously, he looked up at Oscar and protested. ``I trusted you. You bastard!``

"You were supposed to be a man of honour." he scowled. "Of your word...'" he continued. His mood getting more ambivalent and reproachful, as though he had something of value to trade.

As Wendell once again lifted his gun and pointed it toward the target, *Granier* shouted out with a shrieking half laugh and plaintiff cry.

" We've got her! "

a second passed...

" We've got her! " he was almost manic in his protestation.

Almost gleeful. Reveling in his statement. Half laughing and half crying at the same time. He was beginning to shake.

Then a calmness prevailed as Oscar understood exactly what Granier was saying.

The three men stood in silence watching over Granier. Waiting.

" We've got Hillary Robinson." he said with palpable relief... looking up at Oscar Phelps.

II

The three men and Granier exited the church by a small side door entrance which leads to the edge of the canal.

David B. Green

The rain was still pouring and they were going to get wet.

Fortunately, the precipitation also served to keep most people off of the streets. Trent still had the metal case.

In twenty minutes they were seated in a coffee shop on Spuistraat. ***Abraxas Too*** was not that far away, just northwest of the Nieuwe Kerk, but far enough to put some distance between themselves and Prinsengracht. They were all drenched. No-one appeared too concerned however.

As they sat in a booth, they all composed themselves, taking off their wet coats and uniformally committing what had just taken place to history.

A new set of rules had been put in place.

A deal had to be made.

Trent looked around for a menu. Still hungry, he wondered what the space cake was like. He hadn't immediately realized that they were in a weed bar. The menu gave them a handy description of each type of weed or hash and its effects.

Granier studied the menu closely. His bravado and composure back intact.

Coffee shops are not allowed to advertise, so there is no big sign saying "Marijuana for Sale". In some shops cannabis is sold by weight, in others by value. Where it is sold by weight the prices are per gram. There are 28 grams in an ounce. Where it is sold by value, the menu will show the quantity, in grams that you will get of each variety for a fixed price of around 20 Euros.

Trent took a look at what was on offer;

Grass		Hash	
Thai	€ 4.50	Moroccan	€ 5.00
Skunk	€ 5.00	Special Moroccan	€ 7.00
Northern Lights	€ 6.00	Nepalese	€ 10.00
White Widow	€ 6.50		
AK47	€ 7.50		
Super Silver Haze	€ 9.00		

Apart from *Granier* who took some *Nepalese*, the other men abstained in favour of conventional coffee.

Granier had a chip with which to bargain.

$10M in diamonds representing the deposit was paid to Granier. Trent reluctantly handed over the metal case.

$20M would be exchanged at the ABN bank in the early business hours of the following morning and the balance of the $40M provided to Granier upon the successful handover of Mrs. Robinson for which an additional $5M in cash was agreed as ransom. This left Oscar with a small but acceptable retention after fees etc and most of all would sever the association once and for all.

A deal was made. An accommodation for the safe return of Mrs. Robinson.

Oscar demanded proof of life.

Granier gave Oscar a telephone number written on a piece of paper which had been wetted by the rain. It was smudged but he could still make it out.

The prefixed country code was +34. Spain.

Wendell passed Oscar his Blackberry. Oscar dialed. On the third ring tone it was picked up.

The voice answering sounded familiar but was not immediately recognizable.

"Let me speak to Mrs. Robinson." he said.

A moment passed.

"Oscar, it's me and I'm Ok, but they are going to kill me if you don't..." the line was cut off leaving a purr which tailed off.

She was clearly distressed and frightened and almost crying, but Oscar was convinced that he had just spoken with Hillary.

"Who was the man?" asked Oscar, to which Granier replied,

"Oh! That would be your new friend...That would be 'Perry', and if you are wondering, 'Perry' has a score to settle.

He was the '*husband*' of a man with whom you were acquainted who met his death some years back at the *Moore Stairs* in Sydney, Australia.

Oscar looked over at Wendell.

Wendell, thinking that there was little of value that he could add, just smiled a wry smile and continued to stir his coffee.

Chapter Twenty One

Confident that *Granier* would not be so complacent or trusting this time and no doubt would be looking to elicit an element of revenge, Oscar expected the agreed trade in *Andalucía* to be fraught with complication.

Granier would bring his band of thugs from the *Big Easy* and take on some local muscle as insurance. There was a great deal of Russian and Ukrainian influence on the *Costa del Sol* and Granier with his connections, would not have to look far for support.

The exchange would be made in six days time at a location to be determined. The delay no doubt, to accommodate the mustering of this support.

It occurred to Oscar as they let *Granier* leave the shop unharmed and with the diamonds, that he may have badly underestimated him. As an anthropologist he would be expected to be very meticulous and detailed. Characteristics shared with their former mutual friend; The Rt. Honourable Eric Armstrong-Jones.

Oscar and Trent bid a farewell to Wendell and agreed that they should next meet in Nerja at *32-Red* in three days time. Rooms and flights would be reserved.

Wendell had a daughter in Paris to visit and he was due a couple of days off, as was Trent.

The rain had stopped and it was becoming dark. The roads literally were shining with the residual water and the overhead lights reflecting.

As Oscar flagged down a taxi, Trent said that he would prefer to take a walk and clear his head. Oscar understood. They agreed to meet later at the *Sheraton Schiphol* hotel where they had rooms and had stored their luggage. They would take a drink in the bar of the VOYAGER restaurant on the first floor. *Bols Genever Gin* for a brain blast and the strength that it would give them. They had a plane to catch next morning to Malaga.

As the taxi headed off in the direction of the outer ring-road destined for the airport and Schiphol Plaza, 17 kilometers away, the song playing ironically on the radio was by Sammy Davis Jr;

There's some million things
That we could do this evening
With all the night life
And the silver screen

Oh, we got time
And we could take the town in
Or take the fast cab
Baby, down to New Orleans

But what I got in mind
Is a small cafe, out of the way
Oh baby, we won't stay
No and be too late

What I got mind is to disappear
And baby, let's stay right here
Oh, to tell the truth
What I've got in mind is making love to you

At the conclusion he asked the driver to turn the music off and sat back into his seat and closed his eyes.

His thoughts drifted to the CNN Early Morning News Channel that he had watched on the KLM flight coming over. The news readers had been *Betty Nguyen* and *Kyren Chetry*. Both had recently made it on to Oscar's *Top Ten* Newscasters list along with the recent additions of Lorna Dunkley, Lukwesa Burak and Lisa Knights from SKY news and Melissa Theuriau from France 24.

Pleasant thoughts...

...Oscar hoped that this would not be his last visit to Amsterdam.

Trent Alexis on the other hand had other ideas.

He was headed for the 'Red Light' in need of a 'tug'.

He had something very specific in mind.

It involved two girls, both blond, fresh faced and young.

He was still hungry.

Chapter Twenty Two

Oscar was deeply worried about Hillary.

His concerns were shared by his fellow associates whose emotions showed up at varying levels during the time spent at *32-Red* in preparation for the exchange. Mrs. Robinson for all of her quirks, her high filluted and often quite appalling attitude and her eccentric sexual tendencies, was very well liked by all.

Loved by some of them.

She was after all, one of them. A trusted associate on whom each could rely. Dr. Mercer upon learning of her fate, had also volunteered to come over to Spain from Boston, such was his concern. Oscar had thanked him, but respectfully declined the gesture. Gerald was not one for conflict.

It was the early afternoon of the day before the planned exchange. It was very hot; almost 38 degrees after a seasonal early morning shower had cleared the air. Hernando de Carabeo was still a little wet from the rainfall. The outdoor flora had benefited however, which pleased Alberto.

Nerja was beginning to heave with its pre-summer compliment of international tourists. *Semana Santa* was not far off. *Poor Jose.*

Oscar's thoughts drifted. Another time. Another City. Another continent. Another life.

He was sat at the bar side. Looking with craned neck out of the small window that looked over and out onto Carabeo.

His thoughts were locked into a Boston winters evening, perhaps triggered by the offer of assistance from the good doctor. In his mind the snow was coming down steadily on Boylston Street. The flow of traffic was beginning to take conditions into account as it began to screw to a crawl. Plows were out and the metallic grinding noise emanating began to contribute to the normal traffic sounds, which were somehow comforting. The snow was getting heavier and began to fuzz out all the lights that illuminated the sidewalks, giving them quite pronounced halos of neon red and streetlight yellow. Quincy Market and the early evening promise of drinks beckoned and so did the image of the crisp white snow which had once cradled *Lori* and which had become her enveloping shroud, as it began to become fractured by a stream of ever expanding thick red blood which came from underneath her body.

Oscar's insides first began to knot and then to scream. A tear began to well at his right eye. He opened his eyes, shaking his head slowly and he was momentarily blinded by the recollection which had been stark.

Oscar's head began to strain. His neck was sweating and feeling fat. He shook with the stress of the moment and it served to bring him back. He was incredibly tired.

He felt hungry, though knew he would struggle to keep anything down.

He felt like he hadn't eaten for a very long time. He didn't want to eat. He leaned over the bar and plucked from the top shelf an already partially opened bottle of bourbon. He took a long hard pull from the neck of the bottle and winced as the liquid settled hot in his stomach.

The shock served to urgently re-engage him fully with current matters in Axarquia. He felt dull and sleepy and somehow more round-shouldered than usual. Oscar looked at his TAG and realized that now was the time.

Trent, Wendell, Sylvain and Horace were seated in a banquette taking a mostly liquid lunch. Save for the Frenchman who preferred his zumo. Oscar had plans to join them later on in the day, after he had secured the services of a small army of Russian expatriated vigilantes from Marbella to even up the sides. Preparation was all. He achieved this feat without a problem. Favours were called in from his associates at the *Marina del Este* who were only too pleased to help. These people enjoyed bedlam and violence. They were precisely the right profile for this kind of a job. Wherever confusion prevailed, they excelled.

David B. Green

Some time had passed. Oscar was now leaning over the supporting rail at the end of the semi-circular Paseo de *Balcon de Europa* perched at the very end of the cliff-top. He was watching the sea. Blue, crashing and yet tranquil at the same time. He could see an ocean liner in the distance and several yachts and cruisers, quite similar to the *Dolores*. He was at the very nerve centre of the town. Nerja had always been a friend to *Phelps*. At this point he needed her wisdom and guidance more than ever before.

The promenade was flanked on each side by salubrious hotels, restaurantes and bars and of course on the East side by the glorious Spanish white arches which formed the gateway to the view down onto the *Playa de Calahonda*. Abandoned upturned sardine fisherman's boats were stranded next to the rows of active boats ready to be deployed and all...children were splashing in the water as the wash gently caressed their feet.

Oscar looked over to the *Sierra Almijara*, adjusting his eyes to the glare of the sunlight as it tortured so. He reached for his *Bolle* wraparound sunglasses which were hung conveniently by a black chord around his neck. He then turned his back to the ocean and looked at the many tall, wide and green palms and other trees that lined the paseo and made it so unique. He then looked at the two ancient cannons. Memories of the days past, when there was a fortress here on top of the cliffs. There was in the distance, an ice-cream stand with parasol at the beginning of the paseo where it met with the plaza, tended by a local woman, who to his knowledge and memory had been there for years. Behind the stand to the left stood the Iglesia de *El Salvador*. So often the venue for his penitence.

To his immediate right was the life-size sculpture of King Alfonso XII, stood casually, hand on the same rail Oscar was leaning backwards on now.

Next to that was the downstairs entrance to the restaurant, which was unseasonably closed.

Finally, Oscar looked over to his right at about a *two o'clock angle* and just made out the *paseo de los carabineros*, leading across the rocks of the coastline. He had had so many happy days here.

He considered for a moment. Everything that could be done, had been.

In that he took a modicum of solace.

Hillary would be home soon.

Chapter Twenty Three

It was getting close to the time.

The heat was still blistering and the clouds which were very infrequent and distant, were high. The afternoon would not bring relief.

Oscar was seated upstairs at the Black Cat tearoom, drinking not very good, but strong black coffee because he felt like he needed a jolt and writing down some inconsequential notes on the back of an old copy of the Sur in English. He had been studying the availability of flights to Dubai from Malaga and working out the best routing.

Coming up the staircase, emerging from the narrow landing was a very pretty and lithe young woman. She had a small golden brown attaché case of leather and good quality. Her arse conveyed an admirably perky almost feral, *sit up and beg* quality, which Oscar liked very much.

As she sat at a table in the far corner of the room she smiled. White, even teeth. She was very well dressed. She had a good haircut, though her hair was ever so slightly dirty blond in colour and she was clearly in the very best of physical condition and shape. She looked mid thirties. She appeared rich, which made looking good that much less difficult to achieve. She was evenly tanned and not from a bed. Upon closer inspection, she had, he noticed, quite high thick hair which had both body and volume. She wore it in sculpted fashionable bangs over her forehead. Her make-up was slight though expertly applied. She had large eyes of blue. Her dress was simple though elegant and fitted her well. Caressing her body in all the right places. Accentuating and pulling at her sharp breasts and what he imagined would be a very tight bottom. She was perhaps a little sinewy, but still worthy of contemplation in less trying times.

She placed her order for iced tea with lemon and then said *Hello* to Oscar. It was not a shouted greeting. It didn't have to be. She knew Oscar was being attentive.

There was something distinctive about the *Hello*. She had a British accent.

Oscar put down his newspaper.

She took a sip of her libation through the straw and then blotted her lips with her paper napkin. They appeared even fuller and more appealing. Once again she smiled. It was wider now and becoming even warmer.

Oscar's thoughts drifted fleetingly to Mishka and the others.

He got up from his seat. Frowning a little, he made his exit in haste.

There was a soccer match scheduled to start up at the new campo municipal stadium at 6pm and Oscar had encouraged his friends to accompany him and attend. To get their minds off things. They needed a diversion. A distraction.

Only Horace showed any initial resistance. He was not very sport inclined. If it had been *Flamenco* then he would have been at the head of the line. He had a very well developed penchant for the *Marie-Carmen's* of town.

Alberto gave them a lift up to the stadium in his recently acquired *Mercedes* people mover.

The posters on all of the street corners showed that the *futbol* game was between C D F S Nerja and Villanueva de Cordoba Fs Asoc. in the Primera Nacional A division. The sponsor was restaurante Don Miguel. Friends of *32-Red*. Nerja were kitted out in their traditional blue and white striped shirts, blue shorts and socks. The visitors were in all white.

Oscar and the chaps were seated on the terraces behind one of the goals. They were eating *Pippas - sunflower seeds* and building piles of husks as they watched the game unfold. Just like every other supporter in fact, who where made up of mostly an amalgam of loyal expats and locals.

The game did unfold...miserably. At the end of 90 minutes it was a very laboured, uninspired 1-1 draw. Horace and Sylvain had long since lost interest and had spent most of the second half at the bar. Sylvain had temporarily lapsed and would later regret it and reproach himself severely. Wendell had no idea what he had just witnessed and cared little for an explanation. It was a similar story for Trent.

At the end of the game the men walked back down into town. At *32-Red*, the evening was just about to start. The beautiful Senoritas were beginning to congregate at the Tropicana.

Oscar had also had Alberto arrange a few *sure-things* to be shipped in, just in case. He told his friends to mingle, unwind and relax. They did not require much encouraging and Horace was very quickly back in his element.

The morrow was going to be a difficult and exacting day.

Chapter Twenty Four

It was approaching 5pm and Nerja was just reawakening after the afternoon's Siesta. The day had been cloudy and gray. The sun was just showing it face through the dissipating clouds.

It was cool and almost not the weather for shorts. For Oscar and his associates it had also been a tense day. One that had dragged.

None of them had the stomach for lunch and dinner if taken at 8pm would be a conquest.

The exchange was to take place at midnight up at the Caves in Maro. There had been no further word from Hillary, other than that she was *fine*, according to *Granier* when he called earlier in the day from his hotel on Gibraltar. His parting quip had been that *Perry sends his regards*...It served to irk Oscar, which in all probability, it was meant to.

Oscar had arranged for Antonio to ensure his friends at the caves would leave the side entrance unlocked and the alarm disengaged. He had also ensured that the lighting to illuminate the *Chamber of the Cascada* would be activated by a time switch at 11.55pm for a period of thirty minutes.

All that was needed now was the discipline and virtue of patience. The chaps were resting up in their rooms at *32-Red* and Oscar had retired to his apartment at Carabeo 77. He was on the roof terrace and had taken a snifter of *Courvoisier XO* cognac for the strength that it would give him.

The arranged back-up was due to arrive in at 10pm and rendezvous with Oscar, Wendell and Trent at the bridge that straddles the dry riverbed

(*Rambla de Espinar*) and which cuts through the lower part of the village of *La Herradura*.

Despite their vociferous and persistent protestations, Oscar had decided that Sylvain and Horace would sit this one out.

He went back inside and took a seat opposite the *LeRoy Neiman* original, purchased for him in San Francisco. A gift from a friend.

He had made his decision.

Chapter Twenty Five

Wendell and Trent were ready.

Wendell was always ready.

Night had fallen bringing with it a cooling breeze and the three men were in Oscar's silver *Porsche 911 Carrera Cabriolet* headed smoothly east on the A-7 Autovia del Mediterraneo. The leather roof was deployed. They had just passed *Torre del Pino* and where about to make a right onto the N-340 in the direction of *Torre Caleta*.

The sea over to their right was dark and shimmering with the possibility of a liner in silhouette on the horizon and the road was ever winding as it carved its path through the rocky terrain of the *Costa Tropical*. Just after crossing the *Rio Jate*, Oscar powered down as the condition of the road became less conducive to speed.

They arrived at *Rambla de Espinar* on time and a large van of indeterminate colour and without livery was laid in wait just after the *Repsol* gas station. It had Malaga - MA plates.

The hired foreign muscle was also punctual.

Oscar pulled the *Porsche* alongside and turned off the engine. Wendell approached the van from the rear and the door opened. He got in.

The briefing lasted five minutes.

The two vehicles then resumed the journey. They turned off the road in quick succession just after passing the exit for *Maro* to their left. Taking the next right for the *Cuevas*. In under a minute they were pulling into the car park, ground crackling beneath their tires.

Now stationary, they extinguished their lights. Oscar checked his TAG. It was 10.25pm.

In silence. They waited.

After a few moments, Oscar touched very lightly the panel instrument activating the radio and then turned the volume down by patting the appropriate lever with his forefinger... The haunting tones of "Todavia Cantamos" were playing on REM FM. Oscar let the dulcet tones waft to a complete end before switching off. Unconsciously, he had been humming to the sound.

65 minutes had elapsed. Oscar then depressed the button that opened up the roof and they were all fully exposed to the night air.

There was no movement from inside the van parked next to them.

Dressed in his usual garb, Trent had his eyes closed, but was fully conscious of everything and everybody around him. Wendell was looking more vigilant and alert and tapping a tune of some description with his finger on the dashboard. After a minute or so he desisted.

Still they waited.

Oscar allowed his thoughts to drift briefly to the *Queen's Royal Hotel* in Niagara. He reminded himself of the quotation associated with the *lost* hotel. Something about *the guest who never arrives ...is always welcomed back...*

Oscar's cell phone began to vibrate. It was 11.45pm. The number on the screen was prefixed with a + 350. A Gibraltarian number.

"Good Evening" said Granier.

Oscar responded immediately. "Do you have Mrs. Robinson?"

Farren avoided the question countering with; "We are already here...Why don't you join us?" he said rather sneeringly.

The line went dead.

Including Oscar, Trent and Wendell, the head count stood outside the side entrance to the caves numbered ten. The seven 'contractors' were to a man, all of similar height and build to Wendell and looked physically fit. They each had a weapon.

Trent pushed open the side door and it opened without a problem. It was 11.55pm and the ambient emergency lighting was replaced by the more conventional electric variety. Right on cue.

The CCTV cameras high on the ceiling had also been deactivated. No flashing red light was in evidence. Antonio would be rewarded for his efforts.

Wendell moved to the head of the line, pistol out and ready and lead the way through the two smaller chambers of entry and out into the opening of the *Chamber of the Cascada*. The arc lighting was fully illuminating the stage area and the contingent of men in wait could be seen standing there, up ahead in the distance. Oscar could see *Granier*. They did not appear to be concerned and did not look to be that combative.

There was a little posturing initially between the two sets of hired guns as they grew closer to each other, but nothing overly dramatic. Wendell recognized three of the men from New Orleans. Two very large 'brothers' and the bigger of the Caucasians that had been in wait, outside of the *Court of Two Sisters*. The rest, were locals and in total outnumbered Oscar's group by two. Though of course, more could have been strategically deployed elsewhere. They had the advantage of arriving first it now appeared.

Granier said to Oscar who was now only a few yards away from him. "I do hope that this is going to be civilized." It wasn't a question.

"Do you have my Diamonds?" he continued.

Oscar had a case at his side which held the balance of the merchandise in question for exchange.

He tossed it over to one of *Granier's* minders, who caught it cleanly.

"The extra to secure the release of my friend is also in there." assured Oscar.

"Very Good." said Granier.

"Now to the question of Mrs Robinson." he continued.

"Where is she?" Oscar retorted in an enquiring but slightly more aggressive tone.

"Oh...She's not here." Granier responded matter of factly, as if surprised by the naïveté of the question.

"She's in an altogether different place...Perry is looking after her." He said.

Oscar was not encouraged by Granier's statement but showed no outward sign of concern. Though inwardly there was deep burning rage.

Success within Control was his mantra.

Granier continued.

"While it is true that I am somewhat indebted to you for doing me a service by killing the Argentine Doctor and also Sir Barrington in actual fact...The business with *Morag* was, you must understand, less easy to forgive."

He paused for a moment as if collecting his thoughts.

"There is also the question of *Perry* to consider. For this reason alone, it is less easy for me to simply let the matter drop. You must realize that I just couldn't let it go. It is a matter of principal you see."

Oscar's stomach started to churn.

Granier continued in his exaggerated calm and confident mode, when in fact he was neither;

"After we have departed, you will find Mrs Robinson locked in a Confessional booth in the Church of *El Salvador*. She is quite well, you will find."

"Perry is a very compassionate kind of a fellow."

A very long moment passed and Trent was becoming restless and growing very tired of this man *Granier*.

Oscar upon seeing this, urged his friend to remain calm with a knowing gesture of his hand.

Oscar then pulled something from his jacket pocket.

He tossed over to the same *catcher* a small velvet bag.

"There is a three million dollar value in stones in that bag." he said without altering the timbre of his delivery.

"Take it and go." he continued. This would test the loyalty of the hired hands deployed by Granier.

Oscar then passed a similar package to the leader of his own troupe.

There was a stand-off.

As realization dawned, an *entente cordial* had been reached. The support cast had taken quickly their leave, despite *Granier's* futile protestation.

"Who is naive now?" said Oscar.

"You see Farren, you may know a lot about the past, but I know people." he continued. "Those men were looking at either a precarious, potentially grave and doubtful immediate future or an opportunity to get out and secure a longer term, more hopeful less grave future. Faced with that choice, what would you have done?" he said.

Granier again, as he did in Amsterdam, looked disappointed at the frailties of men's minds. It was etched, betrayingly, right across his face. Loyalty clearly had a value and *Phelps* had just met the cost. Inevitably, as with Amsterdam... *the cost always comes before the living...* Even the men from the *Big Easy* had acquiesced. Not a shot had been fired.

"I suppose I shall go then, our business concluded?" said Granier, again in stark naïveté. He really didn't deserve to live; such was his reliance upon the decency of human nature. He was just too methodical and too simple for such a sophisticated man of his standing and tenure within the Brethren of Acadia. Lacking in worldly experience and understanding, like a child with a naive charm. Guileless, unsuspecting and credulous. He lacked the very basics in critical judgment.

The main arc lighting deactivated only moments after Wendell had culled *Farren Granier* with another dulled 'phut!' from his pistol. The body had made little in the way of protest as it slumped to the ground. The side of his head now turned to a bloodied and sticky ruddy gray mush. Only the emergency lighting remained.

Trent picked up the case containing the stones. The three men then hurriedly made their way out of the caves and in moments the *Porsche* had been gunned back into life, booming down toward the town of Nerja.

The town was quite serene for the hour, not too many people on the streets. Oscar parked at the bottom of *Calle Granada* in the *Plaza Cavana* next to the ONCE lottery cabin. They then raced to the front of the church of *El Salvador* passing over the two flat steps and found the main wooden entrance locked shut. The two large lamps positioned high and set at each side of the main doorway served to light up the front of the church. Oscar looked around. There were a few drunken people on the *Balcon* but nobody paid them any mind. No *Guardia Civil* in evidence. Oscar lead Trent and Wendell around the left hand side of the building into a narrow alley way. At the side of the church, down a couple of steps was a sunken office and souvenir shop. Wendell smashed the window and they gained entry.

Upon entering the church it was dark. There was just enough internal emergency lighting to see a way through as they entered the narrow but high church through a door to the immediate left side of the main altar. They ran up the centre aisle between the row upon row of brown wooden pews towards the rear of the main entrance door. As they arrived at the door, Oscar looked to his right and saw laid behind a glass screen, a full size wax depiction of Jesus Christ, complete with a crown of thorns. He moved further down the side of the church and came upon the bank of impressive confessional booths. Trent checked inside the first two and Oscar the third as Wendell indicated that he had found something.

In the fourth booth in the row, behind the curtain at the entrance was a note pinned to the back wall. Oscar used his cell phone to shine light upon the note. It said;

"take a look at the restaurant at the Balcon de Europa…Enjoy the view. Dinner is on me." it was signed *'Perry'.*

As they reached the end of the paseo, both Trent and Oscar were sweating heavily. They took the stairs at the side of the *King Alfonso* statue, down to the restaurant. The door was ajar.

The restaurant did not look active, it never had and the inside fixtures and decor had fallen into a state of gross disrepair. Chairs and tables were stacked up and covered over with sheets. A lectern was upturned and laid on the floor. It smelled fusty and there was a great deal of dust. The great panoramic view window that formed such an impressive and integral part of the Balcon structure was punctuated at its centre by a stark image of terror.

The body of Hillary Robinson was hanging outside.

She was naked except for one shoe and hanged by the neck from a cable which was attached to the bottom of the support rail, secured high above, at the very edge of the balcon.

Her knees were bloodied and the skin blistered and torn. Her face was bruised and swollen and her hands and fingers covered with blood. She had put up a fight.

The wind was blowing her body softly, almost caressing her, as it steadily swung around, high above the sea that was crashing into the shore, deep down below. So that now she was directly facing the three men. It was as if she was looking in at them, through the show window.

The violence and insanity was of a precision and force which met few equals. There were the evidentiary innards of absolute iniquity. The execution had been near flawless and the showmanship impressive.

Horrifically and tragically so.

The tears welled at Oscar's eyes and escaped with rapidity, coursing down his cheeks as he collapsed to his knees in despair. Trent and Wendell rushed to his aid but were pushed away by flailing arms, as *Oscar Phelps* fell apart in front of them.

Phelps was distraught, desolate, crying; sobbing then weeping unashamedly. Loud, ever extending raucous howls of pain and derision.

It was something neither of them wanted to witness ever again.

Epilogue

EPILOGUE

Strawberries cherries and an angel's kiss …

Queen Street, Niagara-on-the-Lake.

Remembrance Day

It was 4 degrees centigrade on Tuesday November 11th. With the wind-chill factor, it felt like -10. Seasonably cold. The wind blew hard into Oscar's face; cutting deep into his eyes, pushing out a tear, no matter it seemed in which direction he was looking. So much so that his head was starting to ache.

Oscar was at the corner of Johnson and Regent Street walking by to his immediate right the Niagara-on-the-Lake Historical lawn bowling club, established in 1877. The oldest in North America, dating back more than 130 years. Oscar could see through the new wrought iron memorial gates, the beautifully flat square that was covered with a fine layer of glistening grayish white frost. His lips were dry and needed a balm. He was conscious of the taught thin hair that had collected in his nostrils and the chill at his ear lobes. He was wearing his large heavy black overcoat by *HILFIGER*, tightly buttoned to just south of the throat, his charcoal *Ralph Lauren* chinos, and high strapped boots by *Kodiak* with a tasteful burgundy silk and woolen backed paisley scarf, knotted high under his chin. In his pocket was his Red Cross of St.George handkerchief. Black fleece gloves by *Columbia*. No hat.

He passed by the *Olde Angel Inn* soon after glancing inside the window of *Captain Swayze's* cottage. No ghost to be seen save for the echoes of the Angel's colonial past.

At the corner of Regent and Queen he turned an acute right and faced the

228

revered Cenotaph clock tower stood slightly elevated on an island in the middle of the street. The immediate vicinity was being cordoned off by industrious town cops and parking marshals.

Oscar looked into the *BeauChapeau* Hat shop which was promoting the *Tilley* winter hat, the 'soft shell' and the 'Audubon' hat, very heavily in its showcase window. Oscar's interest was fleeting at best. The road had been fully cleared of vehicles by 8.49am and the town's municipal workers were busied with leaf blowers, making ready for the ceremony scheduled for later that morning.

Oscar stopped at the *Just Christmas* shop and peered into the window. He caught his reflection and did not like what he found. He had become an old man. Age did not endear. As he peered even deeper, he could then see Christmas tree ornaments and lights. Christmas candles, tablecloths and napkins. Beautifully made Santa's and Angels. Christmas cards and wrap. A toy plastic train was endlessly traveling up and around the road to Santa's workshop at the North Pole.

Oscar took a seat on a bench directly outside the festive store and craned his head just a little to look over at the magnificent gray *Court House* building. He huddled up to protect himself from the cold. Both the Union Flag and the Maple Leaf Flag were in evidence behind him, next to the tower. They were blowing lightly on their respective staffs, their fate to be pulled to half mast at the appropriate time.

A middle aged lady who was rather sprightly, though grossly overweight, had pulled up in a new Toyota van and was beginning the process of laying a series of small poppy covered circular wreaths at the sidewalk in front of the LCBO liquor store, in readiness for the ceremony.

Oscar stood slowly, turning sharply before then crossing carefully the street. He was conscious of his footfall, which was heavy. He sensed he was being watched. Paranoia? He had a feeling that he was seeing a ghost at every turn. Having a vision. He hoped that this would be all that it was. All there was to it. It wouldn't necessarily mean –

At the entrance to the small discreet jewelry store he then stood in wait, patiently, more than a trifle ashamed and in stony silence.

The eleventh hour of the eleventh day of the eleventh month...

Oscar Phelps would be there as always. Standing on the sidewalk with the respectful masses, in front of the *Scottish Loft* and *Hidden Jewels* stores... a slightly more stooped and lonely figure and with a little more grey and carrying an increasingly greater degree of burden in his heart...

Remembering *Hillary Robinson*...

Nerja, Andalucía.

Nightfall. About a month later... December 20XX

...as Oscar looked downwards, the sheer drop from the precipice on which he stood was perhaps seventy meters. It was unyielding.

He wavered a little. His head spinning mildly. His eyes aching as they strained to achieve a clear focus. Perhaps feeling the effects from the combination of mid-morning, afternoon and early evening Gordon's Gin which had blended with the more recently imbibed Johnny Walker *Blue* Label Scotch and the Irish, triple distilled in sherry cases, *Blackbush* BushMills Whiskey, which he had taken in copious amounts from a Glencairn glass that had followed.

The effects of which had served as both Comforter and Anesthesia...

He was conscious that he had been here before.

The Rocks deep below, held a form of *Release.*

It was a 'Release' that Oscar knew could, perhaps should, wait a little while longer.

Oscar still remained fervent in the belief that in this life, he had earned the right to pre-ordain. He took solace in the view recently espoused by his boyhood hero, actor; Michael Caine, who had proclaimed that he wanted to go out in the same way as his friend; David Hemmings.

Immediately after the final take in the final scene of the final act of the film.

A true professional.

Casually, Oscar reached deep into his side pocket and pulled out a black velvet pouch which was pinched together with a string at the open end. It was the pouch of diamonds that had been meant to secure Hillary's ransom. Her liberty. Her life. Her love.

As a single tear made its way slowly down his face, Oscar found himself holding the opened out pouch at the end of his outstretched arm. His eyes were closed tightly and his mouth was pierced shut, displaying thin blue lips that were quivering in pained anguish.

He slowly turned the pouch upside down, releasing the contents gradually... falling silently into the darkness and onto the rocks and into the sea.

When it was finished. When the diamonds had all disappeared. Oscar then let the pouch fall, following the stones into the darkness and into the sea.

His eyes, slowly again, began to open. Re-engaging with the moment. Re-engaging with life and with purpose.

A sharp chill shuddered unexpectedly through his body. It made him fear immediately for his mortality.

Then followed a warmth, almost a glow and with it he could then smell the hint of Hillary's favoured cologne. It was haunting, but also brought a strange sort of comfort. Comfort found in sentimentality, perhaps.

Oscar looked up, deep into the night sky. The moon was almost full. But not quite. Things were never ever quite perfect.

"Courage", "Fortitude", "Positive", "Uncompromising". Oscar thought to himself and found himself mouthing silently the words.

He thought that he heard from a distance, someone; a woman's voice?, asking if he was alright?

As he could know nothing quite so surely anymore. It really did not matter.

Checking himself, he determined that he would not react.

"Maybe," he thought.

"¡Vale! ¡Vale! ¡Vale!"

Personal, Corporate, Musical & Literary Acknowledgements

Red Lights by Georges Simenon

Come Undone - Robert Williams

Firefly - Tony Bennett

Sensa Fine - Connie Francis

Noble House by James Clavell

A Sunday Smile - Beirut/Zach Condon *(Oscar Phelps opening theme)*

The Tailor of Panama by John Le Carre

Our Man in Havana by Graham Greene

Mesrine by Carey Schofield

Amiga Mia - Alejandro Sanz

vivire y morire - Enrique Iglesias

Todavia Cantamos - written by Victor Heredia

Summer Wine - Ville Valo & Natalia Avelon *(Oscar Phelps end theme)*

Waking up in Vegas – Katy Perry

I Saw the Light - Johnny Cash

Mama Do (Uh Oh, Uh Oh) & Cry Me Out - Pixie Lott

I See you See me - The Magic Numbers

Après toi - Vicky Leandros

Chanson Populaire (ça s'en va et ça reviens) - Claude Francois

The SPENSER novels by Robert B. Parker

Caught on a Train by Stephen Poliakoff (Teleplay)

Riverside Blues - King Oliver

Stranger in Paradise - Tony Bennett

The Summer Wind - Frank Sinatra

What I've Got in Mind - Sammy Davis Jr

Scoop by Woody Allen

In Bruges by Martin McDonagh (Selected Extracts)

Test Match Special - **TMS** - Henry Blofeld (Blowers), Aggers, CMJ, Tuffers & the late Johnners et al - Cricket Omni-present

Harbour House Hotel NOTL (Niagara-on-the-Lake) - Ryan Murray

Niagara Historical Society & Museum, NOTL - Clark Bernat M.A.

Markus Former - Amsterdam

Sylvain Charpilienne – Paris

Sunil Vyas - London

Martin Mazza - NOTL

Christian von Hirsch - Bergen

Paul Hayden - Adelaide

Scotty Watson - Auckland

Dirk van Slyke - Houston

Brian Taylor-Walker - Bruxelles

Mercure Hotel - Auckland

Rialto Hotel – Melbourne

Jolly St. Ermin's Hotel, St. James. London – Umberto Michetti

Town of Illfracombe, North Devon

Town of Niagara on the Lake, Ontario

Ayuntamiento de Nerja

Maurice Boland - Marbella

Rancho Manana Golf Club - Cave Creek, Arizona

Tuschinski Theatre - Amsterdam

Court House - NOTL

QVB – Sydney

Watermark Hotel - Brisbane

Le Pavillon Hotel - New Orleans

Cafe du Monde - New Orleans

Mr. Joe Fein of The Court of Two Sisters – New Orleans

June Fallo of The Court of Two Sisters – New Orleans

Philip Auerbach – Switzerland

Alniz Popat – Dubai, UAE & Nairobi, Kenya

NOTL Public Library

BBC World Service

YADDO – Saratoga Springs, New York State

Patricia Highsmith

Step into the World of **Oscar Phelps**
By visiting at;

http://www.facebook.com/profile.php?id=100001634209331

Contact **Oscar**

oscar.phelps.novels@gmail.com

Where King meets Queen
An Oscar Phelps novel

COMING SOON...

The next in the Phelps series:

"Where King meets Queen" an *Oscar Phelps* novel.
(2011)

Selected Extracts...

It was a bitingly cold Niagara-on-the-Lake early October evening and the *Royal George Theatre* was dark.
It was Monday.

Oscar was on his bicycle, meandering but with purpose up Queen Street in the direction of the Cenotaph, after making a sweeping right at some considerable speed at the end of Mississauga Street.

The mistake was in forgetting his *Columbia* gloves. Fleece lined, they would have given great comfort and warmth.

Oscar looked over at the *Charles Inn* which stood impressive in the chill night air and was in relative darkness.

Only the Halloween display of a tired looking, very antiquated and large, red spoke wheels, black hooded carriage with its plethora of assorted size and mis-shaped pumpkins spilling from its broken seat and various other Wiccan images and materials, appeared animated. The six yellow garden umbrellas on the outdoor terrace also looked old and dispirited. Weather worn and seasonally challenged.

After passing the Angie Strauss *Gallery*, Oscar crossed into the road at the Post Office next to the town notice board and continued up the centre of Queen, narrowly missing a black squirrel as it darted out into his path before beating a hasty retreat back to the sidewalk. Oscar reduced his speed so that he could take in fully the atmosphere and energy of the evening.

Feeling alone with the solitude and the latent energy.

The cold air filled and fuelled his lungs as he cycled more sedately, the clock tower and its time displayed, becoming increasingly more visible in the distance. 9.35pm. His TAG concurred.

It was a very dark night, with few stars in evidence and relatively silent. Devoid of any vehicular motion save for the Sentineal horse drawn carriage which was clip-clopping from Queen, turning the corner into Regent Street in the direction of the Olde Angel Inn. Oscar recognized the driver, a very attractive young woman with blond locks tied back and held with a black scrunchy in a bun and decked out in elegantly designed low rider cord jodhpurs of camel, Pikeur white blouse and tailored black sportsman show coat.

A burgundy fleece scarf was well concealed, so as not to ruin the look.

Oscar could not see any passengers in the carriage.

The Stagecoach restaurant had long since closed for the evening, but still the aroma of French fries resonated.

Cork's restaurant showed little promise of life and its open raised patio terrace was abandoned. Bunting still evident on its white painted wooden railings.

Over to the right, the Court House stood in distinction. Proud and fawn grey, lit discreetly and with subtlety to show off its prominence in Classical Revival style. Its facade displaying ornate window heads and keystones creatively carved in the form of intricate faces, with bracketed cornices and then the centrepiece. An elaborate stone balustrade portico supported by strong, heavy, yet somehow graceful columns. The thick winding reddish-brown, green,

237

silver and grey *Virginia creeper* - thought evoking foliage, which had once been a regal summer crimson red, hung resplendent and clinging around the windows and portico that stood beneath the balcony and was supported by various agraffes, had been almost completely shorn for the winter.

As he reached the Cenotaph, Oscar dismounted and left the bike laid on its side in the central median reservation marked out on the road with painted diagonal yellow and white bordered lines. He moved toward the tower, walked up the curb and through the decorative autumnal concrete potted floral bushes and approached the solitary dark olive green door with a window aptly designed in the shape of the Union Flag facing him, reaching down into his pocket for the key.

Beyond the Cenotaph Tower to his left as he peered around the red brick masonry, he could see the Niagara Apothecary at the far corner of the street. Open next in the following year's month of May.

Further across the street was the entrance going down into Simcoe Park and leading to the shallow paddling pool and the Bandstand, while over to Oscar's far right was the imposing and ever impressive *Prince of Wales Hotel*, complete with the flags of Canada,

Ontario and the Union Jack flying prominently, and recently the subject of a visit by the future Sovereign... the next King.

Charles. The Prince of Wales, himself.

Inset to his right, tucked in between the elaborate Designer Dress shops and the yellow fronted, carved Pineapple bearing, welcoming and hospitality signaling, historic, *Owl and the Pussycat* children's clothing store, stood a set of smaller specialist gift and clothing retail stores that also included a new Sotheby's International realtor office...which fate would decree soon lost to the ravages and deep injustices of a Sunday afternoon's fire...their aged hemlock wood interiors taking all night to burn.

Suspended high above the crossroads that linked these historical landmarks were a series of small square yellow boxed and funnel rimmed, perpetually flashing, cautionary *Red Lights*, that jingled in the night air, held together in less than taught unison by a canopied web of connecting cables which were anchored at three corners only, of the merging streets.

The three corners of the streets...***where King meets Queen***.

'It is considered rude to point.' and other hand gestures may get you in serious trouble!!!

...was the advice given to one Oscar Phelps on the overhead displays as he strolled through the Arrivals area of the Dubai International Airport terminal 3, after a grueling 16 hour, 11,000+ kilometer flight from Toronto. Thirteen hours of *Emirates* Airbus A380 flight time routing over Newfoundland, Greenland, Scandinavia, the Ukraine, the Black Sea, Turkey and Iraq before passing Kuwait to the right as they crossed over and into the Persian Gulf, beginning a downward pattern which bypassed Bahrain and Qatar low to the right, while to the distant left stood Iran.

The other three hours, sat on the tarmac in Toronto where courtesy of a passenger who had suffered an ill timed coronary episode and who had as a result, to vacate the flight. The search for his luggage had taken up most of the time.

The A380, the largest passenger jet aircraft ever built, flight number EK 242, had provided comfortable passage to Oscar, who had been afforded accommodation on the upper deck.

The headlines on the three broadsheets that he had read in transit were;-

"8 years later, and no closer to peace in Afghanistan" - **International Herald Tribune.**

"Fraud Disclosure in Afghan Vote Worries Karzai" - **Khaleei Times.**

&

"Pinto turns heads at film festival" - **Gulf News**

Oscar had concentrated his attention upon the latter.

Abu Dhabi: **"Slumdog Millionaire** sensation Frieda Pinto was a picture of poise in her sweeping black *Marc Jacobs* gown at the opening gala of the Middle East International Film Festival on Thursday..."

As he made a left through the bank of receiving doors, carry-on luggage occupying his hands, contemplating a Traditional Balinese Massage at *DreamWorks*; Oscar would soon be en route the World Trade Centre on Sheikh Zayed road.

A little weary from the trip, he was confronted by a mêlée of cab and limo drivers stood in an orderly fashion behind the holding rails, each uplifting a board with the name of their respective target featured prominently.

One of the boards had Oscar's name upon it.

Oscar pointed directly at the holder in both identification and acknowledgment. It would prove to be a precarious start to the day and a new Arabian adventure.

PREVIEW

PROLOGUE

The headline on the tabloid news sheet **7 Days** said:-

"Tears of a Killer"...monster admits murdering child in mosque.

The article, front page, went on to describe in quite lurid and graphic detail, the full horror of the atrocities committed upon a four year old boy by a sex beast, who had admitted to the Dubai court that he had raped and murdered the young victim in a mosque on the holy day of the Eid. The boy's father had expressed a wish for a *death by stoning* capital sentence and Oscar was in absolute agreement and would have happily agreed to cast the first.

Oscar Phelps habitually checked his TAG. He was dining at his preferred outdoor cafe restaurant terrace on the Sheikh Zayed Road located just down from the Crowne Plaza hotel in Dubai. The *Fountain* cafe was principally the IN place for a coterie of local business people to meet and relax, smoke their Shisha pipes, watch each other and take tea and banana cake. The high backed orange brown wicker chairs positioned in the round and which surrounded a series of serviceable sturdy wicker though glass-topped dining tables provided an excellent and most comfortable terraced environment for Oscar Phelps to watch people as they went about their business. Taking their mid-day sustenance while they indulged in various forms of argument, mélange, secrecies and unassuming though possibly nefarious chit-chat.

Oscar leaned back into his chair, brushing away the crumbs from his cake which had accidentally spilled onto his recently acquired silk tie by *TED LAPIDUS* of Paris. A gift from his fast recovering friend, the supremely gifted and enterprising Frenchman, Sylvain.

While taking a sip from his Coca-Cola *light* he then surveyed across from the indigenous to the region ivy, which sprawled like a virus across the expansive wooden cabana that formed the centerpiece of the restaurant, an interesting combination of people who were frequenting at the time.

Some where deeply animated, engrossed in their designer skinned laptops or indeed in each other, scouring notepads, talking into their iphones, texting from their blackberries and they were quite open and incongruous and seemingly oblivious to the humid 27 degree elements. While others were sheltered by various potted trees, pink and mauve flora and artistically pleasing wooden mesh like dividing and partitioning structures that served little purpose other than the aesthetic and spent copious amounts of time trapped in either deep contemplation, a call to prayer or deep and intense, often sinister looking conversation.

From his initial observations, the minority of the patrons were Arabic or originating from the GCC or Indian Sub-Continent. The others were mostly Westerners, African, Asian or Antipodean. They were clearly industriously engaged in the making of deals…*tit for tat* kinds of arrangements, Oscar suspected.

Oscar would not allow himself to get sucked in by the local customs and trading formalities, for speaking personally, he was no tit!

The Westerners where the loudest and least comfortable looking. Over compensating with flagrant bravado and shallow false confidence when it was least appropriate. They looked out of place next to the maturing palm trees which formed a natural boundary.

Theirs was a collectively contrived performance, Oscar had noted with casual indifference and an ever so slight annoyance that bordered upon frustration and tempered angst.

A good majority of the people were comfortably engaged or more aptly, immersed in the practice of smoking. A social pastime of smoking a good Shisha or Hookah, which is basically a water pipe smoking device originating in India. In UAE cafés and restaurants, it is rare for each smoker not to order an individual hookah, as the price is generally low. Indeed, most cafés (called maqha— Arabic: مقهى, "coffeeshop") in the Middle East have hookahs freely available. It was something that Oscar's close friend and Andalucian associate Horace Boylan would have appreciated. He had a very well developed penchant and clearly the appropriate disposition 'for sucking on a Hookah!'

242

These kinds of café are quite widespread and are amongst the main social gathering places in the Arab world and have a similar status to that which pubs enjoy in the UK or a friendly neighborhood bar in North America.

Oscar turned his attention to the Emirati. The clique of four, all bearded, finely groomed and two with designer skins exhibiting *Ferrari & Mercedes* liveried computers, sat in the far corner of the courtyard, dressed rather intimidatingly in full traditional *kandura* garb; three of the men in white and the other in dark grey blue with collar, cuffs and highly stylish *Mont Blanc* cufflinks, accessorized by *na-aal* sandals and with Bluetooth's concealed beneath their *guthra* head-dress held in position by an *egal* resembling a black rope and sporting designer shades tooled by D&G and Carrera that rested comfortably upon their covered heads. *Loaded for Bear...*

Upon closer inspection, Oscar could see that two of them had a *kerkusha with* which they could be seen fiddling and playing with through force of habit. One was smoking a cigarette. *Gauloisse*, from the very distinctive odor, Oscar presumed.

Positioned on their dining table, Oscar could see a book in hardcover; *God's Banker*: An Account of the Life and Death of Roberto Calvi ~ by Rupert Cornwell. It was tucked, though not fully obscured, quite discretely beneath a large green portfolio marked with the Habib Bank AG Zurich logo and tagline.

They were positioned in close proximity to the *al rais* Travel Agency, which had Oscar observed, always appeared to be *closed for lunch*!

Oscar had decreed very early on in this particular escapade, that when the proverbial *"shit was destined for the fan"*, he would be the one walking away casually with a neatly folded *Trib* tucked under his arm. Regaled in a clean white suit by *Canali* or *Bottega Veneta*!

Pristine.

The oval shaped, low rise, blue and white stucco patterned fountain positioned in the centre of the terrace, directly beneath the cabana...was dry.

This scene, this environment, was fast becoming Oscar's milieu.

Set in the early winter of 2009; **"Where King meets Queen"** is the completion of the *Phelps* quadrology.

Following on from ***Brethren of Acadia***, Oscar is moving across previously unchartered International boundaries and involved with a series of new *Associates* who provide him with an entry point into the new *old* world.

The action and intrigue takes **Phelps** and his trusted companions; Wendell, Sylvain and Trent, always looking for an opportunity to finesse, into the UAE, Qatar, Australasia, New York City, Mumbai, Damascus, Muscat, Niagara-on-the Lake, Princeton, New Jersey and Denver, Colorado, where they encounter new challenges and are faced with a series of interesting and fresh personalities to contend with in the form of Ferdy Bray JP, Coral Tobias, William North, Tuppy Waldorf, Caldicott Pelham, Kapil Gambhir, Hitesh Karinde, Karima al Abbar, Eve Newham, Magda Koncz, Katya Black and a possible new love interest in Rosalie Brock.

Featuring the usual rapid fire and discerningly eloquent prose, pithy dialogue and witty repartee, combined with new and rich, often sinister international backdrops of Dubai and Doha and the more typical *Phelpsarian* settings of his more familiar Boston, London, Nerja and Niagara and some of the most colourful, endearing, charismatic, resilient and empathetic supporting characters ever committed to the page.

The *Phelps international* saga continues languidly from within the backdrop of the sordidly overdone killing of Mahmoud al-Mabhouh and the so called *assassination team,* who were using fake British passports in Dubai.

Oscar revels behind the causality of a major mideastern political storm and the questioning as to whether those involved were indeed British nationals.

The action takes place all over Dubai and in the Al-Bustan Rotana hotel in which the actual execution took place. The story unravels and questions just how Mossad were thought to be complicit and commissioned this murder most foul, which leads inextricably, all the way back to the site of the historic Queen's Royal Hotel and its phantoms, which continue to mesmerize so, in Niagara on the Lake.

"Where King meets Queen" offers further proof that in *Oscar Phelps* there is a true contender for successor, in the sociopathic hierarchy, to Patricia Highsmith's wonderful creation of the 1950's & 1960's era; *Tom Ripley.*

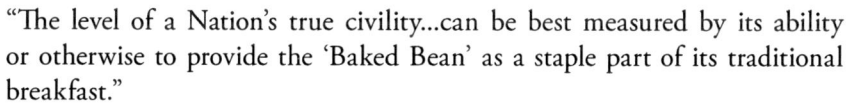

"The level of a Nation's true civility...can be best measured by its ability or otherwise to provide the 'Baked Bean' as a staple part of its traditional breakfast."

- David B. Green-Dubai, UAE - October 2009

If you enjoyed 'Brethren of Acadia', you will find more contemporary escapism within the traditional Oscar Phelps world in:-

The *Oscar Phelps* trilogy

32-Red...An Oscar Phelps novel

"Oscar" is a true Hero to his Associates as he manipulates his way through the World Currency & Corporate Markets, plotting objectives, hatching scams, co-coordinating frauds, with a Charm, Eloquence and ever so slight Schizophrenia.

Protecting his Global Interests. Not Allowing the Barriers of either Principle or the Common Good to Impinge upon his Lifestyle. "Oscar" is pragmatic in his approach to achieving his goals, which in the course of his business take him to Amsterdam, playing the "Ferryman". Boston. Mass, as the "Trouble-shooter". Las Vegas, as the "Playboy" and Salzburg as the "Arbitrator".

From the relative sanctity of his Andalucian Restaurante, "Oscar" will not tolerate or allow indiscretion to breach the Network he has nurtured. A Network from which he has reaped the dividend of a "Very Good Life".

When he receives a "Call for Help" from Hillary Robinson, his London based Associate and some time Sexual Partner, "Oscar" is started upon a path, which leads him to assume his favourite roles.

Fleetingly Proactive in the World of High Finance, Publishing, International Healthcare, Gaming and a renowned Restaurateur. "Oscar" lives his life on both sides of the border of legitimacy. The Threat of Exposure is ever Rife. The Nature of his Solutions often Radical. "Oscar" is a Man on whom his Associates can Rely... A Dear, Dear Boy...

Fraudster, Psychopath, Manipulator, Impresario, Raconteur, Wit, Killer and Friend. All Represent the Enigma that is... *OSCAR PHELPS*.

"32-Red" & "Berlin by Christmas" combine to become...

"The Enigmatic Mr Phelps"

The sequel to the late 1990's set "32-Red", brings Oscar Phelps into the new century with a certain gusto and a very personal mission to be relentlessly pursued. "32-Red" and the previously unpublished "Berlin by Christmas" provide in combination for the delivery of a Vintage Story of Elaborate Subterfuge, Contemporary Murder, Moot Conscience and Guiltless Precision. Woven amidst a Rich Tapestry of Traditional Values and Delicious Amorality. Oscar Phelps is a little older, a little wiser, but still constantly in search. This International Thriller follows the exploits of "32-Red"'s Fraudster, Psychopath, Manipulator, Impresario, Raconteur, Wit, Killer and Friend as he continues relentless pursuit of the song of life. Oscar has survived into the third millennium with enhanced knowledge, decorum and wit. His business "associations" take him now to the Raffles city of Singapore, experiencing the antiquities of Venice, the zest of Hong Kong, the last great bastion of the Empire. To Budapest, Paris, London, Nice, San Francisco, Niagara, Tokyo, Australia and a rejuvenated Berlin. Oscar has a new nemesis, a new "Buffalo" Bertram Keelan to contend with.

This time, a more worthy, more dangerous and ultimately more personal adversary.

Recently widowed, Oscar finds himself seeking to avenge the death of his wife Lori. Killed by a mis-directed act of aggression from an unlikely assailant. Oscar begins his quest with the help of friends on whom he can rely. Plotting his objectives, without conscience, limit or boundary.

Oscar the anti-hero, the "Dear, Dear Boy" will not allow anyone or anything to stop him as he flushes out his prey. With loyal Bostonian henchman Trent Alexis in tow, Oscar moves from within his shroud of sadness, stridently, purposefully, full of guile, with The Wisdom to Remember and the Courage to effect Change.

PREVIEWS

"Berlin by Christmas"

Prologue
December 2003

Oscar was breakfasting with a recent acquaintance, Jeremiah Russo, at a popular Italian eaterie; "Papa Razzi", on the corner of Dartmouth Street and Columbus. The food had been frugal but nonetheless good and the conversation brisk and business like. Which was apt as Oscar was making financial plans for the future, which involved certain lucrative dispositions in Hermon, Maine.

A future, which had its root very much with Lori Kasabian.

It was just after 9.15am, and outside, the Boston sidewalks were covered by a recently delivered layer of very fine snow. It was a bright, cold day and the promise of more snowfall was ominous. Oscar bid Russo farewell and after taking his overcoat, a large heavy black trench coat of pure wool by Perry Ellis from the rack, he made out toward the street. Taking a right from Dartmouth Street into Copley Plaza and then moving on up through James Avenue in the direction of Boylston. Conscious of the fact that he was already a few minutes late for his rendezvous with Lori at the entrance of the soon to be liquidated, FAO Schwartz, from where they had planned to continue on, to look at some new canvasses available at the Camelot Gallery at 221, Newbury Street.

Oscar quickly made haste.

As Oscar turned the corner of Clarendon, he began adjusting his Burberry muffler to close off the wind. Across the road in the distance, he saw clearly, Lori waiving her hand toward him, gesticulating that he should approach. She was wearing a rich dark red dress, which hugged her opulent body very tightly beneath her coat, which was now open and flaying a little in the wind. She was beautiful. She was smiling. She was happy.

Her hair was as it always was, a mane beautiful, thick and lustrous and at this moment it was slightly unkempt from the wind, which secretly Oscar liked very much. Oscar moved faster in approach toward her and Lori began to move elegantly toward Oscar.

Oscar smiled inwardly. A man content and in love. He had made the right decision that day some years ago at the Kronox Bar in Nerja.

As Oscar prepared to cross the street, minding both his step and foothold, he became conscious of a foot scuffed upon the ice on the sidewalk beside him and as it caught his attention, Oscar sensed a danger. There was a tiny pause and then release, its origin was tension, as a man who Oscar thought that he recognized, was now moving just ahead of him and heading straight toward Lori. He was running fast. Building up speed. Lori had not noticed him.

At that moment, the scene unfolding in front of Oscar appeared to transfer into a slow motion mode. The sounds that were common to the street had suddenly become muffled, slurred and distorted. Oscar could see everything about him. He was fully aware and recognized an inherent danger. He had suffered this kind of experience in the past and as with the times before, he felt powerless to intervene. He was mentally paralyzed. Transfixed.

The man was almost upon Lori now and still she was blissfully unaware. Oscar managed a forced and strangulated scream as he shouted out her name in desperation, but to no avail.

In a second, it happened. The assailant drew from his coat a pistol and from perhaps four feet, fired low and into the body of Lori Kasabian. The noise from the gunfire cracked and resonated around the busy commercial area and people, bystanders, city workers, mothers and children began instinctively to duck and dive for cover. Some stood numbed by fear, others cowered into store entrances and a few rushed to the aid of the stricken lady who by now had slumped to her knees on the sidewalk.

Lori's expression had changed. Her face was now pale with shock and she grimaced with pain as she clutched at her abdomen, trying desperately to stop the flow of blood, which was beginning to turn her dress, a dark and sticky black colour. The distinct smell of gunfire, of cordite, held in the air and the perpetrator of the act was seen fleeing the scene at high speed into the distance, slipping along the sidewalks, as he sped in the general direction of the Public Garden.

The snow began to fall heavier.

Oscar saw him go, but paid little heed. As he arrived at Lori's side, she had keeled over further, writhing a little onto her right hand side and hip. One of her shoes had become detached and her black seemed stockings had become torn and laddered. Her clothes were now dowsed in blood and there appeared little way to stem or make the flow relent.

The white snow which had cradled Lori and which had now become her enveloping shroud, began to become fractured by a stream of expanding thick red blood which came from underneath her body as she lay prone. Oscar had seen and recognized this situation before. Oscar moved toward her as she looked out, somewhat bewildered, toward the tops of the buildings with wide open and enquiring, stupefied eyes.

In the background could be heard the sirens from the Emergency Services as they made their way to the crime scene. But it would be too late.

Oscar looked first at his sweetheart and wished the pain in her eyes and face could be his. He then looked down at the entry wound and realized. He clutched her body towards him. Their faces were only inches apart. He kissed her mouth one last time and as Oscar held her in his arms, trying hard to reassure, expressing his love, tears coursing down his cheeks, the final words that Oscar heard Lori murmur as she struggled to find and gather her breath were succinct;

"Berlin by Christmas, Oscar?" she uttered.

Oscar found himself saying in response. "Berlin by Christmas, Lori my love... Berlin by Christmas."

"32-Red"

Oscar was intoxicated by a delirium, his ears whistled, his eyes, after countless preparatory rinses with cold water, found it difficult to focus and the glitz of the Gold and White decor, made his head spin.

Oscar's throat was dry and lubrication would and had not helped. His legs were light and his shoulders felt heavy and tight. He was very aware and uncomfortable of his slight paunch which showed in the mirrors opposite.

He was acutely uncomfortable.

As his money was being counted out in front of him he began to perspire. Beads of sweat formulated upon his forehead and the muscles in his neck began to tighten. Dirt from the wristband of his watch left a tidemark just below his shirt cuff and the buttons on his shirt began to both feel and show unappealing strain.

He wished that he had shaved.

The $25 Dollar Gaming Chips were shoved towards him across the lush green felt of the Roulette Table and in that moment Oscar saw his future. Twenty tan colored chips in the left hand stack accompanied by twelve tan colored chips on the right hand. As he reached to encase the chips safely within the custody of his sweaty clutches, his attention was alerted to the sight of hideously long and twisted, bright red polished finger nails protruding from strong African Female Hands.

The abhorrent and odious talons pushed rather tentatively at a group of $100 Dollar Black and Gold Gaming Chips and ended their journey on number 32-Red.

Oscar looked up at the owner of the talons ... and encountered, Dolores Roberts.

Oscar Phelps, without hesitation, covered the bet...

"32-Red"

May 1997
Prologue

It was the eve of the May 15th, Festival of "San Isidro".

The pueblo that is Maro was oppressive. It was sticky and humid at half past four of an afternoon in an early Andalucian spring day. "Jose" lay in wait in the shadows, he was growing increasingly conscious of his breathing, which was shallow and carried an ever so slight but distinct, wheezing quality. As the hour drew near, his body was becoming awakened by an alarm, which was carried along, sustained even, by his keen sense of purpose. The fear began to resonate as he imagined how his life would change during the course of the next few moments. He began to feel an intoxication which was in danger of giving way to nausea, he reproached himself, his head felt light, it began to swim, his balance was unsure, his condition was not one which could be attributed to alcohol. Though his wish was that it could. He attempted to gather a moist gobbet of phlegm into his mouth but with limited success, he struggled to swallow and he became pre-occupied with this most basic inability, he struggled with his position, which was becoming filled with helplessness and angst. His neck began to ache and his eyes began to lose focus. Then, in the distance, the large heavy doorway squeaked open and he became aware of an alarming scraping sound and then a thud as the elevator carriage began its descent. It was like an alarm clock going off and "Jose" instinctively grabbed at the wall, tearing off a nail in the process. He cursed himself. He was bleeding. It was a sobering curse and one which made him fully aware again of his purpose. He felt for his heartbeat under his shirt and he could not find one. The nausea began to relent. "Jose" had little time nor the inclination to withdraw from his challenge.

The atmosphere is even more oppressive when faced with the spectre of executing your first murder. "Jose" had only his thoughts and the moment. Stricken mute since his heroics in the last war, "Jose" knew his position, recognized and understood the opportunity and that it was unlikely to be repeated. There would be no second chances. He could see fragmented light within and between the passageways of the Caves of Nerja. An impressive array of stalagmites and stalactites. He became conscious of, but was increasingly alienated from the sound of the soprano voice echoing through the labyrinth from the Chamber of the Cascada, as the soprano began her recital. He knew that they were alone.

Upon first sight of Francesca, there was evoked a "chill", in his heart. A heart, which was now beating more and more rapidly. As he scuffled towards the narrow passageway linking his vantage point to the high central column of the Cataclysm Chamber, he came within fifteen feet of his quarry. She was leaning hard against the wooden support barrier and she seemed oblivious to his presence, she was lost in thought and showed little sign that soon, her life would be in peril. She was unaware that she was not alone.

"Jose" stared hard past the myriad of ground lights that skirted the narrow passageway, which coursed throughout the caves, and for a brief moment he became lost in a shallow wave of reminiscence.

There was something about the caves that had attracted "Jose" ever since his first visit in the early sixties. Quests for acceptance, deep foreboding with lost love or perhaps it was just the sense of finality should a mistake be made, a misplaced foothold, an overextended leap. The dividing line between life and death was indeed thin. His heart began to pound. He surveyed the expanse of the ledge and with it; its ability to conceal. He trembled a little, salivating upon his shirtfront, which was now drenched and discoloured with a cold sweat. He looked outwards into the tall and impressive caves and felt profound. He knew that it was time. Slowly he wended his way, quietly and carefully towards her and as he felt for and scaled down the final two steps and onto her level, he became somewhat transfixed. "Jose" peered at Francesca intently.

As Francesca turned in acknowledgment, with the start of a smile, her expression quickly turned to that of puzzlement. Startled, she became a little detached from her circumstances and very conscious of her own breathing. "Jose" without warning, jumped at her, knocking her backwards but not to the ground. Her pocketbook spilled however and emptied its contents. "Jose" pulled back his arm and released a blow so sickeningly hard that it caused Francesca's eye to close immediately and the soft tissue high on her cheekbone to discolour and then seep with blood. As she tried to regain her balance, instinctively she lurched with a growing rage toward him. Again the thud! of his fist closed upon her face. Her nose exploded. Blood and mucus formed a mass and seemed to converge with her thickening lips. She felt the tears come from her eyes. She was beginning to cry. She fought it back. "For Christ Sake!" she mumbled as she began the drift toward loss of consciousness. She felt for her mouth and for her teeth which had become numb and she felt herself falling toward the ground and she was beginning to acquiesce, she was angry with herself and though she was at the point of defeat it wouldn't, couldn't, didn't stop her. Francesca had resilience.

Seemingly without really knowing it, she saw through tearful, heavily obscured and blurred eyes, the image of "Jose" moving again toward her and as he neared she reached out, grabbing for his arm and biting hard into his wrist, moaning and growling at the same time. "Jose" reacted instinctively with annoyance, pulling away, tearing his arm from her grasp as she fought and then with a new found strength he cuffed her venomously across the throat, making her gasp for air. Francesca went down. Slowly she clawed at the ground beneath and somehow, involuntarily tried to scoop the contents of her pocketbook, a last inexplicable attempt at order. As her pathetic form engaged in this final act of dissention, "José" moved upon her and brought his right forearm up hard against her larynx, making a pivot with his left arm. "Jose" took a long hard deep breath. He knelt beside her and he squeezed.

As the soprano drew to her close in the background, so ebbed away the last breath of Francesca Luciani. Satisfied, "Jose" released his grip with a palpable relief and fell exhausted to the ground, alongside her now limp body. As he lay prone, gathering his senses he reached into his shirt pocket and took a swig from his flask of liquor for the strength that it would give him. He listened intently to the silence of Francesca Luciani. The few people, so distant, in the "sala de los festivales" began to applaud.

"Jose" looked down at his work. This had been a beautiful young woman.

The dull gash on her cheekbone had been joined by a fine cut on her mouth, which had now filled with blood. "Jose" was tired and now frightened. Slowly, he placed his hand upon her neck, feeling for a pulse. There was none. Relief! Francesca's prostrate body was relaxed, limp, and without animation. "Jose" hauled himself up and with his feet and knees; he began pushing with all of his might at the body, leveraging it over the edge, where in silence it fell under the barrier and into the darkness held below. Remarkably, her hands and legs appeared to claw at the edge, as if not quite accepting defeat, as the slide into the crevasse began. A relief came to "Jose" as her body sank with a final sense of acceptance, of disappearance, into the depths. No noise, no fuss. Just silence.

Fortified by the knowledge that she was now gone and that his task was fulfilled."Jose" congratulated himself upon his achievement. He began to realize and appreciate fully the situation. With a sense of pride that was masking a quiet despair, he replaced his red beret which had become dislodged during the struggle and spirited himself away.

About the Author

David B. Green was born in 1960 in the small Coal Mining village of Blidworth, located deep in the heart of the 12th Century "Robin Hood" county of Nottinghamshire, England.

He studied English Literature, Spanish Literature, Dramatic Art & Theatre Studies in the late 1970's and was a very useful club and county cricketer at schoolboy level.

David's first novel, - "32-Red" was written in Southern Spain in 1997 and is based upon the Intriguing, Beguiling, and Sociopathic character of *"Oscar Phelps "* and the world he inhabits. The *Phelps* character is an invention of the author's wife.

The sequel to '32-Red', - "Berlin by Christmas" was conceived and written in Australia from a Bribie Island, Queensland base and completed in Niagara-on-the-Lake, Ontario, Canada and in the SAR Hong Kong, China, in the winter of 2004.

The third in the *Phelps* trilogy - "Brethren of Acadia" was conceived and formulated in Montreal, New Orleans, Bergen, Illfracombe, Phoenix, Auckland, Amsterdam & Brisbane, Melbourne, Adelaide and Sydney, Australia during a very dispiriting Australia versus England *-Ashes-* cricket tour during 2006-07. It was completed in Niagara-on-the-Lake in the Fall of 2009.

"Oscar Phelps" is a Rapscallion and Anti-Hero in the classic *Patricia Highsmith "Ripley"* mould. The author's life is often confused with the *Phelps* character in real life.

David is now settled in the Shavian town of *Niagara-on-the-Lake*, Ontario,

Canada after periods resident in Baie d'Urfe on Montreal's West Island, Oak Bay & Cadboro Bay, Victoria, on Vancouver Island, in North Hatley in the Eastern Townships of Quebec, Nerja- Andalucía - Spain, JLT, Dubai - UAE, Amsterdam - the Netherlands and on Bribie Island near Brisbane, Queensland, Australia.

During his formative years in England, David learned about Nottinghamshire's dissenting literary outlaws; Byron, DH Lawrence, Alan Sillitoe. The experience of growing up in a small village community opened his mind and helped him escape into a much wider world. He developed a passion for foreign travel and the cinema, which has remained with him throughout his life.

David is active in the Canadian Professional Theatre & Film Industry as a Producer of dramatic & musical events for the stage. He serves as President & CEO of Delaporte Phelps MagicHour International Film & Theatre Company and as Producer - Magic Hour Theatre (London, England) with responsibility for North America. MHT is a division of MagicHour Media whose credits extend to include; William Shakespeare's 'A Winter's Tale' starring Sir Derek Jacobi and Anjelica Huston & Oscar Wilde's 'A Good Woman' starring Helen Hunt, Scarlett Johansson and Tom Wilkinson.

David's future projects in development include:

Michael Caine...*What's the good of Happiness...* (Musical)

On September 25th 1999, David made his first circumnavigation of the world, following a route established on September 25th 1988 by Michael Palin for the BBC television series; *Around the World in 80 Days*. He has since emulated this journey on four more occasions, east to west and west to east, having traced the steps laid out by Thomas Cook and *Phileas Fogg* in 1872.

David continues to travel extensively throughout all Continents of the World in connection with business, family and cricket watching. He has to date visited more than 65 countries.

"Brethren of Acadia" is dedicated to Karen Ann, his wife of 25 years, for all the love, support, encouragement and tolerance shown in the management of an obsession and for sharing his life, allowing him to follow his dreams and giving him his children.

David welcomes comments concerning the *Oscar Phelps* series of novels and he is contactable at; IHIConsulting@shaw.ca

Niagara-on-the-Lake, Ontario, Canada. December 2009

Brethren of Acadia

Reviews...

"Gripping! I think you're style of writing is in parts like a film script. Very taught, fast moving plot but with flowery visualization."

"The plot, characters are excellent as I thought when I started reading 'The Enigmatic Mr. Phelps' and now 'Brethren of Acadia'. It's your style of writing which is so very different. Staccato. Mickey Spillanish, scriptwritey. What about a TV series?"

- Duncan Hopper - Executive Producer 'A GOOD WOMAN' & Author of the Stageplay; 'Whatever Happened To Lyn Roe?' & 'Marilyn the Musical'

Brethren of Acadia

An Oscar Phelps novel
© David B. Green 2010

"The Enigmatic Mr Phelps"

The Oscar Phelps novels
© David B. Green 1997, 2003, 2005 & 2010

Crime Writer

The Enigmatic Mr Phelps

The thrilling international crime drama
coming soon to a Cinema near you, detailing the continuing
life & times of anti-hero and international sociopath;

Oscar Phelps

By
David B. Green

A classic crime mystery thriller with all the ingredients of the genre... containing beautiful and sensual women, explicit sex mixed with a good dose of violence and action.

Every time a trusted associate is in dire need of a solution to a distinctly sticky problem, Oscar Phelps is the one to whom they turn. Every time a random thought is suppressed and a radical idea abandoned, Oscar Phelps is the one to take another look.

The attractive, high maintenance, mature, blonde, sex addicted and highly charged professional lady from Berkley Square breathed a sigh of relief when Oscar agreed to blindly offer his assistance to her request.

The Axarquia region of Spain and in particular a small bar/restaurant in a small coastal town had become the spiritual home to a band of highly unorthodox, ethically challenged, roguish and clandestine individuals bound together by a familial alliance with one Oscar Phelps. They shared an allegiance. An allegiance to greed and a lust for life which would continue unabated, irrespective of legitimacy polarity.

The strangulated remains of a once beautiful Italian girl, secreted on a hidden ledge in the caves of Nerja form both stark tragedy and a compelling opening to this story of power, love, honour, treachery, envy and greed and all set against a cavalcade of exciting and glamorous international backdrops.

Problem is, when all is said and done, there is always a loose end to tie up, a trailing link to a past indiscretion that comes to challenge the status quo. A new foe to be quelled. The radical and ultimate solution rests firmly in the domain of one Oscar Phelps.

But that's not the worst of it. The real tragedy is that those closest to Phelps were the ones to both benefit and lose the most. The one's whose greed and angst ultimately cost the real prize.

This is the fast paced story of intrigue, of what went wrong, how it was corrected and the consequences and betrayals that surfaced.

* * *

From the first frame, we know that Oscar Phelps is our killer and yet we have an empathy to the point of almost cheering him on. There is no attempt to mask. No attempt at self-doubt or loathing, or even conscience getting in the way of progression and loyalty. Avoidance of the truth is not on the agenda. Reality is just a blur. Style the reality.

From that knowledge comes a sit-back-in-your-seat old school thriller. Because we all realize that Phelps is the doyen of his clique. The sociopath we all ultimately know should get caught, but clearly know he will not. The international man for all seasons who will stop at nothing to achieve his objectives. We sit back and watch and learn as he exercises his charm and beguiles for the two hours it takes the story to unfold onscreen. We yearn for the chase to relent and for the nemesis to be revealed and taken care of.

As we watch, we follow Oscar and his closest associates operating in open and flagrant revelry as they occupy their favorite haunts, milking the vulnerable and protecting their interests. Oscar has humor, delivers hubris and tells jokes and whispers anecdotes as he leads social activities as a pillar of society on both sides of the Atlantic.

He moves effortlessly below the authoritarian radar of entire global communities on high alert, literally getting away with murder after murder and leaving a trail of destruction in his wake.

We fall in lust with Hillary Robinson, the savvy and engaging 40 something Mayfair sophisticate and world traveler, who knows how to take care of herself and just prefers others to do it for her. Vivacious, sexually charged, shallow and hugely intelligent, she's one step away from what she sees as her rightful position at Oscar's side. And she's just found a barrier standing in the way to her achieving it.

We get swept up in the shenanigans of the Rt Hon. Eric Armstrong-Jones, the London Aristocrat so often ignored by the task force, as he battles away in manipulation of the financial markets. Knowing that Oscar Phelps, his friend and ally will always provide safe haven, solace and support.

As the clock ticks down on Francesca Luciani, who refuses to play the victim, we witness a story of despair and naiveté as she invites the inevitable. She moves into a neighborhood of self doubt and petty recrimination, never to surface. She puts forth an ultimatum; she invites a solution from which she is destined never to recover.

'Buffalo"Bertram Keelan in pursuit, is always one step behind and two steps too slow and just not clever enough to outwit or to make a long standing impression.

As the pursuit of truth intensifies and with it the network of intrigue extends beyond international boundaries, delivering a range of deviant personalities and eccentric characterizations and personas in support, we find woven a complex tapestry, which both opens up and envelopes the world of Oscar Phelps.

The story fixates upon the flawed profile that Oscar exhibits and his distorted sense of loyalty.

When 'Buffalo' Bertram Keelan finally arrives uninvited, confident and brazenly intrudes within Phelps' ultimate place of sanctity, impinging upon the people and the moment. Oscar treats him with a form of largesse. He sees captured within the bravado, not strength, but exactly the opposite. This is a smiling slow witted man asking for direction, without a hope of success. No threat. And that is why Oscar throws open the door to invention, without the possibility of escape.

* * *

This story is an urgent and exciting whisk through time, location, people and emotion and what happens when a beguiling and enigmatic man influences the people around him to an extent that defies probability, but leaves open the gateway to possibility. Offering further proof that in *Oscar Phelps* there is a true contender for successor, in the sociopathic hierarchy, to Patricia Highsmith's wonderful creation of the 1950's & 1960's era; *Tom Ripley*. Stylish, with psychological depth and insight. Hypnotically haunting. The detail is dark and somewhat disturbing. Phelps exudes characteristics of the suave and cynical, whilst obviously highly sophisticated and infinitely debonair. He is a combination of consummate villain and unmitigated blackguard. His appeal is indisputable.

Fleetingly Proactive in the World of High Finance, Publishing, International Healthcare, Gaming and a renowned Restaurateur. The Threat of Exposure is ever rife. "Oscar" is a Man on whom his Associates can Rely... A Dear, Dear Boy...Fraudster, Psychopath, Manipulator, Impresario, Raconteur, Wit, Killer and Friend. All Represent the Enigma that is... *OSCAR PHELPS*.

Like **The Talented Mr Ripley**, this film is built around three heavyweight leading roles that intertwine through colliding storylines with a rich vein of idiosyncratic support characters and sub plots that bind the story together. Fuelled by the terror and mystery of the inevitable consequences of betrayal and murder. With the violence and gritty period authenticity of **Michael Caine's** depiction in **Get Carter** resonating throughout and the rich and glorious dialogue of **Le Carre's *The Tailor of Panama***. It is told with irreverent black and sardonic humour, underpinned by characters you will adore and a degree of clinical menace, detail and sobriety you will appreciate, not observed at this level since **The Day of the Jackal.**

This story maintains its dark, disturbing and ultimately charming though harrowing appeal, right from the haunting opening *Sunday Smile* theme and long after the end credits and the *Summer Wine, Oscar Phelps* theme, have faded into the distance.

INDISCRETIONS OF A FORLORN APRICOT

Chapter one.

"Take that you bastard!" said Joan Fontaine, her strong little fist connecting with my chin. Lightning exploded in my brain and I went down for the count of ten. As consciousness returned, my mind drifted back to my boyhood in Birmingham. I thought of the poignance of first love, the unforgettable spring when Birmingham's air, soft, richly thick and grey, and fragrant like an unwashed bedsock, made my heart beat faster. And she came running towards me, my little Beryl, her little fist outstretched and her high, childish voice crying to me, "Take that you bastard!"

My reverie was cut short by the emergence of Louis B. Mayer from the bathroom. I understood at once that my career was ruined. I had caught the great L.B. in a compromising situation with my wife! It was unforgivable. I knew then that my contract would be dropped and I would be relegated to spending the rest of my life on tour with Katharine Cornell.

End of Chapter one.

That's the kind of thing to give the public.

George Sanders (6th September 1959)

Dear World, I am leaving because I am bored. I feel I have lived long enough. I am leaving you with your worries in this sweet cesspool. Good luck.

Wish Me Luck As You Wave Me Goodbye...

Oh, Firefly, why can't I
Latch on for you no how
Oh, how I love you but gee
While you set the night on
Firefly, shine a little light on
Shine a little light on
Shine a little light on me

"I have Graham Greene's telephone number, but I wouldn't dream of using it. I don't seek out writers because we all want to be alone."

"I find the public passion for justice quite boring and artificial."

-Patricia Highsmith

I have a theory that you should do everything before you die.

I admire people who do things.

My theory is that everyone is a potential murderer.

Don't worry; I'm not going to shoot you, Mr. Haines. It might disturb Mother.

- ***Bruno Anthony***
from *Strangers on a Train* by Patricia Highsmith

"Work...The greatest restrictor of Men's Minds."

- Anthony Aloysius St.John Hancock - whose ashes were
brought back to the UK from Sydney, Australia in an Air
France hold-all and in deference to his fame and knowing love
of cricket, his ashes travelled back in the first class cabin...

'If your approach to life is that it is an ordeal to be survived…then chances are, you will survive it, and little else. "Good Luck! in the next one…'

- David B. Green, Niagara on the Lake, ON. March 27th 2010

Robert B. Parker in *discourse* with David B. Green
Concerning the literary characters of *Spenser* and *Oscar Phelps*...

Postmark Boston MA, August 13th, 2005
August 12th, 2005

Dear David Green
Thanks for your letter, and for your thoughts on how I should proceed
with Spenser. Any references in any of my novels to anything of yours is
in fact a coincidence and was not intended.
As for finishing my works after I have gotten off the bus, I have decided
never to get off the bus. But if I change my mind, even in death I work
alone. It doesn't somehow strike me as seemly to reference, upon request,
Oscar Phelps in a future Spenser.
Good of you to think of me.
RBP

Postmarked Niagara on the Lake ON, August 19th, 2005
August 21st, 2005

Dear Bob Parker,
Many thanks for taking the time to correspond with me again and for your
note in response to my enquiry. The content of which is both understood
and fully appreciated. In death I would also not want anyone to continue
the Phelps series.
The coincidences in several references in this year's Spenser are indeed,
strikingly remarkable. Perhaps I am looking too hard? I appreciate as
ever, your continued encouragement for my Phelps endeavours and Thank
you again for seeing me through a period of great personal transition
during the period 1996 thru 98, when the Spenser novels helped keep me
centred. Thank you also for the signed copy of Small Vices and your note
of support for 32-Red and Berlin by Christmas.
I wish you continued success with Spenser, which remains in my view the
standard by which this genre is measured and with your other featured
characters of Stone and Randall. I also wish you continued good health
and happiness and I thoroughly appreciate your thinking of Oscar
Phelps.
DBG

January 18ᵗʰ, 2010
Robert B. Parker, the best-selling mystery writer who created Spenser, a tough, glib Boston private detective who was the hero of nearly 40 novels, died Monday at his home in Cambridge, Mass. He was 77.

The cause was a heart attack, said his agent of 37 years, Helen Brann. She said that Mr. Parker had been thought to be in splendid health, and that he died at his desk, working on a book. He wrote five pages a day, every day but Sunday, she said.

Robert B. Parker RIP

"Life is a tragedy for those who feel, but a comedy to those who think."

- Walpole

David B. Green

BRETHREN OF ACADIA
...a Second Face in February

The Enigmatic Mr Phelps

"32-Red"

Berlin by Christmas

The Oscar Phelps Series

Brethren of Acadia
...a Second Face in February

The Enigmatic Mr Phelps

"32-Red"

BERLIN BY CHRISTMAS

David B. Green

The *Oscar* Phelps Series

From the Publishers
Amsterdam based PR & Media Group - Molitor 5901 Boekerij & 32-Red
Productions are pleased to make - Brethren of Acadia - available globally via
our commissioned publishing house; AuthorHouse in the United States, who
manage distribution worldwide through the Ingram Book Group

Brethren of Acadia continues the Phelps tradition for delivering international intrigue set against a backdrop of exciting global locations and dusted with an occasional murder, rampant and explicit sexual episodes, violent conquest... providing for a highly entertaining and thoroughly absorbing read. Crammed with an intense & refreshingly eccentric honesty, this leads often to the characters of menace evolving to become an ensemble of people, for whom you will wish to cheer.

"I think your choice of actor to portray Oscar is spot on - a very good performer, good-looking enough to be likeable and attractive, yet with the quirky streak necessary to portray the sociopath that is Oscar.
Can't wait to see the film!
Two tickets, please, in the balcony.
What is more cinematically appealing than a likeable rogue?"

- Stanley Morgan
actor in the James Bond movie **Dr. No**(1962) playing the Concierge in Les Ambassadeurs gambling club in London who provides the first introduction to Sean Connery as James Bond 007.

WATCH OUT FOR *OSCAR PHELPS* AT THE MOVIES... SOON TO BECOME A MOTION PICTURE

David B. Green is the author of the *Oscar Phelps* series of International Crime Fiction novels. He is English and lives in Niagara-on-the-Lake, Ontario, Canada.

Step into the World of *Oscar Phelps* by visiting at;
http://www.facebook.com/profile.php?id=100001634209331

Contact *Oscar*
oscar.phelps.novels@gmail.com

David B. Green is the author of the Oscar Phelps series of International Crime Fiction novels. He is English and lives in Niagara-on-the-Lake, Ontario, Canada.

Jacket Illustration & Formatting by Lloyd W T Green

LaVergne, TN USA
10 February 2011
215930LV00002B/4/P